BILL LONG GAME

Bruno Phillips

Billy's Long Game
BOULEVARD *editions*
London 2009

BOULEVARD *editions*
is an imprint of
Erotic Review Books
ER Books, 31 Sinclair Road
LONDON W14 0NS

Tel: +44 (0)20 77365800
Fax: +44 (0)20 7366330
Email: enquiries@eroticprints.org
Web: www.eroticprints.org

© 2009 MacHo Ltd, London UK
© 2009 Bruno Phillips

No part of this publication may be reproduced by any means without the express written permission of the Publishers. The moral right of Bruno Phillips as author of the designated text has been asserted.

Erotic Review Books is a publisher of fine art, photography and fiction books and limited editions. To find out more please visit us on the web at www.eroticprints.org or call us for information on 08000262524 (UK only). Overseas +44 1905727476

ISBN 978-1-904989-58-5

Bruno Phillips

BILLY'S LONG GAME

a story

Bruno Phillips has been by turns a psychiatric nurse, adman, scriptwriter and yacht's cook.

He is a frequent contributor to the Erotic Review.

He divides his time between London, Cornwall and France.

BILLY'S LONG GAME

A Story

CONTENTS

Preface   *p.7*

Chapter 1
Where Have You Been to Billy Boy?   *p.9*

Chapter 2
The Minstrel Boy to the War Has Gone   *p.57*

Chapter 3
Oh Stay, the Maiden Said and Rest   *p.89*

Chapter 4
'Tis to Glory We Steer   *p.113*

Chapter 5
On Yonder Hill   *p.137*

Chapter 6
Where the Girls Are So Pretty   *p.157*

Chapter 7
Away You Rolling River   *p.183*

Chapter 8
Like a Bird On the Wing   *p.207*

Preface

I am told no one is interested in history. Well, I lived through a lot of it and found it all interesting enough. Although the most fascinating affairs with which I was involved were with women. In other regards I tried to influence matters as little as possible. As for the women, they were nearly always memorable and usually great fun. Seduction was not my forte. Being seduced was. I found that if a woman wants your cock, she'll make the running and all you have to do is say 'Yes'. Who knows how they decide what is exciting enough to make them open their legs. Some people say 'listening to them' is good. Others think danger is the trigger. Whatever it is, or was, I seemed to have it. Women often told me I was 'not very sympathetic', or even 'heartless'. Later on in life I was sometimes cursed with the epithet 'sweet', but only by young girls who didn't know much. It's not important. Actually I think it is sexual indifference that attracts women. As with cats, indifference does not alarm and it arouses their curiosity.

Anyway, this isn't history, but it is a story.

Chapter 1

WHERE HAVE YOU BEEN TO
ALL THE DAY BILLY BOY?

Once upon a time my name was William 'Billy' Jones. I was a Cornishman. My mother, as I recall, was a bright and affectionate woman who lacked only an education. My father was Arthur Myddleton, 3rd Baron Broleigh. He was an amiable old devil who gave my mother and me a home, though denying me his name. So I took it anyway. If I have left any bastards myself, they should know they have the blood of English gentry in their veins, well leavened with that of Cornish peasants. In pursuit of accuracy, the Broleighs were really only successful yeomen whose founding father, dynastically speaking, emerged from the early days of the industrial revolution and threw money at one or other of the early nineteenth century Governments.

From the almost but not entirely Honourable Lord Arthur I learned a bit about books and a lot about horses. From the Cornish I learned to survive.

My mother was housekeeper to the Myddleton family. She was the sole girl in a troupe of five brothers; most of whom were substantial tenant farmers down through Cornwall and up along the Devon border. The eldest brother happened to farm Broleigh land and my mother was barely sixteen when she went into service at the Manor House.

Lady Myddleton died in childbirth. My mother thought well of her as gentle and considerate. The son, Walter, had just reached his third birthday when I was born. How my father seduced my mother is a mystery. Or possibly it was the other way round. These were not things you tackled your mama about at the end of the nineteenth century or even now. I think she might have, in the old terms 'set her cap' at him, given the context of their relations. Still, Broleigh was first stuck with a young motherless heir and subsequently a bastard child. He dealt with it much as might be expected. A wet nurse for Walter in infancy and then my mother was deputed to look after young Walter until she became obviously pregnant. She and I were banished to her brother's farm and a suitable arrangement made until after my birth. After that, in my recollection nothing was said, in the sense of circumstances being fully explained. I remember asking if my uncle was my daddy. No he wasn't, my daddy was an important man who couldn't be with us but looked after us. For a while he sounded like God. I spent my baby days and nights very happily at my uncle's farm. This was home. My cousin Jenny was my companion and friend. Mother returned to her duties but came home most nights although not always.

It's hard to recall when Walter first impinged as a truly obnoxious creature. He early learned his role as heir to the title. As child of the housekeeper and hence somewhat privileged interloper my place was more equivocal. From around four years old I was made his playmate and began to spend more time at the Manor. This was when Mama told me to 'Regard Lord Broleigh as your father and Walter as your big brother.' To be kind, Walter had no mother. My own mama had 'brought him up' to a certain point. I think he genuinely liked her, although he was very often rude to her. Whatever the case, there was hostility between my half-brother and I from the moment we became sentient.

He was an accomplished bully. Whether psychological or physical he was able to judge the precise amount of pain to inflict before the evidence outweighed his protestations of innocence. Jibes about my 'absent' father, invitations to ride the nursery rocking horse prior to being shoved off it were typical assaults. Insults regarding my own and mother's social status were routine and refined over the years. To the tenants he conveyed a supercilious courtesy. They didn't like him, but he dared not contradict his father's genuinely enlightened estate management. In any case Walter was not much interested in such matters, and at the age of eight was sent up country to boarding school. I realised, as I grew older that our father was starting to train me as his estate steward. Flattering as this was, my dealings with Walter did not bode well for any sort of future after he inherited. Meanwhile, Lord Broleigh continued to treat me with a sort of rough affection and increasing responsibility.

Arthur Myddleton called me 'boy' whenever he addressed me, and 'the boy' when speaking of me. 'Time you learned to hold a shotgun boy,' or to my mother 'I need the boy to ride over to Pengelly farm for the rent.' None of this went down well with Walter. Especially since he had ground to make up on his return for the school holidays. We had come to blows a couple of times; not to his advantage, despite greater age. Instead of combat he sought ways to implicate me in mistakes. Luckily my father was astute enough to see through this. My tenant friends and relatives would back me up and these sporadic attempts at incrimination ceased. This lasted until my fourteenth birthday.

With the insight of all bullies, Walter latched on to my close friendship with Jenny. He had often attempted to suborn her, through gifts and slighting references to myself but without success. At seventeen he was pretty much a full-grown man. On the pretext of an errand he needed done, he persuaded her to ride with him. Some sort of assault was attempted. I happened by the farmhouse just after her return.

'Well' snorted Jenny, seemingly less frightened than angry. 'I told him he could put that pathetic thing away since I'd seen better on our pig.' My mother and aunt giggled despite their concern. My uncle looked stern. 'His Lordship should be told.' For some reason I demurred. 'Let it be Uncle. I'll see to Walter.' Our eyes met. I had no plan in mind, but he must have seen something that convinced him.

My return to the Manor also coincided with Walter's. We met in the stable-yard. 'Hullo peasant,' was his opening gambit. I said, melodramatically but sincerely, 'Touch Jenny again and you are a dead man.' His attempted dismissal was half-hearted. 'Like to like peasant. Sod off and raise some brats.' Entirely by accident, he had hit upon a quite important insight. Though close and perfectly aware of the 'facts of life' as are all country-bred children, Jenny and I had always had a relaxed sibling relationship. Growing up together meant we had shared childish confidences about each other's 'things' and 'places', but we had no sexual or romantic consciousness. Then came the assault, which changed everything.

To start with, I saw Jenny in a new, sexually charged light. No longer my pretty young cousin and chum, she had been re-cast by Walter's lust as a desirable woman.

She too, appeared to have acquired a new demeanour. On our subsequent rides out onto the moors, she was less the tomboy and more the girl. She held out her hand for me to help her dismount, leaned into me as I lifted her down. Her glances became more sidelong and demure. On one of our rides she suddenly said, 'Dear Billy, I feel so safe with you. I mean, protected.' In consequence, I found myself fantasising about her to the point that when masturbating, it was her face and figure I had in front of me.

Throughout the Autumn I was given more and more responsibility. Broleigh took me round to meet the Estate's fishing boat skippers in Mevagissy, the mine manager in Camborne and our land agent in Truro. 'This is Mr William Jones,' he would say. 'He rides and shoots as well as any grown man and has my confidence.' I was flattered, but wondered what he had said or would say to Walter, who was shortly to leave school and must expect to take some part in managing the Broleigh lands.

One very good reason for Arthur Myddleton to have confidence in me was that I was related to many of his tenant farmers. My paternity might have been a taboo subject of conversation but it was well known nonetheless. Nor had my mother's pregnancy been especially adversely regarded. Women generally became pregnant before wedlock, and it was understood that if marriage was impossible there were correct ways of doing things. In my mother's case this was continuity of employment and fair treatment. The Myddletons had always been good landlords in a practical way. Housing stock had been invested in, rents reduced in hard times, farms were consolidated where sensible. There was a genuine sense of goodwill and only Walter cast a shadow on our cordial way of life.

Every year, there was a traditional Christmas Ball held late in Advent. Church and Manor combined to offer our small community a celebration. Walter had returned briefly from his school, and had then gone up to London where his father maintained a house. Jenny had come over early to help my mother bake the pies so central to any Cornish event. I was busy arranging the buffet tables and cutlery. Jenny came into the great hall. The local pipe and fiddle band were setting up under the double staircase. I remember Jenny had on her best dress and there was flour on her cheek. She came over to me with a sprig of mistletoe in her hand and said 'Well Billie boy, it's time to kiss your loving cousin.'

Her breath was sweet as a mare on clover and her lips softer than feathers. It was over in a moment and she danced away laughing. I do remember standing still in the bustle and a member of the band called out 'Lucky Billy.' However the rest of the evening passed only she remains in memory. That is what a woman does. She creates an overwhelming complexity of reaction through her breath, lips, voice, eyes. What was lucky? She had told me she loved me.

When we next saddled our horses and trotted out through the winter wet lanes and onto the moor we had ceased to be children. There was a new note in her laughter and her touch on my arm had become almost proprietorial.

Ultimately of course the kiss repeats itself. The clash of tongues and the press of bodies enhance the deep breaths and flushed faces. Ah yes, they were provoked by our shared and challenging cross-country duel in which the Tors and tracks of the Moor were conquered. Her courageous mare and my noble stallion stood panting in the yard. We led them into the stable and sponged and rubbed their glistening and silky flanks. They smelled as only a horse smells. Jenny's mare trembled and 'whickered'. My stallion, a marvellous black horse called Nigger snorted and a huge erection flourished below his belly. Jenny turned to me:

'He fancies her, Billy. What do you think?'

'I think he does.'

'Do you fancy me in that way?'

'I do.'

'Is your cock as big as his then?'

'No, but big enough for you I hope.'

Then we kissed again as my hand slipped down to her crotch. Ladies in those days mostly rode side-saddle. Jenny, as a country lass, wore men's riding britches. Her breasts were familiar, if tactile and enticing objects she had permitted me to admire during their development. Her groin remained speculative, as mine did for her other than the childhood sightings. Her fingers struggled to unleash my cock. She manoeuvred to allow access to the buttons and folds of her lower garments. Both objects achieved we became mutually amazed: myself by the light but curly bush of brown hair at the base of her belly. She by the thick hot rod of muscle she grasped in her fist. Whatever people say, the sight of a good-sized erect cock causes most women to lose their natural sense of decorum.

'Oh my, Billy he's so big.' She stared down and two red spots flushed on her cheeks. It was a sign of desire I came to know well. She was right of course. Nature and the Baron's genes endowed me with an unusually large organ. It was to provide me with a great deal of entertainment over the years. In those days of course I was just at the beginning of the wonderful period of seemingly unlimited potency attendant on youth.

Jenny's exclamation was not mere untutored maidenly surprise. With elder brothers she had long been familiar with the male part. Nor do country girls just exchange hints on cheese making in the playground. She assured me, mine was far more impressive than anything she had seen or heard of. Her fingers tightened round my shaft and she began to fondle and pull, whilst staring down at the swollen, open-eyed, purple glans as it emerged and retreated in her grip. As a regular masturbator, there was no danger of my coming prematurely – as is so often supposed of young sexual tyros. I cupped my hand over her vulva and with my fingertips, rummaged gently through the hair, parting the lips. I found heat and moistness. She gasped and parted her legs further. Even among the aromas of the stable there was a waft of something ineffably erotic rising to my nostrils. She sighed, lifted her face for a kiss and our mouths locked together. For what seemed hours we stood embraced, caressing cock and cunny. I found by experiment that insertion of my fingers into her cunt and subtle stimulation of my thumb at the top of her slit caused her to murmur and wriggle appreciatively. Eventually she took her lips from mine and whispered 'Would you like me to have Billy boy in my mouth?' This became her pet name for my lucky prick.

Later, she confessed she had learned about the pleasures of fellation from her brothers. From the age of about twelve, she had regularly masturbated or sucked them in exchange for three pence usually. She said she treated it as fun. It also saved her from any more difficult sexual encounters. 'If they want to tup they can try a sheep' was her practical summation.

She sank to her knees and opening her mouth wide, took my cock in as far as she could. Then, cupping my balls with one hand she began to suck and jerk simultaneously. I gazed down on her, and held her head gently between my hands, feeling her ears and liking the scent of her dark silky hair. Occasionally she took my cock from her mouth and laid it against her cheek, smiling conspiratorially up at me.

Eventually of course I had to give way to the excitement. My shudder and involuntary groan should have warned her; possibly it did, but she allowed me to push my cock further into her mouth as it jerked convulsively and I bent over her, her forehead pressing into my stomach. I felt her cough and splutter and released her. My cock pulsed in her fist and a second spurt of semen splashed with the vigour of youth onto her lips and cheek. She was not deterred, but laughed and licked my glans at the same time blowing out some of the viscous liquid. 'My goodness Billy, such a lot of spunk you do have.'

After this, our walks and rides were seldom conducted without at least one and sometimes more, mutual pleasurings. Jenny admitted she loved 'Billy boy' as much as its owner. She became almost insatiable in her demands that I 'get him out' for her to play with. This of course was delightful for me. She became sanguine about swallowing my semen, but liked very much to have me come over her belly or breasts. In such scenarios she would often prefer for us to masturbate in unison so that we came together as she heaved her hips and worked her vulva with cries of 'Squirt me Billy, squirt,' her eyes fixed on my flying hand as mine was on her fingers.

I learned under her tuition, to manipulate her cunt to orgasm and much enjoyed it. Her scent was hugely erotic to me and I would carry it on my fingers as long as possible. She would not however, allow me to kiss her 'there'. I was permitted to inspect her as she lay legs wide, lips spread – and indeed to do the lip spreading myself. But if I brought my face too close, eager to taste the juicy flesh, she would push me away with a sharp 'No Billy, no.' I asked her why and she simply said: 'It's not right.'

This was more disappointing than what was I suppose, a mutual decision not to fuck. Her reticence over cunnilingual sex was not paralleled in relation to any other activities. Not having 'babbies' was her major concern. 'I'd love a fucking,' she told me, 'but babbies are not for me at this age.' She confessed to having deflowered herself with the handle of her hairbrush '...as soon as my monthlies started. I'd really like Billy boy in my cunny.' She sighed once as we lay half-naked on a warm rock on Bodmin Moor and she idly fondled her object of desire. Then: 'If you like, you could do my bottomhole - the hairbrush felt quite pleasant in there when I tried it out.'

Her attentions and the concept caused an immediate erection. As she turned away and knelt to take my cock in her mouth I pulled down her drawers and inspected her arse from the rear. Her bulging pudenda and flushed cunt lips swelled amid the hair that also grew up inside her thighs and straggled more sparsely between her buttocks to the puckered mouth of her anus. This had not occurred to me as a possible destination. My classical reading had given me some idea of sodomy – as had the jokes of local youth, but I had only thought of it as buggery and for homosexuals like Oscar Wilde. Still, the idea kept me amused as I fingered her wet cunt and later, tried to get my cock into her bum. It wasn't successful so she sucked and jerked her Billy boy to his second ejaculation of the afternoon.

Time passed pleasantly in this way. We found a method, involving lubrication of course, with goose fat as it happens, for me to bugger her, but she never took to it. His Lordship was giving me more and more responsibility and I was out on the estate a good deal. Jenny's household indulged their only daughter, so that her domestic duties were comparatively light. Excepting the kitchen gardens, or a few root vegetable and bean fields, the farms had virtually ceased arable agriculture long before and converted to livestock. Women raised chickens, ducks and pigs. They made sausages, cheese and preserves. Milking was also useful work for girls ('It's how we learn to wank boys,' Jenny said) but over early. Accordingly, we would spend some time together almost every day. Our friendship was no secret. It was quite clearly supposed by everyone around that she and I had an 'understanding'. In fact, I am sure her family encouraged her to visit unchaperoned, since I was obviously a catch and were a baby to happen matters would be agreeably settled.

Whether this was anything to do with Jenny's decision to fuck me I don't know. It was either my, or her, fifteenth birthday – we had long regarded them as shared, and we had been out for a long and as it happened, sex-free ride. When we had settled the horses, Jenny came up to me and kissed me. I noticed those two red lust spots on her cheeks. 'Fuck me Billy,' she whispered, and snuggled into my arms. I had long learned not to ask questions at moments like this. She seemed almost feverish as she stripped off her riding britches and drawers and opened her blouse. By the time I too was naked from the waist down she had spread a horse blanket on a bale of straw and was lying with knees up and thighs splayed. Her fingers parted her vulva lips. Her cunny looked hot, wet and darkly flushed. I got between her knees, and she reached out for her 'Billy boy'. As if she sensed a hesitation she said: 'Don't worry, I want it and my monthlies are on.' Later, I was to discover that intercourse during a woman's menses was taboo not for effete aesthetic reasons, but because the religious knew it reduced the chance of pregnancy. Luckily, I never became victim to the ancient superstitions about cleanliness and thus with various free-spirited women, had many spontaneously good times in the years before easy contraception.

As Jenny had suggested, her loss of virginity was a technicality. With the help of her eager hand, I thrust my cock into the hot and slippery tunnel that was its natural home. She had half sat, propped on one elbow to watch, so far as she could, my penetration. Now I was in, she fell back with a satisfied whimper, leaving her hand at her groin. Her vagina was tight and I could feel it contract. She closed her eyes and repeated 'Oh, Billy boy, oh.' She drew her knees further back and with my shins against the bale edge and my arms under her calves I began to fuck into her. She pushed back, our pubic bones ground together. If I had worried about babies before, I certainly didn't now. This was it, what Nature did. I smelled the horses and heard them stamp as if in approval. My balls slapped her bum and there was a burning wet mouth round the root of my cock. We grunted and sighed and groaned to each other until she cried out 'Now Billy, I'm coming, spunk me, spunk me!' Her hips lifted, I could see her teats dark and stiffly jutting from the pale mounds of her breasts and the suffusion on her neck. My cock swelled, convulsed and squirted. Jenny subsided with a long shuddering sigh.

It was at this point that his Lordship came upon us. We heard him go 'Humph, hah, see you in my study William,' and with heavy irony, 'at your pleasure of course.'

So quickly had this interruption occurred, I think Jenny hardly noticed it. She certainly took no alarm. Rather, she just lay on the bale, legs akimbo, giggled and said, 'Well done Billy boy that was lovely.' My cock slithered from her cunt. I noticed it was streaked with mucus and blood. Her slit closed its lips and a small trickle of semen hung down between her buttocks. I too felt quite unperturbed by the prospect of an encounter with his Lordship. Something else impinged much more profoundly on my consciousness. That was the realisation that not only had I now reached a man's estate; but that my relationship with this woman was also on a quite altered plane.

In his Lordship's study that evening, he tried to look serious and failed. He offered me a brandy and said, 'Mr Jones, your mother and you are a great help to me. Sexual congress with young women is a natural thing but it has consequences. You are too young, useful, and I believe intelligent to have to deal with these at present. I know a bit about women. Take my advice, and learn other methods of pleasuring each other. If you must fuck, get out in good time. She'll thank you for it and you'll not mortgage your future. Incontinence is the curse of the poor classes,' he added mysteriously.

II

Looking back over the years, I feel that I did not serve Jenny as well as she deserved; in the general, rather than sexual sense. The proper course of things would have led to our marriage two or three years later. A baby would be born a little less than nine months following our honeymoon in London – to everybody's satisfaction. I would have formally become Estate Manager for the Broleigh family.

Events certainly started that way. Who knows what Jenny herself told her family. I do know that her parents and brothers, always cordial and polite, became notably jocular. Previously, our dealings tempered familial connection with professional reserve. I would for example, accept a glass of ale or cider as we discussed farm business, but do so standing. Afterwards, to evoke the concept of a friendlier but still formal event, I was invited to tea or even Sunday luncheon. It struck me as a brilliant piece of etiquette, that 'tea' – the substantial meal of huge quantities of pies and cakes, offered about 5.30, involved only myself, Jenny and her parents with a brother or two as available. I wondered if they had any notion I had an image of my lover's lips around their indifferently proportioned organs. Sunday lunch demanded that my mother attend. Fortunately, Lord Broleigh favoured a large breakfast served at 11 a.m. followed by a ride out, much claret, sleep and supper around 9 p.m.

Jenny herself had also subtly changed. Our personal and sexual relationship continued as before; with the exception of having full congress during her periods. Following my father's advice, these encounters were supposed to conclude with my pulling out, but mostly she would say 'No Billy boy,' and pinion my buttocks with her heels. She remained adamant about cunnilingus and our occasional experiments with anal sex had been failures. 'You're just too big Billy,' was her verdict after I had grunted and she squealed for several struggling minutes. *Tant pis* I thought. She would roll over onto her back and we carried on as before.

The change was in her more public displays of affection. These were small enough. Her arm linked in mine as we walked down Molesworth Street in Wadebridge, a kiss on the cheek when I arrived at her home. The use of the term 'my Billy,' or even 'my William,' when referring to me. These terms were often accompanied with a wink, especially when she added the 'boy' to the Billy. Even to my youthful awareness, the signs were that Jenny and I were tied for life. It was a perfectly pleasant idea. Apart from a vague idea of travel to France, Italy or Greece, I had no defined longings or dreams. Winter came and went and autumn arrived again. No one seemed in a hurry to force issues. Occasionally my Uncle or Aunt would make comment about '... doing up that cottage when old Hoskin dies,' and Jenny would give me a little look whilst I tried to adopt an expression indicating indulgent if manly acquiescence.

Walter had left school. Mostly he stayed in London but his occasional return to Cornwall was marked by audible rows with his father. As effectively Estate Manager I was often witness to these. It was painful to watch my father wilt under the scorn of his heir. The issues were of course solely to do with money. Walter and I barely spoke. 'Sucking my father's estate dry?' was a usual insult, when not asking 'Is the lovely Jenny still a good fuck?'

This meant little to me other than as a jibe until the day Jenny came into the stable yard at a gallop and flung herself off her horse with a cry of 'Oh William.' She was dishevelled and very distressed. It seemed that Walter had come across or maybe laid in wait for her as she rode out. From her account he had made another and very serious attempt at rape. Between her sobs it was hard to discover the detail. I comforted her as best I could and took her back to her family. Her father and brothers stormed and roared and looked around for shotguns. I managed to persuade them that the assault had not compromised Jenny's virtue and that in any case I should, could and would deal with the issue. Jenny seemed to recover quickly. She refused to say more than she had first told me. I did not press her, but I didn't forget. Luckily for Walter he had made a hasty escape to London. I was tempted to tell Lord Broleigh, but decided to keep my own counsel.

November was a bleak month. It rained and then began to snow. Walter had returned home and had become especially awful. With the Jenny episode in mind I had one confrontation with him. It wasn't entirely satisfactory, but as he was looking down the barrels of a cocked twelve bore, both that and the threat of making a formal complaint to the local magistrates forced an uncharacteristically meek response.

His father refused point-blank to give him access to the estate finances, or to have any dealings with the tenants and businesses. So Walter would get drunk after breakfast – usually prepared by my mother to streams of abuse about the state of the eggs or kippers – and then ride off to Wadebridge or on the moors.

One day, late in the afternoon, Arthur called me into his study. 'Walter's not back. I'm worried.' I went out into the stable-yard and found Jenny waiting for me. She began to explain that the weather was too bad for our usual ride. I said, 'Walter's missing, Arthur wants me to look for him.' Walter was a reckless rider as well as drinker. Knowing his habits I called into the village pub and learned he had been in a bad mood and galloped off onto the moor. Jenny insisted on coming with me.

It was getting dark and snow had started. On the edge of the moor I saw hoof prints leading off toward the Tor we knew as Brown Willy. Well, we found Walter, if only because his horse trotted out of the gloom and whinnied in recognition of Nigger and Jenny's bay mare. Up the slope, amid a pile of peripheral stone at the base of the Tor we found my half-brother. He was a mess. One leg was twisted oddly, his brow was swollen purple and an eye was bloodied and closed. Red oozed from his ear. I went down on one knee and felt for life. His eyes opened. One of them saw me. His hand lifted feebly and rested on my wrist as if with affection. Jenny stood behind me; I could hear her breathing.

Walter made a sound. It was possibly 'Hey, hey'. It might have been 'Help me.' Jenny leaned forward and spat directly into his face. She said 'Let him die, he's an animal.' Blood trickled out of Walter's nose and the corner of his mouth, merging with the spittle. 'If you love me,' said Jenny, 'you'll kill this filth for what he did to me.' The import of her hatred did not register immediately. Then I realised that Walter's second attempt on her might have been more successful than she had admitted. Something had been communicated by the vehemence of her tone. The killing was easy to do. I held him under the chin and behind his head. I think he believed it was meant to be soothing, or maybe he heard Jenny's command. His fingers tightened on my wrist. I was thinking, 'What did he do, was it with her consent? Did she enjoy it?' No answer would have made any difference. I knelt on his chest, snowflakes settled on his bruised and bloody face and I pulled, twisted and heard his neck snap. His body went limp and some sort of sigh escaped his lips. It didn't seem very much.

Then I felt Jenny's fingers in my hair and she dragged me up and into her hot mouth that was sour with lust. 'Oh God Billy, you're a real man.' I think she would have fucked me there and then. Her hands were on my buttocks and pulling me into her. The snow fell harder and the horses stood by, tossing their heads and eager to get home.

We got Walter across his horse and took him back to the Manor. I found it strange that I felt more sympathy than anyone else did. Even our father, although much saddened seemed, in some indefinable way, relieved. Jenny could hardly stop her eyes glittering with delight despite a serious face. She waylaid me that evening as I transited between the Manor and the home farm on some administrative errand. 'I love you Billy, I know you love me too – you were so wonderful.' I stroked her hair and kissed her lightly. 'Enough said, Jenny. I'll see you in the morning.' I wondered why I had been so cool. Perhaps it was Jenny's palpable excitement at the whole event.

Not so long after the funeral of his legitimate son, Arthur Myddleton, Lord Broleigh, Baron, of Broleigh Manor in the Duchy of Cornwall had a stroke. I had been to Wadebridge in the dogcart – the estate could not afford a car. As I trotted old Hannah up the drive I saw the doctor's impressive, if noisy, Renault outside the front door. In the hall I met my mother coming down the stairs with the doctor. He looked grave and she distraught. 'A stroke' she blurted out, 'Arthur, his Lordship, has had a terrible stroke.'

Terrible it was. The poor old bugger had lost the use of most of his limbs and all his bodily functions. He could communicate only in grunts and with a rolling of eyes. Once a burly and florid six-footer, with a decent quantity of lard as befitted the middle aged landed gentry, he shrank seemingly in an instant into the pallid decrepitude of an ancient. My mother immediately took on the role of full time nurse. I assumed not merely the day-to-day detail, but the absolute control of the estate's management. After a short while, the solicitors and accountants who, as it turned out, both held the mortgages and were the executors of the estate, came to the Manor for a conference. They were surprisingly courteous and affable. We had expected to be given notice and asked to leave the house. Far from that, whilst no one mentioned our intimate connection with his Lordship, there seemed to be a tacit recognition of our unique status.

Mother's offer – almost demand, to continue the nursing responsibility was accepted with enthusiasm. In turn, I was asked if I would be content to assume formal control as estate manager, subject of course to my responsibility to the estate's executors. Only later did I realise this was rather a compliment given I was only seventeen years old. We were both offered a small salary in addition to our right to live rent-free in the house and subsist on whatever commodities we chose to produce. The terms were hardly generous and represented something of a bargain for the estate. On the other hand, they were adequate and we had a home, work and income.

The twist in the tale was that the estate was to be broken up as quickly as possible, commensurate with financial prudence. Farm rents were not very exciting whereas land values were rising and tenant farmers became increasingly interested in acquiring freeholds. The fishing, mining and quarry operations were also beyond my competence and our resources. This left only the 'home' farm, a few hundred acres mostly devoted to mixed sheep and beef and the Manor, for me to run. We had some woodland for game that I impressed our new 'landlords' with by proposing a commercial shoot. The initial meeting and subsequent encounters left me feeling quite excited by the prospects before me. Not least because I persuaded the executors that some form of motor transport was necessary and so learned to drive and cut a dash with my relatives, and of course Jenny.

She herself was duly impressed. I felt her family became slightly less warm. There was nothing tangible, but I think now, that as probable successful bidders for the farms they began to see themselves as serious landowners on the cusp of gentryhood. My mother and I on the other hand were effectively hired hands, whose tenure almost certainly ended with the death of his Lordship, their erstwhile landlord.

Moreover, whatever I might bring to the marriage, land was not part of it. With three brothers in Jenny's family alone, another male without land was not an asset. Country people are very astute about inheritance and even if my mother and I were unsure if any provision had been made in Arthur's will, her relatives would have shrewd ideas. In that matter I fear we were naïve and the executors were not going to enlighten us. Meanwhile poor mother devoted her life to her Baron and I got on with my job.

Inevitably these new circumstances affected the frequency and nature of our encounters. Our walks and rides on the moor became rarer luxuries. The abandon of our lovemaking mixed urgency with comfort. Jenny was never the clinging type, but she seemed to realise the pressures we were both now under. We had never gone in for a great deal of 'I love you' declaration. Instead, we had sexual passion and jolly camaraderie. Now, we found ourselves saying 'I do love you, you know,' on occasion, especially when we were parting for a few days. There was too, a wistfulness that infused our physical encounters and led often to our lying embraced but silent and tender in the aftermath. We never discussed the future or plans and she stopped taking my arm in Wadebridge High Street on the odd occasion we were there together. Sunday dinner stopped, partly because my mother was committed, but teas also became rarer and there was less proprietorial joshing.

So maybe it was life rather than my poor manners that took me away from Jenny. After a couple of years, with the estate reduced to its most basic elements it was clear that there was little but subsistence left. Yes, we could farm but we faced bigger competitors – not least the newly elevated yeomen of my own family. I sounded the executors on the prospects of a sale for the home farm to myself possibly, or an uncle. This was gently rejected on the grounds that it added value to the Broleigh estate and I could not afford the house as well. What finally emerged was a plan whereby they would be looking for a wealthy buyer to acquire what was left of the estate and take it over when Lord Broleigh died. They advised me that my mother would have a position during his Lordship's lifetime and in accordance with his will, a small pension after his death. My own future was in my hands.

These matters and events carried me through to 1912. It was my nineteenth birthday. I had a real decision to make. Should I struggle on as a farm manager, or tenant somewhere? How would my life shape itself as the years went on? I could see little except the round of seasons and the hard repetitions of nature's cycle. For sure, there were the rewards of family and community. Jenny would be there, increasingly surrounded by children, her haunches spreading and her fingers covered in flour as she pushed me away with an 'Honestly Billy, not now.' But I was a young man with unsatisfied ambitions. In the outside world beyond the Allen Valley there were presentiments of war, a society of elegant men and women, literature and theatre.

To be fair to myself I was honest with Jenny up to a point. We went for a walk and I said 'The farm isn't going to be mine, ever. When the old man dies, mother will be pensioned off, the estate sold and I won't have a job. I would like to marry you Jenny, I love you, but I have nothing to offer and I think your family must worry about having another man around to claim a share of what they have. I must find a new way of life. But I promise to come back for you if that's what you want.' Actually, this is not quite how I said it I am sure, but it serves. We both had a little cry if I remember and she said she understood and of course she'd wait as long as possible – an interesting caveat.

Then I went to mother and we had a long and candid conversation. She agreed with me. She tried to persuade me that Jenny and I and the family had a future, but could see how awkward it would be for me without land. She confessed herself glad I had not fathered a child and was quite gratified that her Arthur had advised me on this matter. 'If he'd taken his own advice life might have been different,' she said. It certainly would have but I chose not to tease her. Whoever had the idea, the army suggested itself as the best option. I rather think mother came up with the game plan. 'It's time you claimed your rightful name,' she pronounced. 'Your father is Arthur Myddleton, Baron Broleigh and if there was any justice you would be the Hon. William and inherit the title. That's worth a commission in any army. What's more,' she continued warming to her theme 'I shan't have my son trailing about at the beck and call of folk below his station. And that includes his uncles.'

Mother's scheme was perfect in its simplicity. Before his stroke, Arthur had been in correspondence with the Colonel of a local Regiment about a commission for Walter. On the Broleigh letterhead I wrote a letter to this gentleman. In it I explained my father's circumstance and gave the news that my elder brother had been killed in a riding accident. I expressed my desire to obtain a commission, notwithstanding reduced circumstances, and enumerated my skills as horseman, shot and my experience as a manager of men and matters. In a masterly touch of my mother's we secured the envelope with the Broleigh seal. Altogether it was a fine piece of work. We consigned it to the Royal Mail, and despite a real regret for my mother and Jenny, I recall even now, the pure frisson of anticipation about the outcome. At that moment I became William Myddleton, son of Lord Broleigh from Broleigh Manor in the Duchy of Cornwall. Perhaps I should have mentioned, the name is pronounced 'Brule', when one is in the know.

We received quite promptly, a polite but non-committal acknowledgement from the Colonel's ADC. It included a short expression of sympathy for his Lordship's misfortunes and an assurance that should the Regiment or the country need recruits my letter would be on file.

By 1912, the 'authorities' were, in their strange British way, fumbling about with preparations for something inconvenient or possibly threatening to happen abroad. True, there had long been rumblings of concern, especially in relation to Germany, but the rural public at least were not much interested. Various politicians and bits of the armed forces, notably the navy had long smelt danger. Now, the idea that 'chaps' might be needed had percolated to various bodies. It is hard to realise that in those days, not only did we still resist the idea of a serious standing army; we still relied heavily on our landed aristocracy to recruit additional forces.

At the end of that year – or maybe very early in 1913, I received a letter inviting me to attend the Army Recruitment Office in Exeter, at my convenience. It referred to the reply I had received from the Colonel the previous year. Exeter was over sixty miles 'upcountry' and involved a rather lengthy train journey. Nonetheless, this was the summons. A few weeks later, I packed a few necessaries for what I pretended would be a two-day trip but privately knew would be much longer, and had one of Jenny's brothers drive me to Camelford Station in the dogcart to catch the train. Dear Jenny, she came out to kiss me goodbye and her cheeks were wet with tears. I told her this was not goodbye, merely a scouting trip. I went through the same with my mother just before.

'Women eh?' said Jenny's brother as we trotted away. Then: 'She'll be right presently, we'll look after her.'

'You'd better.' I said. 'Or I'll come back from hell and kill you all.'

This manly exchange created a very friendly atmosphere so we parted company at the station with genuine cordiality.

III

One thing my nineteen years had failed to provide was much experience of cities – or even large towns. Truro was the most urban place I had seen, and that only once. Exeter was foreign territory and I felt an alien in it. Even the accents of the people were strange to my ears. The noise and smell of combustion engines filled the crowded streets. The colours and styles of people's apparel made me feel very much the rustic. Having found the recruiting office, I was somewhat reassured on this last point. If I felt rustic, most of the half dozen or so attendees were out and out hayseeds. The sergeant in charge was a weaselly-looking old veteran with what I later learned to be a Cockney accent. He took my letters with scant attention. A moment's perusal modified his indifference somewhat. 'Ho,' he said 'a hofficer.' 'I hope to be.' I replied politely. 'Ho do you?' he said, and to the room at large: 'This young gent'opes to be an hofficer.' Six pairs of eyes glowered at me. The sergeant handed me back my letters. With heavy irony he said 'If you wait 'ere, sir, I hexpect another hofficer of suitable rank will come to deal with you. Hin the meantime, sit down and try not to upset anyone.'

I found a seat next to a rather pleasant looking young man who seemed better dressed and less coarsely made than his companions. He gave me a brief smile and said: 'Meredith, hope to get commissioned.' In low tones we exchanged further particulars. I gave him a brief resume of my Myddleton identity, but without trying to impress. He was a very agreeable fellow. His family were originally Welsh landowners who had turned to the law in Somerset, where he attended Wellington School, and had held rank in the Officers Training Corps. He had known and detested Walter. This was a momentary worry. Luckily the age difference meant he would not have had conversations with Walter that could have complicated my enhanced identity. Nonetheless, I had to explain why I had not followed my brother to Wellington, and did so in terms of duty, decrepit estate and so forth. The whole culminating in parental illness and tragic death of sibling. Well, it wasn't so far from the truth...

Myself having neither a public school, nor officer training education I supposed his own background would surely make his commission a certainty, but he felt my connections and equestrian skills would be equally influential. In the event, we both achieved our aim. We lost touch quite quickly after basic training, but I heard bits of news. Poor Meredith had been 2nd lieutenant barely a year when he was killed; by all accounts leading the usual pointless charge over a few yards of bog, waving his revolver at German machine gunners. I know this because I was billeted with my cavalry squadron just behind the lines. One of Meredith's fellow schoolboy officers came by on his way to the field hospital with casualties on a cart and recognising my regimental badges, gave me the news. Now, as then, I give thanks that my ability with horses kept me from many of the horrors of infantry warfare.

I don't know whether our life expectancy was better – though suspect it was, but we had two great reliefs. We had more respite between attacks and the ineffable excitement of a charge or a skirmish on the back of a strong horse gave a powerful illusion of immortality. Even if immortality was a delusion, our life among the horses brought a sense of old-fashioned decency to our lives amidst the awful machinery of war.

This was a long way ahead – if not as far as we had thought. Officer or not, we recruits went through the basic training along with everyone else for at least six months. Meredith sadly, did not master the horse and so returned to the infantry. I was humbled a little to find that some of the hayseeds I had looked down on, were excellent troopers and quite my equal in the saddle. Luckily, I overcame the poor impression created on my arrival in the Exeter post and became good friends with one or two of them. My upbringing had created a man of expectation, but not a snob and so I found it easy to adapt my social stance as needed. This was indeed useful, as however competent one felt on a horse, learning to become a cavalryman was hugely demanding. Potential officers were thrown quite as easily as ordinary troopers and there was much to learn in the mastery of combat skills from horseback. In our modest West Country Yeomanry regiment we had less pretensions than more grand bodies of illustrious Dragoons, Hussars and so forth; not least because we had no ceremonial duties or traditions. Nor did we give ourselves the airs of Sandhurst 'gentlemen cadets'. We were an odd mix of regional historic custom and what shortly became known as 'pals regiments', usually under the auspices of a local aristocrat or regular regiment.

I don't think that in the end we made less competent soldiers. Given the sketchy training with which we all, regular or volunteer, were hurled into in the shambles of unprecedented battles, the Sandhurst officer was no more likely to succeed than the Cornish corporal.

Despite my pretence or maybe self-delusion that my visit to Exeter was merely a 'scouting trip', it was the end of my life as a Cornishman. By the time my war was over, all that was left of my childhood and the people who had helped me grow up, were a few affectionate, slightly sad letters from those early months. These mementos are long gone. Yes, but I was twenty - the future had come upon me, I was a cavalry officer – albeit the most junior possible, and war was imminent. Before the war happened however, Colonel Sir Warren FitzMalpas' wife did.

There is a long tradition that army life is full of lecherous women, sexually voracious and manipulative in their pursuit of gratification and influence. This 'canard' comes often from the anecdotes of the colonial era. The truth is more modest, but nonetheless recognisable. The Army is a man's world. It is extraordinarily close-knit.

Women who choose to become part of it and thrive are those who must be highly competent in their desire and ability to manage relationships with men. Possibly even, they seek out the heady sense of adventure that attends association among the military. Those who might dispute this should read almost any 'Great Romantic Novel' of the past two hundred years.

So the Army is indeed sexually charged. Its women face the necessity to form and break relations at the behest of circumstance. Their menfolk appear and disappear, perhaps forever, quite abruptly. These same menfolk often enjoy experiences and connections of extraordinary intimacy with their fellows denied to 'the wife at home'. We must also acknowledge the possibility of such social machismo failing to deliver the fantasised promise at closer quarters, leading to female discontents.

As it happens, Lady Julia FitzMalpas was a true military daughter and wife. Her Papa was a General and had a decent Boer War but sadly, died of typhoid at Mafeking. Her husband had been a Captain in her father's Regiment and so she had the luck – if that is the word, to be born and married into the life. Her chap also inherited a title, which helps the career, no end.

Poor, dear Julia, there you were, sprawled on your marital bed, my Commanding Officer's sacred territory. Your pretty little bottom – striped red from the vigorous horsewhipping you often demanded, was lifted and as I worked my cock up your rectum you were shouting 'Yes, bugger me, bugger me, bugger me.' Possibly you represented my lost and unfulfilled desires for Jenny – was the shared initial some strange trigger to my desire? In this memorable and indescribable sexual experience, love, hate and regret commingled. The hours we spent together drinking gin, in the ritual dance of the regimental calendar, when we shared our personal reminiscences, as we met thrillingly at some dangerous rendezvous: well, they were all remembered as I shoved my cock into your arse for that last time. That you thrashed around and said many grossly obscene things gave me great joy. Men make a serious mistake if they fail to comprehend the desires of women and ensure their satisfaction. Yours dear lady, were notably abandoned and most often involved rapine by squadrons of impossibly hung cavalrymen.

As a Regiment we got along quite well together. The NCOs were a decent lot. Even my cockney sergeant turned out to be perfectly pleasant to deal with. In fact it was he who first warned me about Julia and her accomplice, Lieutenant Grant the Colonel's ADC. This trio was responsible for the tensions that slightly undermined our happy band of brothers. Nothing can remain secret in a barracks, so it wasn't very surprising to me shortly before our passing out parade that my sergeant approached me in the bar of a pub we frequented in Exeter on leave days. He lifted his glass to my health and said 'I think you should know Mr Myddleton, that Lady FitzMalpas has an eye for young troopers and especially hofficers. Hunfortunately so does Lieutenant Grant.' He went on: 'I mention this only since hit 'as been remarked that you appear to 'ave a well developed personal weapon.' I laughed, but his warning was well meant and timely.

The predilections of Lady F were the subject of ribald, if sotto voce jokes although no one claimed personal experience. Grant's liking for handsome young troopers was also known. The Colonel's situation was sometimes speculated on. Was he complaisant, complicit or carelessly ignorant? General opinion was, that Grant and the Lady were each other's panders and it did not do to fail them. There were several stories of young hopefuls who had found their lives a misery and careers foreshortened following a refusal of service or debacle in execution. This suggested a less than honourable role for our senior officer as instrument of the will of others. He was not a very nice man and something of a bully. I had no trouble with him at any point; due I am sure to his perception of my social standing. Poor Meredith however, had his life made miserable by the jibes and critiques he seemed singled out to bear. Hardly a Mess Night passed without FitzMalpas's cruel commentaries on Meredith's shortcomings and Welsh background.

I, on the other hand, was treated with as much courtesy as could be expected between a Colonel and an aspiring subaltern. I think he also approved my horsemanship and capabilities with sword and pistol. Whatever the case, shortly after my Commission came through Grant appeared as emissary with an invitation to dine '*intime*' with Sir Warren and Lady FitzMalpas. I quite liked Grant. He was noticeably effete and I played up to it by occasionally quoting Ovid to him. Relatively early in our acquaintance he made some remark, rather wistfully I recall, along the lines of 'I expect you are a lady's man...' I concurred with a laugh saying 'procul hinc severae', and he took it well. His company was worth having, as he was sharply witty and well read; nor is it a bad thing to keep in with your Colonel's ADC.

I had seen Lady Julia previously, only at a distance. She quite liked to come and watch our training in the practice ring of the barracks. She would her clap her hands at something well done or make a moue for a clumsiness. She had a good seat on a horse herself, side saddle of course; and I had noticed her coming and going from outings on Dartmoor when she sometimes diverted to the barracks for purposes of her own. She had also attended the regimental sports day and I remarked on her special attention to the boxing matches; which caused her visible excitement.

The FitzMalpas' personal quarters were some three miles from our barracks in a large house in the Bovey Tracey direction. I rode over in my dress uniform and arrived thank God, just before it started to rain. Grant was in the library and he poured me a sherry. We chattered amiably for a quarter of an hour or so until the door opened and FitzMalpas came in with his wife. I think it was lust at first sight for both she and I. Though I had been without sex for over six months, the town tarts did not appeal and I was still pining a bit for Jenny. The occasional wank doesn't count. It is not to my credit to admit the appearance of Julia rather obscured erotic memories of my cousin.

Lady FitzMalpas was one of those petite girls with small features and boyish figures who often exude a particularly powerful, even dangerous sexuality. Her hair was fair and done in a chignon. Her dress fashionable, but I observed that her body seemed to move inside it rather than it conforming to her motion. Her eyes were somewhat slanted, green and very catlike, her nose pointed and uptilted. Her mouth, at first sight quite small, revealed as she spoke a sensual shape, sharp little teeth and a tongue that she used frequently to moisten her lips. She greeted me in a low voice, but looked at me very directly and appraisingly. I clicked my heels and bent over the gloved hand she offered. I caught an exotic scent, later discovered to be patchouli.

Dinner was a remarkably enjoyable social event. Colonel F was on good form; jovial, quite interesting in his anecdotes and observations. Julia proved herself well informed about military matters and of decided opinions in relation to international affairs. She offered the view that whilst it had been good to reach the Entente Cordiale, the Frogs were unreliable allies and it was a great shame we had fallen out with the Prussians. Her husband listened indulgently and grunted 'Something in what you say m'dear, but don't say it in front of the politicos next week.' This was in reference to a forthcoming visit by a junior minister at the War Department. My own contribution was to be a good listener and to amuse the company with tales from deepest Cornwall.

FitzMalpas had known my father many years previously and very briefly when they were engaged in some scheme to ensure the election of a favoured local Tory. He expressed sympathy for Lord Broleigh's illness, and even more for the death of my brother. 'I hadn't realised he had two sons.' He observed. 'I don't think he quite got over my mother's death giving birth to me.' I said in a sombre voice. The gathering looked into its soup. 'Quite, most sad, poor show all round,' said our host. I successfully fielded a couple of leading comments about inheritance.

At this point I felt Julia's foot pressed on mine as she lifted our spirits with a teasing remark about how she had heard of the passionate nature of Celtic girls. I laughingly indicated that she was right and she smiled and her tongue flickered between the sharp white teeth. Colonel F snorted and said: 'Not the bloody Welsh I think, all chapel and hymns.'

Julia withdrew after dinner - good Devon beef and a generous supply of claret - and we three men settled down with the Stilton, port and brandy. Our talk was mainly about the prospects for war and the likely fate of the regiment. In truth we were really not a proper regiment, rather a battalion of volunteers with a few regulars left over from the Boer and Afghan wars. The noble peer who had originally given his name to our corps was long dead. In addition, less than half our number were qualified as mounted troops and were light horse rather than heavy and so Hussars rather than Dragoons; the rest being straightforward light infantry. FitzMalpas thought it entirely likely we would be broken up on deployment with the cavalry joining an appropriate regiment and the infantry amalgamating with the Devon & Cornwalls, or even the Wessex. 'Heaven forbid they end up with the Welch,' he remarked. Quite why he so loathed the Welsh nation was never clear to me. 'How d'you feel about the war?' he asked me. 'Bad do,' I replied 'but we can't let the Kaiser and his cronies get away with it.' He concurred.

Eventually, Julia put her head round the door to remind the Colonel he had an early start. I bade everyone farewell and Julia gave me her hand and I felt her thumb caress my fingertips. It wasn't the cold that made me shiver slightly as I rode back to my quarters.

A few days later, Grant appeared in the Mess and handed me an envelope. 'It's an invitation,' he said 'or rather, a request.' I opened the envelope. In a neat but schoolgirl hand on the Colonel's notepaper Lady F had written: 'Dear Lt Myddleton, the Colonel and I shall be greatly obliged if you will escort me on a ride into the moors tomorrow from 0900hrs. Lt. Grant assures me this will not conflict with your present duties.' It was signed Julia FitzMalpas.

I said to Grant 'Of course, should I write a reply?'

'No, I'll tell her.' He took my arm, and leaning toward me said softly 'It was the Ovid that made me recommend you. I think I was very unselfish. Don't be surprised by anything and be careful dear boy.' In my room that night I pondered a letter from my mother.

I had made just one trip home, a week or two earlier and just after I received my commission. It was not very successful. My mother was having a difficult time with Arthur and my visit to Jenny was circumscribed by the presence of brothers and parents. It was as if the family had closed ranks to shut me out. Even Jenny showed little inclination to find a private moment for us. We all exchanged uneasy pleasantries, my uniform was admired and I returned early to the Manor. I was sitting in the library about to get drunk. Then I heard Jenny's tap on the window. I let her in. She was breathless and clearly upset. I held her, making soothing sounds as with a small child. Eventually calmed, she accepted a proffered brandy. Light returned to her eyes. 'It was just horrible today,' she said. Then, 'I've so missed you Billy, and my Billy boy,' she added smiling shyly. The upshot was that one hungry kiss later, her skirts were up, her drawers off and she was on her back on the rug. Her cunt was hot and wet and she bucked up to meet me. Her fingers dug into my back and she swore in my ear 'Fuck it to me, Billy fuck it to me.' I had never known her so wild. After a short while her breathing became frantic 'Now, oh now, shoot me, give it to me.' Finished, she held me down on her with her hands on my buttocks and her knees drawn far up so I could feel my cock pressed to the end of her cunt. Her tongue caressed my ear and she whispered 'Good Billy boy, very good.'

Then, abruptly, she pushed me from her, produced a handkerchief from her skirt pocket and stuffed it between her legs and pulled up her drawers. I reclothed myself. She looked into my eyes and said softly 'I'll never not love you Billy.' I could think of nothing to say. 'Nor I,' were the only two words I could speak. The next thing I remember was being alone again. So I finished off the brandy.

Next morning I had a visit from her eldest brother. I had a hangover and was not at my sharpest. Without many preambles John said 'We all know that you and Jenny had an understanding, but it's only fair to get things clear.' I agreed. He continued 'The fact of it is James Corey from St. Manion has been visiting. Jenny and he get on and he's going to come into a fine farm. We all think well of you Billy and now you're an officer I expect you'll make a good life but we're thinking there needs to be an engagement so it's all on a proper footing.'

He stopped, breathing a little heavily. This speech had been an effort and he avoided my eyes. 'Fair enough.' I said. 'What does Jenny think?' He looked at me defiantly. 'She thinks same as us, else I wouldn't be here and she would.' Hungover or not, the situation and its resolution was quite obvious to me. 'There's a war coming,' I said. 'Jenny's future is the most important thing. You must do what's best for her and the family.' There was a silence. 'I'll write her a letter.' I said.

John stuck his hand out awkwardly. 'Thanks Billy.'

I went into the library and wrote my farewell letter to Jenny. If a little formal and cold, it was not merely to spare her feelings. Despite her last clandestine visit, deep down I think I still suspected her of deception in the matter of her rape by Walter. I was also angry she had not the courage to tell me of James Corey herself. Both emotions were ignoble but the alternatives were either to make her feel bad through an over emotional farewell, or to become engaged. I signed it, rather spitefully in retrospect, 'Your ever fond cousin William'. Then I packed my small valise, said goodbye to my mother and walked the six miles to the station.

On the same day as Julia's invitation, mother's letter arrived. It was a curious mix of regret and reproach. Jenny had been upset. She was upset. It seemed to me that these women were very inconsistent. Did they want me married or not? Why should I be married in any case? I now had a career in the army, as an officer. A few large brandies in the Mess restored my sense of purpose. I wrote a rather silly letter to my mother making pompous reference to '...Getting on with the affairs of men.' My ride with Julia must have been in mind.

Next morning, I showered, dressed myself in my best civilians and went out into the yard to saddle my horse. Sadly, I had been unable to bring Nigger with me from Cornwall. The estate trustees had offered me other mounts, but the stallion was too well bred and valuable in stud to be let go. Here, the regimental farrier with whom I formed a close understanding, had found me a spirited and delightful gelding, also black but with a white blaze on his forehead whom I christened Minstrel. The two of us formed a partnership that would take us through my war service until my capture and save my life more than once. Odd as it may seem, if tears come to my eyes when I think of the past, it is Minstrel's memory that brings them. Animals have their own magic. Horses are very special. They have strength of will and body. They are noble of bearing. To win their confidence and affection is to achieve much. Minstrel's morning snort of welcome and the feel of his muzzle on my cheek as we greeted each other meant as much to me as the smile or kiss of any woman, well, almost.

Nonetheless on this spring morning in 1914, the smile that Julia FitzMalpas gave me when we met outside the barracks held its own promise. She rode an Arab, smaller than Minstrel, but powerful and lively. It seemed almost too big for her slight frame. Her command of her mount was clear, even as we trotted gently through the byways toward the moors. She was very congenial and approved Minstrel and my evident rapport with my animal. Horse matters provided comfortable discourse until we reached the open country. I confessed relative ignorance of Dartmoor, which pleased her and with a cry of 'Follow me,' set heels to her horse and was off at a gallop. Minstrel was eager to follow, so we kept pace a little behind and went high and deep across the wild terrain. Even as a Cornishman I had to acknowledge Dartmoor's grandeur – although I still felt Bodmin Moor held greater magic with its stone circles, ancient settlements and Celtic ghosts.

After some time of galloping, trotting, picking our way through rocks and bogs, we arrived mid morning, at a small tor. Julia jumped down and sprawled on a rock, face turned to the sun exclaiming, 'Oh, this is such fun, how free one feels.' She was quite right, one did. The choice for men in such situations – other than leaping on the girl with grunts indicating endearment with intent, is either to say in a soothing but manly way 'Oh yes, yes indeed,' or to quote a decent piece of poetry. Out of some inspiration, I reached for a bizarre piece of Shelley and sitting down nonchalantly beside her responded:

" Cease, cease - for such wild lessons madmen learn

Thus to be lost, and thus to sink and die

Perchance were death indeed!

– Constantia turn, in thy dark eyes a power like light doth lie."

She sat up and said 'That's awfully good Lieutenant Myddleton. Except my eyes aren't dark.'

I said, 'I know that, they are the most fantastic greeny-yellow cat's eyes, but they hold dark secrets.'

'Are you a madman seeking wild lessons, William?'

'Why else be a cavalryman in the age of machine guns?'

'I have a reputation you know.'

'That is no concern of mine.'

She sighed, lay back on her rock, head cradled in her hands, a dreamy look on her face. 'William, I am thirty years old and my husband rather older and frankly, though he is indulgent to me and less beastly than his troops suppose, he is utterly uninterested in sex. I think he possibly has a yearning for Captain Grant or something younger of the sort. He does however value his dignity. If you are to do more than follow me round on a horse and recite poetry you would do well to remember that.'

To receive an explicit invitation to fuck your commanding officer's wife is a matter of interest; 'Bien entendu,' as my French friends would say.

I searched for a suitable response and said: 'I'm at your command, madam.'

Still in the same dreamy voice, eyes closed, she replied: 'Take down your britches and show me if what I've heard is true.'

Without doubt, the general sexual climate of the late twentieth century is open to and possibly determined by, the overt physical demands of women. This does not mean that back then, as is evident, that women were not able to declare and fulfil their lusts – albeit with some constraints in order to avoid discovery by hostile third parties.

So I stood up and aware of Julia's heavy lidded gaze released my tool from its confinement. It had been fairly interested by her Ladyship's remarks anyway, so that by the time I had it '*en plein air*' it was quite enthused.

'Mmm, I think he will do very well,' was Julia's verdict. Then she said: 'Let's see how well he'll ride.'

In a few practised movements she had stripped off her outer garments, lowered her underwear and in a quite pragmatic manner, knelt in the mossy bed of the ground about her rock, presented her bottom to me like a mare on heat.

Every cunt like every cock has its own character. Hers had a neatness and sensuality, that reflected her face, yet the texture, colours and odour of the hothouse. Her buttocks were those of a boy – except for the curves that only a woman's hips provide. I held those enticing orbs apart and presented arms to the anemone mouth of her wet slit. 'Go on Lieutenant Myddleton' she demanded, 'fuck me.' So I did.

Unlike our later encounters, she said little during the proceeding. That she had a climax is certain. The body's movement tells you this, even if the words can be simulated. If it doesn't one has no business making love to women. This was definitely a test. I waited until her spasms had diminished and then thrust forcefully, allowing my cock to pulse out its release deep inside her. This caused her to sigh and reach her hand under her body to feel my balls. I took my weight off her but kept us joined until she indicated it was time for me to withdraw. Her fingers escorted the exit of my prick from her cunt in an affectionate sort of way. I had no thought of her possible pregnancy. Her cunt – only my second, had been an interesting contrast to Jenny's in some hard to define sense - leaner and more voracious if less rich and generous. We lay on the rock for a while, breathing deeply; the sun and breeze competing for our comfort, our naked loins still exposed. Our horses grazed companionably nearby.

'I have been a very naughty girl.' Julia suddenly remarked. She rolled onto her stomach and sighed: 'You must punish me. My crop is just beside you.'

I struggled to stand up, pulling at my britches. 'No, leave them off, I deserve to be beaten and fucked.' Julia's voice was harsh with command and supplication. There is objectively, little dignity in the sexual games we play. I hopped out of my lower garments and found the riding crop. Julia lay prone, legs slightly apart, her twat still wet and with a little froth and juice around the lips and fur. The sight prompted me to toy with her. I laid the crop on her spine and drew it down, so the leather loop stroked between her buttocks, over her anus and along the cleft of her vulva. She shuddered. To beat a woman had never been much of a fantasy for me but I took a tentative stroke, then a second more confidently. The quiver, the moan, the simple beauty of the female form in willing submission was, I must confess, thrilling.

We went on with this charade for some while. She urged me to greater force and her buttocks grew more and more lined and reddened with the blows of loop and shaft as she heaved her body up to meet my whip. Her cries of pain or pleasure disturbed the horses, which whinnied in disquiet. Their concern communicated to her and with a gasp, she subsided, murmuring 'Thank you, enough, I am contrite.' For myself, I had regained an erection – lost for a while as I concentrated on this strange new role and the breeze cooled my balls. She looked up at me with a dulcet gaze I learned was a consequence only of her having been conquered. Her fingers reached to stroke my cock. 'Wank off William, so I can watch.'

I doubt any man will rebuke me. I said: 'No Julia, get back on your belly, I am going to fuck you again.' Her green eyes glowed and her tongue snaked out. 'Oh you dreadful man, you brute, you will hang for what you will do to me. Rape, buggery even, you will sodomise me you swine and I deserve every thrust.'

Buttocks up, her arsehole wet from sperm and her own juices, Julia was both an easy and accomplished conquest. As my cock worked its slithery passage into her receptive sphincter we exchanged stimulating badinage. It was much along the lines of 'Oh fuck me you bugger' and 'You love it you fucking whore.' More caring sentiments were blasphemously expressed as: 'Christ I love you, you beautiful man' and 'God Julia, you are the most desirable woman.' I have no idea what Julia felt at the climax. My penis was deep into her rectum, she was sobbing 'Oh you fucking bastard.' I shot everything in one huge moment, she collapsed and so did I. The horses grazed calmly and seemed to have accepted the situation. Our brief affair provided a pleasurable education for me and I hope genuine reward for her.

There you are. A bastard Cornish boy is now a Cavalry officer possessed of a noble name, in the favour of Colonels and their wives. Within six months his cock won't be in a pretty woman's cunt, it will be shrivelled in his britches as he charges the guns of the enemy.

IV

Speaking of which, life was not all flogging and fucking Julia. We did much serious training, largely wheeling and charging in the prescribed historic manner; waving our sabres and dashing at dummies with our lances – though we weren't Lancers specifically and the British army wisely soon abandoned this antiquated device. Unlike the French, Germans and Poles. It occurred to me that in a war where machine guns and concrete fortifications were likely to be the norm, cavalry warfare of the old style would be somewhat anachronistic. I raised this one night in the Mess. The Colonel 'humphed.' 'Haig would disagree' he said. 'The Cavalry's job is to exploit the confusion of bombardment and support infantry attack.'

Our adjutant, a Captain Maynard spoke up and said he thought I had a good point. He spoke with the authority of a man who has seen action. 'The Hun isn't the Boer, the equipment is different and what's more the terrain of Northern Europe is not the veldt. Frankly, I think the coming war will test mobility to the limit. What there is must come from motorised movement.'

He also mentioned that he had been impressed by witnessing a flypast of aeroplanes. He was convinced that war would be mechanised. This response carried weight and I was able to advance my theory about light cavalry being used much more to harass, skirmish and behave in fact more like the Boers had – as highly mobile guerrillas. I pointed out that Dartmoor and surrounds had interesting features to exercise in this way. Bogs, walls, stands of trees and so forth. Pompous old cuckold he might have been, but Colonel FitzMalpas wasn't stupid. 'Very well,' he conceded at the end of our discussion, 'let's try your and Maynard's ideas out.'

I was delegated to evolve a training programme. The Colonel and Maynard got the cooperation of the Devon & Cornwall Light Infantry based in Okehampton and we ran three or four weeks of exercises. There were some veterans of the Boer war, and they were of great help. The whole thing went well. Our chaps loved being guerrillas and the Boer war veterans had fun too, replaying battles with the old enemy.

In consequence of this success I won an early promotion to full Lieutenant and command of a squadron. It also won me more favour with the Colonel and hence even better access to Julia. My last coup was to find a trooper for Grant to play with. He was a pretty boy from Teignmouth way and I found him one day in the stables, sucking off a lance corporal. I told the kid to report to Grant and warned the corporal he would lose his stripe if I heard any more of this beastliness. A few days later in the Mess, Grant sidled up and whispered 'He's a really charming young man, awfully good of you Myddleton.' My reward was Grant becoming a more than helpful go-between, in making assignations with Julia.

The weather that spring was as delightful as the political and international scene was stormy. The army was perfectly sure that war was on its way. Matters military kept us busy and gave greater urgency and risk to Julia and my affair. In fact, I am surprised rumour of it did not get back to the Colonel since it was probably common gossip in the Mess and beyond. Luckily, in early June, the Colonel was summoned to London to confer at the War Office. The morning of his departure Grant alerted me, and in the evening I was in my mistress's bedroom stripped naked and about to tie her to the bedposts prior to the dose of beating and buggery she so much liked.

Julia had two other foibles. She would not kiss me and she would not engage in oral sex of any sort. The kissing I could cope with, but the oral sex, or lack of it, was a disadvantage. At least Jenny had loved my cock in her mouth.

This night, I determined to show her what she – or to be honest, I – was missing. Her bed – the marital bed, was a good old-fashioned four-poster. We enacted our playlet; she knelt at the foot of the bed, with cries of 'Oh you brute, sodomise me if you must with your great thing.' It nearly made me laugh listening to these quaint vulgarities of lust. Later, before learning the languages, the expletives of foreign girls were much more arousing simply because the specific meaning was unknown, if easily guessed. That said, ladies of good breeding who talk dirty are always of appeal. It's not the dirty talk, so much as the loss of control combined with the refined accent that excites.

Julia stretched her arms out on either side so that I could tie her wrists to the posts. In this position, her chest supported on the bed, I could spank and roger her at will. She did look charming I must say. Her neat little tits, the nipples already engorging, her slender but shapely hips and between the spread and taut thighs, the swell of vulva and suffusion of her cunt lips. I took her hairbrush and with an oath of 'Cuckold me would you? Slut, bitch!' in some imitation of Colonel F's tones, began the pleasant task of bringing a glow to the ivory orbs of her bum.

When she had reached a state of pleading excitement, instead of plunging my cock into the orifice of choice, I took her by the hips, tucked her thighs under my arms and upended her. She shrieked with astonishment and began to struggle. Although a strong girl, her frame was small and slender whilst I was a very fit hussar of over six foot. Adjusting position and grip for maximum comfort I brought my face and her hot little slit within grappling distance. She writhed her torso and called me a fucking bastard who would be shot for what I was doing. 'Yes dear,' I replied and began to guzzle her. It was like consuming a bowl of warm oysters. My nose pressed into her little bumhole, my tongue dived into the tunnel of her cunt, my lips gathered in the flesh of her vulva. I love the taste and texture of a woman on heat. Soon enough her shrieks of protest turned to moans of pleasure and whispers of entreaty to go on.

I became aware that my cock was rigid with lust and swayed very close to her face. A small adjustment in grip so that I was hugging her round the waist, allowed my member to come within reach of her mouth. I moved my hips to allow the erect muscle to slap her cheeks. It occurred to me she might bite it off but it seemed worth the risk. She took the bait. I felt her lips on my glans, then her sharp teeth round Billy boy's neck. In this manner she very expertly pleasured me whilst I paid full attention to all her most sensitive places. Sensing she was near orgasm I allowed my own climax to follow its natural course. Her moans and leg waving increased and mingled with choking sounds as my semen spurted into her throat. She was however in the throes of her climax and we gulped down each other's juices with enthusiasm.

When I released her from her bondage, I expected either rebuke or some form of post-coital relapse. Instead, as I stood over her, she grabbed my wrists, pulled me down on top of her, rolled me over and ended up astride me. 'No one has ever, ever done that to me,' she said fiercely. I could see a froth of semen at the corners of her lips. Then she laughed, leaned forward and kissed me intensely, her mouth almost painfully hard on mine, her tongue pushing deep. Mingled with her saliva and the taste of her juice were the texture and flavour of my sperm. The bitch was disgorging it back to me! How witty, how just, I thought and holding her head between my hands cheerfully returned her kiss.

Later, we sat in the Colonel's study and drank his Napoleon brandy. She had on only a peignoir and I was in the Colonel's best silk dressing gown. We were taking an awful risk. On the other hand we had a genuinely stimulating conversation – mostly about the forthcoming war; but also about the Suffragettes for whose ambitions she had great sympathy. I liked her at that moment, more than at any other. She was intelligent, funny and deserved better than Colonel FitzMalpas. Slightly drunk, we returned to the bedroom where she made me put on her peignoir – it barely fitted around my shoulders; she herself wore nothing but my boots. We looked ridiculous but it felt hugely sensual at the same time, perhaps through some hint of sexual transgression. I gave her a thorough and affectionate buggering.

Julia spent more and more time in London. Then in the autumn of 1913 she left Exeter for good. Grant gave me an envelope. 'Lady Julia was very fond of you,' he said. In the envelope was a banker's draft for two hundred guineas. The note with it read simply 'to Lieutenant Myddleton, with gratitude for your company and best wishes.' Well, the money was very agreeable and would settle my mess bills, dress uniform and Minstrel's cost. I supposed I was piqued by her casual dismissal but I realised there was little else I could have expected.

Real war was not far away. Franz-Ferdinand met his fate in Sarajevo. Various political manoeuvres ensued; but we didn't believe anything other than the series of declarations of war between Germany and assorted foreigners. In the Mess, whatever the foreign secretary's hopes about conferences and diplomacy, to guarantee Belgium was to guarantee war for us British and indeed, our Empire.

This was duly declared, as we all know, on August 4th 1914. We hung about as the preliminaries got underway. Luckily, as a perceived 'almost regular', with a squadron of acceptably trained cavalry to look after, I did not have to deal with the problem of the well-meaning fools who rushed to become volunteer cannon fodder. Eventually we were given our movement orders that we were to entrain for one of the Channel ports. The exact one was not revealed to us ostensibly for security reasons, but maybe because they didn't know. In the end it turned out, for some unknown reason to be Weymouth, but we had a jolly few weeks in London since our lines were on Putney Heath.

I have to say that throughout the War – as I experienced it, we were all mostly ignorant about events outside our own small sphere, or as derived randomly from gossip. I was comforted decades later to read a famous British general of the Second War, admitting the same thing from his elevated perspective. At this juncture I recall there was some concern about the British Expeditionary Force having a rough time and I know that despite propaganda, the mood was increasingly dour.

Just before Christmas 1914, our Movement Orders came through and we began the process of dismantling our lines preparatory to the march out. The months without Julia had largely been occupied by regimental affairs. But then I had a sudden but bitterly poignant resurrection of regret at my treatment of Jenny and my mother. I sat down with a bottle of port and struggled to write both those marvellous women a suitable letter of contrition and love. By the time I had concluded and sealed the missives it was gone midnight and at least two bottles of port had evaporated. I doubt either bottle produced, or letter said much of value. There was apology and vague hints at restitution. I went across to the barracks post box but on an impulse called in first to the stables to see Minstrel. He greeted me, with a soft snort and nod of the head. I put my arms round his neck, leaning my cheek into the strong muscle and silky hide. He lowered his head and suffered me to cry in his dignified and uncritical presence. Then I went back to my room and burned the letters in the grate. Fuck it all.

We can never know the future, but in my defence I must

again stress a belief that mine did not lie in Cornwall as a family farmer. Many years later, during the Second World War, in fact, I met in a bar, a WREN from Cornwall who knew Jenny as 'Auntie'. Judicious cross-questioning and declaration of some local knowledge revealed that Jenny had nursed her grief for her vanished lover for only a little while. She became engaged to James Corey and quickly had the first of several children. The marriage was a happy one. Well, that is always good to know. Poor mother's fate I knew about; but then, at least she never had to face loss of home and poverty.

The Authorities may plead exigencies of war, but my own thought is they haven't a clue. I offer the whole of World War One as primary evidence. Two days before Christmas, we marched out to some obscure camp up-country, in which we would merely replicate our present routines. Apart from sobbing wives, camp followers, publicans and so forth; there were some sniffles and growls among the ranks, whose hopes of one last Festive leave in familiar if not familial territory, had been dashed. For myself, it was a moment of huge relief. I had no Julia to amuse. I was freed from the burden of dealing with any more visits to Cornwall and the difficult combination of love and reproach women manage so effectively.

We secured the horses in their quarters on the special train and ourselves ditto. People waved their handkerchiefs but we paid little attention. We were on our way to war in a strange world across the English Channel. Much as our ancestors had done with similar reluctance, for centuries past. There might have been a brief moment of enthusiasm as a result of some well-reported account of Hunnish atrocity. However, despite the general middle class and city mob jingoism, we Westcountryfolk never too eagerly subscribed to the causes of our leaders. Foreigners were best left to their own devices whilst we got on with the seasons' demands.

Chapter 2

The Minstrel Boy
to the War Has Gone

The winter of 1914/15 was a miserable one. We fooled around on Salisbury Plain in a holding camp, living mostly under canvas until about March. There was a requisitioned semi-derelict manor house as a Mess for officers; and as cavalry we at least had barns as stables for the horses. I spent more nights in the relative warmth with Minstrel than I did in the draughty and leaking attic that was my quarter. Then we were shipped up to Putney on the edge of London. Accommodation was even worse as we were in tents, but the weather had improved and there were public houses and theatres to hand.

There were also tarts; but with respect to that fine breed of girls I never fancied a dose of clap. It might be thought that a handsome cavalry officer would be an honoured guest in any drawing room or even boudoir. Sadly not, the war was not going well and the girls – especially the pretty ones, fresh from their pre-War Suffragetting, in various ways made it clear that our place was across the channel. The few invitations we received were usually to the salons of twittering spinsters who had organised knitting groups for 'comforts.'

Eventually, we entrained again and found ourselves in Weymouth. Colonel FitzMalpas was not with us. He had acquired or been posted to a staff job in London and took Grant with him. For all I know Grant took his little trooper too, for I never saw the boy again. The benefit of losing the despised FitzMalpas was that Captain Maynard had been made up to Major and was now, effectively if temporarily, our CO. In Weymouth, he took me out for a drink one night and confided that he thought it likely we would be absorbed along with other Yeomanry units into a Division in Northern France, probably near the Belgian border. He was gloomy about the war, which had become bogged down in the trenches. Not only the French plan (the famous Plan XII) to attack Germany had gone astray. The Schlieffen Plan of invasion had also, after early success, been stalled. The 'race for the sea' had turned into the historically familiar and appalling contest of endurance.

In his view, the role for cavalry was now very dubious. Horses were regarded mostly as decreasingly useful substitutes for motorised transport. He had even heard of cavalry being dismounted and given bicycles. With the armies dug in for miles across a terrain of shell holes and barbed wire, the idea of an effective mounted attack was ludicrous. Even our guerrilla role looked problematic. Such adumbrations had at least the effect of preparing me for the worst. Maynard's briefing was also the last time I had a coherent idea of the strategic picture until a couple of years later. He was more encouraging in a morbid way about my, and his, chances of rapid promotion. All officers at the front were being killed or wounded in numbers. 'Keep yourself in good odour and you will get on,' he observed as we made our way back to our billet. I reflected that staying alive was the essential trick.

We lurked about in Weymouth for a few weeks. The sojourn was made bearable by there being decent riding country to hand so I kept my squadron, men and horses, fit with extended gallops and small exercises on the Dorset Downs. We finally embarked on a scruffy transport into which the horses had to be loaded by harness and crane. Minstrel endured uncomplaining as always. I stayed as close as possible during the entire process and made sure to visit him several times in the miserable hours we spent rolling around the Channel. I should comment that not only did I love my horse, as any man of sensibility would cherish their animal; I loved him as my companion. In this harsh – to be harsher, world a man's horse represented the softer, more homely virtues alongside the utilitarian ones necessary for survival. There is a bond of mutual support and dependence. There is too, the simple sensual need for someone or some thing around which to put ones arms, which smells of life. I knew many soldiers who adopted dogs, cats, pigeons and rats in their pilgrimage through battle.

The voyage was not pleasant. It was late April and the Channel was whipped up by strong winds. At that time, submarines were not a recognised danger and we all supposed the Royal Navy – in our case represented by a noisome and ancient coal-fired vessel with a very small gun, would protect us against any assault by the German equivalent. Quite why we had to begin our voyage to Boulogne from Weymouth, when other ports might be suggested as nearer, remains a mystery of the military planners' arcane craft. Eventually, in a dank dawn, we disembarked at Boulogne and after more hours milling around as our 'receiving authority' pulled itself together, were sent off to Etaples in a mixed convoy. This moved slowly enough for the horse-borne to easily keep pace with the lorries.

As the biggest clearing-house for the British Army in France and with a terrible reputation, it is surprising Etaples functioned at all. In such situations, the subaltern begins to fully earn the trust his men should have in him. Our officer complement was slender. Other than Maynard the true regular and myself now formally secured as such having joined and earned my commission 'before the War', all our officers were Officer Training Corps types from University or very often, school. There were few trained cavalrymen among them. Maynard's orders were sketchy and in truth only carried us to this point. He beetled off to find a senior officer who might sponsor us. I drew on my early days on the Broleigh estate to suborn farriers, influential NCOs and friendly officers of equal rank to our cause.

Among the first helpful people I came across was an advance guard of Indian Hussars. They were a congenial group and their Colonel – old Indian Army, and his Subaldar, gave me a friendly welcome and briefing. There was a big attack going on at Ypres and their troop had been instructed to ride up in support. He invited me to bring my two squadrons of cavalry over to their lines where we could share facilities. In any event, since they would only be with us for a day or so longer, we could take over their quarters by right of occupation. These were hardly more than a row of tents and some tethering posts; but at least there was feed and established lines of contact with the relevant quartermaster. I introduced myself to him also and found he was a fellow west countryman, albeit a Devonian, which helped in these foreign parts.

I rode over to Divisional HQ and reported to Maynard. He looked down in the mouth. I told him we'd found quarters and he replied 'Well done Myddleton. I'm afraid you'll have to take command of both squadrons. I have orders to get our infantry up to Ypres within a day. They don't need cavalry, but you'll be deployed elsewhere shortly.' I explained further about the Indian hussars. He shrugged 'That's nothing to do with me but I'm a little concerned that you are under rank for two squadrons.' The upshot was he saw his Divisional Commander and had me posted acting temporary Captain. The brevet and its insignia were easier to get than food, being handed out by an adjutant on the spot, together with a hurriedly signed form designed for the purpose. This told me a good deal about the casualty rates, the force of necessity and Major Maynard's kindness. I also received authority to make up a suitable number of NCOs to help manage my enhanced command; with the usual caveats about channels and confirmations. I made sure I had a stock of stripes though.

Maynard vanished from my life and I returned to my unit. The troopers cheered ironically when told the news; but the new NCOs were pleased and assured me they wouldn't let me down. 'What next?' one of them asked. 'We wait,' was the reply.

A few days later, just as we had become settled, organised and were beginning to become involved in the embryo football teams, social events and so on that grow from large communities like ours my orders arrived. We were to proceed to a place called Aubers, and report to the local battalion HQ.

The journey to Aubers was leisurely, covering some 60 miles and several days, but not very pleasant. It rained, the roads were hugely crowded with men and materiel; and it has to be noted, refugees. Most were from Belgium, but many were French fleeing from the German advance. We did not feel very welcome and there was no sense those of the locals we met saw us as protectors. Damage to the area from shelling was relatively slight, but food was scarce and as always, the army was regarded by the civilians as a predatory mob: quite correctly in truth. Or when not predatory, a source of subsidy. Nearer the front, destruction to buildings, absence of civilians and noise from the rolling bombardments became very marked. With such flat country, the growing bleakness was highly visible over distance and the more unnerving. Although we were three hundred plus mounted men, we clung tightly to our two abreast formation like lost schoolchildren.

'I thought there'd be lots of lovely *madamoiselles*,' observed my newly promoted Cornish colour sergeant as we jogged along side by side at the head of our column. 'Chance would be a fine thing,' I replied, 'We'll have to hold our own for a while Prout.' He gave a short laugh 'That's the problem Captain.' Candidly, even masturbation had been a scarce pleasure since leaving Exeter. Whatever Shakespeare had to say about the deleterious effects of drink in relation to desire and performance; cold, discomfort and fatigue are the most effective antidotes to sexual arousal.

From my own perspective, the attack at Aubers Ridge early in May was a success. Its overall military impact was, I believe less happy. Our apprehensions prior to engagement were also about gas, which we had heard on the grapevine, was being used by the Hun. We reported, we were treated courteously as comrades in arms, and I was glad to find a battalion CO who had sensible views on the use of cavalry. He said 'Our job is to set up a diversionary attack here, so the Frogs can biff the Hun further down the line.' The scheme was for us to exploit a gap in the line to the north and do what we could to create confusion to the enemy's flank and rear. Infantry and artillery would make a frontal assault. The combined effort it was hoped would delude the Germans into thinking it was a major attack; and so forth. I was able to impress this Lt-Colonel with our potential. He knew FitzMalpas, which was a bad point, but cheered up when I concurred with his distaste and even more when I told him of our training programme.

'Did you come across Malpas's wife, Julia? Sulky filly but, y'know...' he asked at one point. I told him I had. We laughed and he poured me a brandy and we peered at maps for a while and agreed timetables. We had about eighteen hours to prepare. I had no battle experience, and all my troopers, junior officers and all but three of the NCOs were equally innocent.

It did not make sense to put both squadrons in at once. I had to carry everyone with me and so held a joint briefing for subalterns and NCOs together. The upshot was to divide a single squadron into three sections, a subaltern paired with a more experienced NCO. I would lead a section for the first incursion. The remaining two sections would await orders to join any engagement as needed. It was as sensible as we could devise and depended entirely on whether we could find our way through a small valley, behind the brow of a hill and into the rear of the German artillery position without detection. The idea was simply to be able to bring up more force or retreat swiftly as events determined. Even we tyros had learned, if only from reading of the Zulu in the Boer War, the futility of hurling large numbers of people at superior firepower. As von Clausewitz observed, 'never attack the enemy unless you are very strong.'

There is a lot of flesh and blood in a couple of hundred men and horses. The trick is to keep them alive and fighting as a group when one small bullet can finish any one of them. The Germans had a lot of bullets. It should be recalled I had neither training nor handbook of cavalry tactics for this enterprise. What I did have was a native countryman's cunning and fieldcraft. Landowners, poachers, badgers, foxes, deer and now Germans; it's all fair game and involves being as sneaky as possible. For the rest, our plan worked as well as could be expected. We trotted off in line, at about midnight. There was a half but overcast moon. During the next two or three hours, and dismounted, we worked our way along the valley and up the small hillside that was our objective. By dawn, we were on the flank of the German positions and could actually look down on the small vale in which their howitzers were emplaced. I recall watching the gunners rouse themselves and begin preparations for the routine morning bombardment.

At the anticipated hour, they duly started to fire the artillery. Ours replied from over the hill although, for once as planned, accurately aimed aslant from our route. I had also disposed our two Hotchkiss machine guns to divert enemy attention from the line of attack. These opened up exactly as needed. Since the cavalry were undiscovered I had called up the full attack squadrons. We two hundred gallant brothers, our horses snorting and stamping, were poised just below the crest of our sheltering hillock. We came to the brow of the hill, and without the bugle nonsense, but sabres, pistols, carbines and so on at the ready, charged down on the German battery.

It is often imagined, especially by film people that 'the enemy' is taken by surprise on these occasions. That surprise is very transient. We had several hundred yards of hillside and field to cover, by which time the Huns had in place their infantry support and light machine guns. Numbers of our horses and men went down, but we got to the emplacements and I am glad to say did the job. I have never personally had a problem about killing for a purpose. I have no detailed recollections except that of firing my revolver at close quarters and using my sabre with satisfaction as my opposer fell bloodily away. After which I withdrew a little and watched my squadrons, enthused by example, gallop about and deal death by gunfire and sword.

Having reduced the opposition, I ordered half my forces to retreat whilst my own and another section spiked the howitzers as best we could with grenades. We were also fortunate to capture several prisoners, although I was forced to shoot and kill an officer who had feigned surrender to one of my lieutenants, then drew and fired his pistol. Luckily only slightly wounding his captor.

This little passage of arms had some pleasing results. We returned behind the lines a happy and remarkably undamaged band of cavalry. In consequence of the action, my CO won great credit for a well-accomplished diversion and inventive use of his troops. He in turn was grateful to me for my part in the enterprise. He got a full Colonelcy as precursor to his final apotheosis as a Major General. I had my Captain's rank confirmed and, to my surprise, in due course, an MC; this based on the fact I had led the initial charge, indulged in personal combat with, and stayed to spike the guns of the enemy to the inspiration of my troops. I confess I had not been quite observant enough to note how well others of my squadron had performed. That said, in consultation with my colour sergeant – for whom I did obtain a medal, there were mentions in despatches and promotions for as many as we could reasonably justify.

Minstrel of course had behaved brilliantly and we snuffled noses and rubbed each other's faces with great affection when we had returned to quarters, washed and fed and all the rest. In cavalry combat it is vital to have a horse under you that will not shy or panic, but carries you unflinchingly as far as your courage demands and beyond. In that first action I experienced the excitement borne of confidence; how I could fire my revolver, swing my sabre and simultaneously, turn my horse merely through willpower, the touch of a knee and mutual understanding.

What to say of the next months of seemingly unending danger and tedium? So far as I could tell, the front changed little. Inspection of historical maps supports this impression. My promotion, medal and the goodwill of my Divisional Command helped me keep together the best of my squadrons. Our action had won us esteem. If the generals and staff officers took little account in their strategic world the executive officers in the field did. Far too many of the regular cavalry were being turned into surrogate infantry and needlessly sacrificed. Our small and diminishing group of three hundred — 'the hayseed gallopers' became our sobriquet - earned a reputation with the fighting colonels and their subordinates. We galloped – or more often slowly walked up and down between Ypres and Arras for the next year or so. The advantage was, we spent more of our time wandering about than we did in combat. In those contexts we managed to inflict more damage than we suffered. That said, I could never become inured to the groans and bloodied flesh of men and horses that accompanied every engagement. As much as the men, I cared for the horses. Vets were scarcer than nurses, so it was always my first task to find out where they were based.

On the positive side, with nurses in mind, I managed to form a brief liaison with a very pretty Scottish nurse in the nearby field hospital. My very dog-eared, illustrated copy of Fanny Hill had become as neglected as my prick. We had come back from some minor skirmish. I had brought two of my men, strapped to their horses. My presence was also due to the fact I had felt a burn and blood on my upper thigh as our enemy fired their irritated shots on our intrusion. After the men had been carried off I mentioned to the nurse in charge, that I had a small wound. She was a vivacious but practical girl who took me to some alcove in the field tent. I dropped my britches and drawers and she cleaned and dressed the very slight bullet graze close to my groin. The feel of fresh air, the proximity of a female hand inevitably encourages erection. Helen, for that was her name, laughed and said 'I think that will do for now.' As I pulled up my drawers, she added 'But your problem would repay more attention when we're less busy.' We arranged to meet in the late evening when the front would be quiet and she would be off-duty. Our rendezvous would be a small row of field ambulances just beyond the casualty tent. There were moments when you felt the British Army had got it right. No other military force had arranged for nurses to be at the front line with their own accommodation.

I found her by the last ambulance in the row. Whatever romantic novels suggest, young men and women in war, who have been without real sex for months, don't waste time in flirtation. The only thing she said as she preceded me into the back of the van was 'When was the last time you had a woman?' I told her it was with my CO's wife over a year before. She laughed, said 'Good' and then her arms were round my shoulders, her mouth crushed to mine and her thighs clinging to my waist. She was a lithe thing and I had no trouble getting my hands under her buttocks to support her. Beneath the long linen nurse's skirt she was naked. My fingers felt hair and moistness. There was the unique aroma of a woman on heat. Somehow, we got her bottom against a stretcher frame and liberated the object of her desire. We were both laughing and panting with lust at the same time. Then I got my cockhead into her cunt and she put her face into my neck and gave a long low sigh of release. I helped her ride up and down on me. Her cunt clasped and sucked me from root to tip. Her breathing became stertorous. 'Do it for me Billy, do it,' she panted and used her calves to drag me hard in. As she began a muted moan and her cunt quivered, I let my spunk shoot up into her accompanied by an ill-suppressed exclamation of my own.

For all I knew, every one of those ambulances was populated with nurses and soldiers. When we had begun to breathe easily and she had taken my handkerchief to stuff between her legs she said 'Look for me when you get back again Captain Billy but best of all, just get back again.' Then she patted me on the cheek and was out of the ambulance and into the dark like a little fox.

II

One morning, late in 1916 we were billeted near Arras. As usual the poor PBI were suffering the assaults of artillery, gas, machine guns and the ludicrous demands to 'go over the top'. My 'Company of Cornwall Hussars', as I had managed to recreate us informally in military circles thanks to my perceived connection with the Broleigh pedigree, was summoned from our retreat in a grisly and collapsing cluster of barns and small farmhouses. In addition to the erratic deliveries of awful rations sent by Command, we had managed to secure a more reliable supply of dubious - but with culinary effort - edible, pieces of meat from our local resources. These were represented by an old peasant couple who still clung to the one habitable cottage and kept a few chickens and grew swedes. To my sergeant's disgust there were no generous minded 'madamoiselles' in sight. We were therefore as positive about our situation as could be expected.

Over lunch in their requisitioned, but wrecked chateau my superior officers explained rather apologetically, that we were slated to join a major assault further to the Southeast. This attack was to follow Haig's usual wheeze of an artillery bashing, rush through the softened up enemy with the infantry and mop up with the cavalry; or some such thing. Reconnaissance had identified various salients, small valleys and clumps of woodland that represented a possible weakness in the German front. Also they might hold forces that could embarrass our flank but were not on our main line of attack. I took these orders and various speculative maps kindly provided back to my gallant band. Only at this distance of time is it possible to strike a light-hearted note.

The Battle of the Somme as it proved to be, was a scruffy affair for us. Still, it was rather better for my chaps than for the 20,000 killed on the first day alone. We wandered south, reported in and since we had arrived deliberately early, sought permission to run a reconnaissance. This was grudgingly approved; and then only I think because we were peripheral to the main assault. The terrain was a nightmare. That which had not been dug or blown up was at best mildly undulating. If there had been trees they were mostly now mere stumps. In our sector there seemed to be the remnants of a small orchard, a farmhouse, a barn and two or three chicken sheds.

By this time we also had the occasional piece of photographic air reconnaissance and some off-cuts were made available. These were recent and gave us a good idea of enemy positions, topography and all that sort of thing. I studied the main plan of attack. Nothing I saw led me to suppose that on attack day plus one, or however our timing was described, we would be other than highly exposed.

On the other hand to be shot for cowardice was not in the plan. I called for volunteers for the first effort; this being something like opening artillery salvos plus infantry assault. I picked chaps whom I knew to be single and with less than a full company we stocked up with ammunition, polished our sabres, groomed horses and generally got ourselves organised. I was holding an inspection on the evening preceding the attack. Some general drove by with his entourage and stopped to enquire who we were and what we were doing. 'Cornwall Hussars, Sir.' I replied. 'Mmm heard of you.' Was his brusque reply. 'What are you doing here?' 'Flank attack sir.' 'What's your name captain?' 'Myddleton sir.' 'Chap who got the MC at Aubers?' I nodded. 'How did you do it?' 'Good men, good horses, right tactics.' I replied without thinking. 'Hah!' he exclaimed, setting boot heel to horse 'I can see your men and horses have the first two right, let's hope you do it again.' He must have seen my face because as his car moved off he looked back at my fading salute and shouted 'Strategy Captain, we must have the right strategy.' I thought to myself, 'Too sodding right General, the strategy is to kill the enemy, not your own troops.'

In one's memory it is of course, the small and personal things that stay. I recall, on the same evening, an ensign came up with a message from the passing general. In official language, it wished us well and at the bottom was a scrawled note 'Good luck Myddleton.' Then the bombardments started and in due course we worked our way on foot, leading the horses to our incursion point. Eventually the guns decreased and to our right we heard the shouts and shots of troops moving across no man's land. These noises were followed with the rattle of machine guns and the explosions of grenades and mortars. It was dawn and it was our turn.

So we galloped off across some muddy fields and between broken trees, and shot and slashed some dismayed Germans before they managed to realign their dreadfully effective machine guns from inside the sandbag bunkers and kill everyone in sight. I seemed to be the exception, although others must have escaped. Poor Minstrel fell as we left the small shelter of a henhouse and tried to reach our objective. We were taught to use our horse's body to give cover to our own fire. No machine pistol for me, just the revolver and I managed five shots with two results. As the helmeted and revengeful looking infantry advanced I wondered whether to reserve the last bullet for myself. Believe me, we had been told seriously worrying stories about how the Germans treated helpless opponents. Then Minstrel lifted his head and whinnied piteously. His hindquarter was dogmeat. I crawled up to his head and whispered 'There boy' to him. At which point several bayonets and cocked rifles were very close to my person.

I don't suppose German infantrymen were any more ghastly looking that ours. Oh well yes, this lot were. Their Neanderthal faces grimaced down beneath those awful kettle type helmets. Bolts worked, bayonets dug into my tunic. Then salvation: an authoritative command and the simians fell back. I looked up and saw a German cavalry officer at the head of a troop of Uhlans. He had his pistol out and pointed it to the infantry mob. I rose slowly, hands in surrender, my revolver dropping into the mud. Our eyes met and I gestured to Minstrel whose wounds, breathing and whimpers were clearly those of an animal in terminal distress. The German officer nodded, but turned his pistol in my direction as warning. I picked my weapon up, brushed mud from the muzzle, knelt and placed it behind Minstrel's ear. I whispered my farewell and pressed the trigger. The Webley, army officers for the use of, was a basic old thing, but covered in dirt and close to like this, nothing better.

On my feet again, I gave the officer a smart salute. There were tears streaming down my face, but he knew why, and it was nothing to do with being taken prisoner. He gestured me forward and one of his troopers led out a riderless horse. As I mounted, the officer turned to me and said in perfect English 'Well Captain, I think war is no longer for cavalry.' I managed a weak smile and replied, 'Then I am glad it is to you I fall captive. Thank you.' He nodded courteously and I noticed he had a bloodied bandage around his arm and was riding one handed. Seeing my glance he said: 'Shrapnel.'

Rittmeister Friedrich von Eisen of the 2nd HKK Corps and the Pomeranian Light Horse turned out to have been educated at Oxford and apart from being of very similar age to me was a legitimate Baron; if you see what I mean. I played up to this by revealing my own 'pedigree'. We got on very well from the start, and as his wound was serious enough to require sick leave, he determined, on discovery of my Broleigh title, to take me home as his personal prisoner. The price to be paid was my full cooperation during my interrogation. I had no great trouble with this. I did not relish being a prisoner of war in some dreadful forced labour camp. Since what I knew was of minimal value there seemed no point in being over heroic and merely parroting name, rank and number. Accordingly, I spent a couple of militaristic days answering their questions as best I could. At first they were disinclined to believe my ignorance. I pointed out that having a title did not get me access to the staff tent. They were interested in my Cornwall Hussars, which they claimed to have heard of. I had the impression, that as with the British regular line officers, cavalry was no longer taken very seriously. At best we were gallant fools. What led them finally to accept my evidence was their complete amazement at the profligacy with which we hurled men at their front line. This seemed so devoid of any deliverable results, let alone coherent plan that it was no wonder people like me were permitted to charge about at random with our own private armies. Given such reassurance as to their prospects for victory, I was returned to von Eisen for further detailed inquisition.

To him I gave my own parole as officer and gentleman, this quaint idea being still accepted among cavalry officers and the German upper classes. He told me his pragmatic purpose in taking charge of me was to have an intelligent aide during his convalescence. Nonetheless, I was lucky to have him as my mentor. The fate of too many prisoners of war at German hands was miserable indeed, there being no Geneva Convention and a brutalist tradition inherited from Bismarck's 'blood and iron' beliefs.

We began a leisurely and not always uncomfortable journey out of France, into Belgium and northeast across Germany. 'Freddie' as he liked to be called was an entertaining companion. We swapped biographies – carefully polished in my case, and discovered a shared liking for the racier classics. Freddie confided that he had inherited an extensive collection of erotic books, prints and paintings from his father; many of them quite old and rare. Their provenance was not always quite clear in terms of either authorship or acquisition. This collection was housed in Freddie's home, which was a small *Schloss* or large hunting lodge near the Pomeranian lakes south west of Danzig. The family had once had much more extensive properties. Freddie's uncle had contrived to mortgage these in a series of ill-judged investments when Germany had a fit of empire building in the C19th. This created a degree of anti-semitism in the von Eisen tradition, since it was perceived to be a Jewish run bank that had foreclosed the loan. Equally, Freddie was a liberal intellectual at heart, somewhat baffled and frustrated by the political clamour that attended the management of his country's affairs. He fell back on his Prussian heritage and if he had a hero it was Frederick the Great. Somehow, this connection and his Oxford education led him to feel affectionate toward the English whom he regarded as rather like cavalry. That is to say, possessed of a heroic history and sound values, but no longer relevant at least in Europe in the face of Teutonic advance and the decline of our industrial strength.

Our transit was spasmodic. Freddie carried enough authority to secure adequate accommodations and transport, though both were scarce. My obviously British uniform was the object of only mild enquiry. Most traffic was heading toward the Western Front. Until one reached the epicentre, when it flowed toward the East. Germany was not in a good state so far as I could tell. The people looked poor, hungry and sullen. This was in contrast to the troops, who looked pretty smart, bouyant and well fed.

I think it was in Leipzig where Freddie and my relationship took a brief and curious turn. We were lurking about in a moderately decent hotel reserved for officers; awaiting a train to carry us further toward Danzig. Despite the evident deprivation of the civilians, it must be admitted, the military in general and officers especially were as careless and self-indulgent as circumstances allowed. We had a filling sausage and cabbage dinner. There was plentiful beer and schnapps; a bottle of which last we took back to our room. It was the middle of July, the weather hot. We stripped to our underwear and sprawled out on the twin beds of our shared room. Inevitably the discourse turned to women. We exchanged reminiscences and preferences; speculated on the dispositions of ladies and peasants. The verdict being that the ladies were ultimately more inventive and depraved but trickier to manage. Freddie said that in his experience Polish girls were very tricky whatever their social pretensions. As I lay on my back, nursing my Schnapps, Freddie declared: 'I have had no real sex for two years.' I blearily remarked that Leipzig must be full of tarts. Freddie was incensed. 'Toothless old hags or innocent German maidens. All I want is to have a fuck with some pretty girl, or at least my cock sucked.' I commiserated. Freddie said: 'You actually fucked a real and pretty nurse only a few months ago.' This was inarguable, since I had mentioned it in some general conversation about life behind the lines, so I muttered about luck.

There was a silence. Freddie said 'You seem to be a lucky man. You were lucky to meet me, for example.' I agreed with this.

'Otherwise, you would probably now be in some terrible camp for unlucky English soldiers and picking turnips. Or perhaps dead.' This too was inarguable. I was by now so drunk I had passed into that clear stage where everything is understood. 'I like you,' Freddie observed. 'I think you have a pretty mouth.' I rolled over onto my side and saw that Freddie von Eisen had his drawers off and his cock in his hand.

'Das Ewig-Weibliche zieht uns hinan' [the eternal feminine draws us upwards] as Goethe said. In my case it drew me over to Freddie's bed and 'going down' rather than up. In truth, cocksucking is very pleasant, in the right context. Women do it all the time and most agree they get a lot of fun from it. Most men have probably fantasised about sucking their own prick and even tried it. This is achievable by some. There in Leipzig I had a charming young man to whom I owed a good deal and upon whose goodwill I depended. His cock was shapely, clean and in any event I liked the chap. He was my own type. All these retrospectives are secondary to the confession that I gave Freddie von Eisen a rather competent blowjob and quite enjoyed it. I swallowed most of it too. Freddie passed me the schnapps bottle. 'Bloody good old boy,' he said and in a moment he was asleep. How typical I thought, my own alcohol-stunned desires nudging at my loins.

I was relieved not to have to put my liberal pragmatism to the test in relation to buggery. This may seem somewhat hypocritical, given ones willingness to roger women wherever they are willing to receive a stiff prick. My own aesthetic preferences apart I nurse the idea that girls are better engineered for this sort of thing. Freddie agreed. We planned to complete the rest of our journey in a relatively few days after which Freddie assured me of female company.

As chance determined, we were denied the railway north via Berlin due to the demands of war on the railway system and found ourselves in Dresden en route for Stettin. Frankly, I had little idea of where I was at the time but having checked a map, and my memory, I am sure this is correct. Dresden was certainly a place that I recall. Freddie was pleased about our avoidance of Berlin. He feared imbroglio with 'higher authorities' he said and that he would be made to take a staff job despite his injury. His keenest desire was to get back to his Pomeranian retreat where, he told me, he gave a home to his sister who was in residence and a female cousin due to arrive who would be very pleased to meet an English officer. I confessed my original attachment to Jenny. We agreed that female relatives were perfect. They avoided the issues of unknown heritage and obviated the problems of 'family rivalry' and 'introductions' and 'getting to know each other'; nor did you necessarily have to marry them. Moreover if you married a cousin life simply continued and property stayed where it should.

III

Tales of abandoned conduct in country houses are not merely lubricious fantasies. They can be, but they are based in solid reality. Wherever you have a moneyed and leisured class, you have means, motive and opportunity for sensual indulgence. Sadly, the poor have only the miserable consequences of their brief moments of pleasure in less inspiring circumstances to repay their human impulses. I perceived this early in life. Lord Broleigh may have denied me recognition, but at least the old bastard gave my mama a home and kindness and myself an education and a name. Even though the education was careless and the name involuntary.

So in a fine mansion on the outskirts of Dresden I found myself during the course of one evening, both dressing in and divesting myself of borrowed evening clothes as guest of the City's garrison commander. My English origins were perfectly understood and were considered irrelevant to the situation. Apart from our Royal Family being Hanoverians and Saxe-Coburgs, many of the upper classes felt that Britain and Germany were historic allies, especially against the French. Throwing the Frog out of Canada and defeating Napoleon were notable examples. These historic events translated into mutual respect between the officer classes.

So the sentiments expressed were of regard for our respective nations' qualities and hopes for future reconciliation through sensible political action. We swapped toasts and shared concerns about quite what would happen with Russia. My German had progressed well, due to Freddie's insistence on vocabulary. I was also fortunate so many educated Germans spoke English.

I was in conversation with a very jolly young woman called Cosima. Her husband was a pilot in the nascent but by now highly regarded German air corps. I complimented her by saying something about heroes and beautiful wives. She smiled prettily and thanked me but sighed and said 'I think he loves his aeroplane more than me.' I took a manly but sympathetic tone and explained that in combat, planes and horses represented one's chance of life. Cosima sighed again and fluttered her eyelashes. 'Yes, but your horse is a living creature made to be ridden and desirous of love. A plane is just metal.'

The spontaneous dialogues of seduction rarely repay inscription. A sympathetic look, the touch of a hand, nudge of a foot, shared confession of loneliness and suppressed passion. It is set up in minutes, confirmed in seconds. Hence at midnight in the boudoir of a well-connected German air-ace's lonely wife I pulled off my underwear and let my growing erection feel the air. It being summer, the weather was warm and Cosima had stripped naked. She was not conventionally pretty. Her features were somewhat out of proportion. Her eyes were sly, her nose too flat and wide, almost Negroid and her mouth too wide. But those eyes were lascivious, her voice made for saying suggestive things and her smile full of promises. Her skin too had an extraordinary milky quality. She lay on the bed, one knee raised, thighs modestly together. Her languid eyes, parted lips and rapid breathing conveyed her eagerness. That is, if being naked did not. I was equally impatient and my erection complete. Cosima reached out for it with a husky laugh. 'My, are all English officers so well armed?' Her fingers closed round the neck of my shaft and it pulsed in her hand as she pulled me toward her. I knelt astride her whilst she squeezed and pumped at my cock, gazing at the shiny head and open eye with interest. 'I am so glad you are uncircumcised,' she murmured just before her lips closed over me. I let her play for a while, wondering what her style would be. 'Let's fuck,' she said after a while. Between her spread legs I poised over her so she could rub herself with my cockhead, which she did in a very self-indulgent way. Her pudendum was virtually hairless, the vulva showing flushed between her white thighs. Then I was into her hot clinging cunt and enjoying the gasps she in turn made. She responded to my kisses with odd little tongue darts and nibbles at my lips with that wide and mobile mouth. I let my weight press her down and allowed my cock to jerk its full length inside her. Her fingernails dug into my buttocks and her heels ran up and down my calves. She had her eyes shut and was breathing harshly but made little movement of her own in response to my thrusts. Her body was soft and there was flesh to spare on her torso but this made her a comfortable ride.

It was pleasant enough work but I felt the urge to surprise her. I put my hands under her buttocks and rolled us both over so she was on top of me. My cock was still in her cunt but only by a couple of inches. Her eyes opened wide and she stared down at me and laughed. Then she drew up her knees and straddled my hips, fumbling for the by now liberated organ as she did so. It slid very readily back into the moist and welcoming lair and Cosima began to ride me with real energy, her hands on my chest and her breasts, tipped by dark stiff nipples, swaying as she jigged and squirmed. Her lips were parted in a secret smile and she was hissing and muttering to herself. My German was not up to the task, but it sounded like a running commentary about how much fun she and a special bit of her was having with a special bit of me. I did catch something about *Englische Offizier* and *grosse Schwanz*. She seemed very content, if not much involved with my caresses of her breasts and thighs. I enjoyed it though. That pale skin and its malleability in the palm. She'd be fat soon enough but for now her plumpness was perfect. This was altogether enjoyable and I relaxed and let her carry on. My cock was on good form and showed no signs of over eagerness. Cosima's gallop became a longer slower series of circular motions. I could feel her cunt gripping me, sucking at my cock head. She reached one hand between her legs and began to rub her pudenda. She was far away in her own sensations and I was merely her imagination. I took a grip under her buttocks and bucked up into her, in time with her movements. Amid the usual and final cries of '*Ja, Ja ich komme!*' we shared a juicy moment before collapsing into each other.

I'd like to record that we enjoyed several more bouts until dawn. The reality was simply that after a tender period of embrace and mutual congratulation we parted, albeit on the warmest terms. I returned to the room I shared with Freddie. He was fast asleep, but the lady's stocking I noted on the floor required no explanation. I picked it up and tucked it under his pillow, before climbing into my own bed. It did occur to me to wonder exactly how he managed the encounter, since his wounded arm was in a sling and one of my duties was to assist his dressing and undressing. The solution to that problem was explicable, my interest was in the position adopted for intercourse; probably the same as mine I concluded, though there were other possibilities.

The next day we set off for Stettin. I have to say, by this time I think I felt I was in fact a German cavalry officer. It must be remembered that the German army and its officer class enjoyed a unique status and power. There was a bureaucratic civilian machine, but whatever social resentments might have existed, that bureaucracy was mostly, staffed by former soldiers. Hence Freddie von Eisen's title, military rank and adequate paperwork sufficed to obtain for us pretty much whatever we wanted. This included my wearing a borrowed uniform. In the few checks to which we were subjected during the last phase of our journey, only Freddie's papers were requested. On the single occasion where my identity was quizzed, Freddie's production of his authority to escort me, with the explanation that my British uniform had been destroyed, was accepted with nods and smiles of amusement. He told me later, that his frequent reference to me in such encounters was not that I was a prisoner, but that I was of German origin and had returned to my native country to serve the Reich.

From Stettin we had to make our way on horseback. Whilst the motorcar was of course established up to a point, this did not extend to general availability on demand, least of all in war. Moreover, gasoline did not feature very often in the services available from Pomeranian villages. Over a few days of not especially memorable or comfortable travel we reached the von Eisen estate. I have to say that despite Freddie's company and my very lucky situation, there were moments of ennui and gloom. That it was summer still, gave a verdant appearance to the landscape. In reality, not only were the midges often a misery, but the dreary, flat, dark, arable land interspersed with gloomy pine forest and odd patches of swamp nearer lakes and streams, depressed my Cornish spirits. In addition, we had to deal with the sullen and inadequately provisioned services of country inns, that even Freddie's rank, affable manner and money could not improve.

Good old Friedrich von Eisen, as we rode up the long and overgrown carriage drive that led to your hunting lodge, I recall your apologia. 'Now then William, this is a poor house. My proper estates were long ago sequestered by Jew bankers.' I made a response and he said 'Well, after we beat the French in 1870 and decided your Empire was also something to copy, my grandfather made some investments. I don't know the details, but this little place is all we are left with thanks to the jewboys.' My suggestion that to play catch-up with the British Empire was possibly a mistake was not well received. 'You are all such smug bastards you bloody islanders,' was his response. Then he added 'if we lose, and we won't, it will be because our government is a traitor. But as regards to empire overseas, you're right. Keep all those places only your Navy can reach. The Prussian future is on the great lands to the East. There is our empire.'

Despite the neglected air of the drive, the derelict gatehouse and wild shrubbery, lawns and kitchen gardens, the 'lodge' itself was a marvellous and very large example of its kind. Turrets and

Gothic windows adorned the façade. There appeared to be no one around as we trotted up to the front entrance. This was a covered portico with a wooden and ornately carved canopy and pillars. The main doors were also of heavy wood with panels of painted wood faded by age. Then two or three peasants appeared carrying sickles. Freddie greeted them and they backed off, with sycophantic but to my eye unaffectionate expressions. The front door opened and I had my first sight of Freddie's sister,f Viktoria von Eisen.

Clad in men's riding clothes she cut a dashing figure. Tall though slenderly built her aquiline features were handsome rather than pretty, framed by tight drawn plaits of the Wagnerian sort. She immediately struck me as looking like a more masculine version of her brother. She gazed on us sternly for a moment, then her face became animated with a truly beautiful smile of recognition and she dashed toward us down the steps of the *Schloss*. We, or rather Freddie, worked our way through the usual confusions and babble of questions that attend a surprise arrival. I took it on myself to lead the horses away and find the stables. The sullen rustics seemed to have vanished so I appropriated two stalls, dealt with the tack and made sure hay and water were available. I had just finished when I became aware that Viktoria was standing at the stable doors. She regarded me with a quizzical but not unfriendly expression.

'So you are our noble English prisoner,' she said in German. I laughed and nodded assent. 'Friedrich says he likes you a lot.'

'I'm very grateful to him.'

'Guests, even grateful ones should not do the work of stable hands.'

I followed her back toward the house, remarking 'I didn't see any stable hands. Anyway, I like to look after my horses.'

'Gerhard, our steward, has had to go to the town. We are very short of staff for obvious reasons. There are only those foul Kashubs who are useless and untrustworthy. The local peasants...' she added over her shoulder answering my unspoken enquiry.

We reached the house and joined Freddie in the drawing room. He had opened a bottle of schnapps and we toasted each other amiably. Freddie put an arm round Viktoria's shoulder and gestured to me 'Willy here will become a good Prussian and be of great help to us.' Viktoria smiled 'Yes Friedrich my dear, I think he will.'

I wasn't so sure about the good Prussian bit, but thought it quite possible to be useful.

Over the next few weeks, as summer turned to autumn I gradually assumed the role it was most naural for me to play; that of estate manager. Gerhard the Steward seemed content with this, being elderly and more of a butler than anything else. We were a happy sort of household. Viktoria was amiable and often went riding with me when I was out and about on estate business. She was very supportive of my policies despite her prejudices. We also talked easily if inconsequentially about literature, and our two countries. She and Freddie were very obviously close and the sounds I heard frequently in the corridor outside my room at night suggested assignations that were not usually associated with close relatives. That said, I felt a welcome part of their social life and we habitually had long dinners of great merriment.

Of the War, we had fragmentary news of unreliable quality. In the autumn of 1916 the Germans were giving the Russians a hard time. We also heard talk of the Austro-Hungarians being severely knocked about. In the West, despite optimistic newspaper reports, there was rumour of large losses on both sides and a general stasis on the front. In West Prussia not far from the Northern Polish border and the Baltic we felt ourselves very insulated from the distant '*Sturm und Drang.*' Although even here, returning and often limbless wounded brought their first hand accounts. There were also hints of political turmoil. Frankly, I never got to grips with the complexities of German politics. What little I knew came from Viktoria's curious blend of socialism, class arrogance and Prussian pride. She had approved of Bismarck and was dubious about the Kaiser. She loathed the communists but respected Rosa Luxemburg. Freddie cared nothing for politics and maintained Junker aloofness from the machinations of office seekers.

By the time winter arrived, I felt I had taken the Estate properly in hand. I had set myself to learn Polish, so that I could better communicate with the Kashubs. That was not their first language, but although they were German assimilated to a degree their innate Slavic hostility was evident. It was never clear to me where they originated. I think, from their stories that they were a displaced tribe who had wandered in from the East millennia before. It was their misfortune to be in territory constantly in flux between German and Polish dominance. By being open about my English origins and treating them with courtesy and where possible, generosity, I managed to establish a degree of trust and win some cooperation. It was to prove a highly worthwhile investment some two years later. Meanwhile, despite the general shortage of food, we achieved a level of self-sufficiency on the estate that enabled us to enjoy a better standard of life than was increasingly the case in the towns.

It was a reasonable existence to which I had rapidly become accustomed and I was not much troubled by worries for the future. In any case, over the weeks I became more intimately bound up in the von Eisen family's personal lives. Relatively early on, Freddie had taken me into his library and showed me his astonishing collection of inherited erotica. I can remember only a few items offhand, but he had a very nice privately printed edition of Lucian's *Dialogues of the Hetairai* and what he swore was an original of Millot's *Ecole des Filles*. He had too, many of the more famously licentious works of English and French writers including, *inter alia*, *My Secret Life* and *L'Ecole des Biches*. I wondered about the school preoccupations in these works.

There was also an impressive inventory of artworks and photographs; the former from an eclectic range of both well-known and anonymous artists; some original but mostly decent quality lithographs or prints. The photographs were more from the Parisian dirty postcard school, but there were some interesting renditions of Sader-Masochian bent. Other than that, there were shelves of vases and statuettes – some evidently of specific erotic function, such as elaborate phalli and dildos as well as the Greco-Roman decorative ware. We were in this study one evening idly looking through some volume or other, when Viktoria came in. She joined in the conversation in a knowledgeable way and then said, 'I think Willy would like my pictures.' Her large and challenging catlike eyes fixed me for a moment.

One never knows what to expect in such a situation, certainly not the astonishing prolixity of her highly gifted and totally obscene sketches and watercolours. If the Marquis de Sade had briefed Hieronymous Bosch or Breughel this would have been something near the mark. Freddie and Viktoria were either side of me, like the Tenniel griffons in *Alice*; their interested scrutiny palpable as I pored over the folios. It occurred to me that this was some kind of test or initiation. In sum, what we had was a facsimile of German mythology; the *Ring Cycle* or something like it. Except in this, Viktoria as quite identifiable Lorelei, river maiden, Princess, Goddess or whatever was necessary. She was mostly naked and engaged in sexual struggles of various types; on occasion assisted by nymphs. The leitmotif of her situation was evidently the phallus. Whether assailed by dwarves and trolls or rescued by Nordic gods, possessed of breasts or not, our valorous maiden's antagonists all flaunted an enormous and erect penis. In some contexts she herself was the phallus-equipped mistress of revenge and pain. Her victims nonetheless wore their tumescence proudly. No orifice remained unfilled. The vulvas of her main subjects and those of her subordinates were always represented shaven, with the colours of a fine sunset: this was lividly apparent even in her pencil sketches. I may also have caught glimpses of Freddie's facial representation but cannot be sure. The finale in her narrative gallery portrayed the apotheosis of our heroine surrounded by a prostrate assemblage of defeated enemies, adoring acolytes and eager suitors. She held aloft an oval chalice, from which she tipped a viscous pale liquid onto the upturned faces of her audience.

Bear in mind, although a sexually experienced young male, I had not before, come across quite this level of erotica. The problem was simply how to respond. My German was not up to the subtle task of conveying appreciation without committal. I fell back on the English of 'Extraordinary, quite extraordinary'; coupled with wide-eyed looks to left and right, a spontaneous grasp of Viktoria's wrist and other gestures expressive of loss of words.

The test had been passed. Freddie made ebullient comments about the talent of his sister and how he had reassured her his English officer was a man of spirit. I think he meant 'one of us'. Viktoria gave me her appraising look but leaned into me as I released my grip on her arm. She whispered something in

German I failed to catch but nodded to anyway. I think it had the word '*schön*' in it, which was good.

These are of course, the remembered truths. In reality it may have been different although I don't think by much. After all, how many British officers spent some of the ghastlier years of World War One in a Pomeranian hunting lodge with a charmingly dissolute Prussian aristocrat and his sexually obsessed sister? The exposure of Viktoria's private collection of fantasy was certainly a key moment that led to over eighteen months of intense and often exhausting involvement. On the other hand, it certainly passed the time.

Chapter 3

OH STAY THE MAIDEN SAID
AND REST

One matter on which Freddie's word had yet to come good was the promise of ample female company. By the Yule of 1917 my neglected cock had only had a few lonely walks with its owner. Matters were not helped by my growing infatuation with Viktoria whose presence of itself guaranteed an erection. The revelation of her artistic impulses fuelled my desires further.

I think the first snows had begun when Elisabeth arrived with her single servant. This latter was an old biddy who rather endearingly, became in time the bosom companion of Gerhard the Steward. Elisabeth herself was a distant cousin of the von Eisens. Small and vivacious, she had almost Latin looks. These had been acquired through an interesting mix of Austrian Jewish and Catholic antecedents conjoined with a more conventional Prussian heritage. Her arrival was occasioned by familial concerns about the situation in Bavaria, where there were signs of dangerous political volatility.

She arrived with two cartloads of valuables sent for storage in Freddie's care. Cordially received, 'Lissa' as she became titled fitted very well into our ménage. Freddie sidled up to me after dinner and said, 'I think you and Lissa will do very well together.' He was probably right so I agreed. I could hardly tell him that I was in love, or at least in lust, with Viktoria, though he would not have been surprised. I had never taxed him with his evidently incestuous relationship. I supposed that would prejudice my situation. Freddie had his unstable side.

Lissa's arrival changed the social situation completely. Viktoria, although unfailingly affectionate to her relative in public, betrayed a different facet to me one evening quite soon after the new arrival. Lissa had retired and we three were sitting drinking schnapps in the study. A comment was made, about Lissa being pretty, or possibly her arrival bearing possessions. Viktoria turned her large feline eyes on us both and remarked, 'To be a bit Jewish may be regarded as a misfortune. To be also a bit Catholic appears as carelessness.' We laughed a great deal at this, if not for the same reasons. More soberly, we men hurrumphed and voted Lissa a super girl. Freddie called her '...a genuine Eisen'. Nonetheless, Viktoria's comments made subsequent events much less surprising even if her predilections had not been established in her art.

My use of the term 'Yule' was deliberate. At Viktoria's instigation, Christmas was abandoned in favour of 'Yulefest'. As I have already noted, her idea of Germanic political tradition borrowed from many sources and I was never very au fait with the details. In this matter, she admired an Austrian called Schonerer and even more, a nominally Christian-Socialist, but self-declared pagan, Karl Lueger. Freddie thought them both mad and vulgar, but indulged and to some degree shared his sister's prejudices. These can best be summarised as pantheistic, nationalistic, favouring of social justice delivered to a happy and obedient peasantry by a natural ruling class.

With the snow settling, the logs chopped, cured meats in the larders and fresh game in the icehouse we could settle down to a secure winter. Our Kashubs were cooperative, thanks to my application of reasonable farm labour management principles. It is always better to give than to have stolen and most tenants deliver more for a fair landlord. We rode out in the mornings, and sat around reading in the afternoons. Lissa, who turned out to be only eighteen was well educated and possessed of charm and spirit. Short, dark and petite, her features were distinguished by the large and submissive brown eyes of a houri. I began to wonder how easily she might be seduced – although Viktoria's presence continued to distract.

One's own memory may wander, and what follows is more a composite of two year's libertinage than orderly narrative. Hence the specifics of the Yulefest orgy whilst broadly accurate are also representative of how matters were conducted thereafter.

Quite what led to the sudden change of pace in our social relations is also mysterious. I can only assume Viktoria was waiting for a fourth player for the game. Subsequently, whilst making me perfectly free of her person, we never fucked without Freddie's presence.

So it was that one cold and snowbound evening Freddie and I were drinking some of his Napoleon brandy in the study after dinner. Gerhard and Birgit had turned out to be a very competent pair of cooks and their work deserves recognition. Viktoria had led Lissa off for what we assumed to be a womanly tête-à-tête. Then the door opened and Viktoria entered. She was naked, except for a pair of thigh length, black chamois leather riding boots. Her hair was unplaited and in disarray. In her right hand she carried a crop and with her left, on a dog chain that terminated in a thick black leather collar, she led a completely unclothed Lissa. I greeted this scene with total astonishment. My encounters with Julia meant I was no stranger to the scenario suggested by this presentation. It was simply the suddenness with which it occurred and the social elaboration of its conduct.

So we began as we continued. Viktoria became our mistress of games wherein very subtly, Lissa and my status as subordinates, was made explicit in a new way. Shamefully, Lissa suffered a double penalty of being a young woman with a suspect heritage. Whereas, my history and gender allowed me a high degree of equality in the roles I played. To be frank, to play more sadistic parts on occasion. Lissa, although apparently content in her compliance, never had the opportunity to dominate.

Over the years, I have pondered the nature of male and female relations in their physical context. My upbringing and experiences predispose me to somewhat of an elitist view. How women proceed socially is one thing. I am completely in favour, as have been all women of my intimate acquaintance, with their right and ability to engage as equal beings with political, economic and legal affairs.

In our sexual relations I believe more basic rules apply. I will confess to prejudice in favour of pretty women with good figures over puddings with no figure at all. Having a cock or a cunt casts us immutably in a primitive but still promising physical relationship with each other. Male cocks get stuck into female places. The symbolism is inescapable. Darwin and Freud had something to contribute about these aspects of our sexual relations. Promise comes from the natural style and pleasure of use combined with the potential for sensual inventiveness by men and women. Elitism derives simply from the idea that the only thing to distinguish us from primitives in the sexual act is aesthetics. None of us wish to see ugly things. Nature can make the mating displays of her creatures beautiful or silly or ugly. Humans can do the same for each other. Later in life I had the opportunity to reflect on the differences between the roles of protagonist and observer.

Which recalls my first sight of Queen Viktoria and her slave Elisabeth. Her Majesty proud and arrogant; her lithe and athletic body completely depilated, her pudenda's swelling enticement offering clear sight of clitoral ridge and inner lips between slender thighs as she posed wide-legged. Her captive was demure yet defiant with the soft ivory curves of the maiden and a dark luxuriant bush at her groin. Forced to her knees, Lissa offered her buttocks to her mistress's pleasure. The riding crop rose and fell; the sound of leather on flesh mingled with gasps and cries. As in all these matters the affair must be well judged. Lissa's flushed face and increasingly engorged nipples betrayed her pleasure in the skill with which her pain was delivered. My experience with Julia came to mind. The lashing over, Lissa turned her face up to the mistress who straddled her, and with the chain drew her slave's face into the regal crotch. As victim, the girl was remarkably enthusiastic. She licked and suckled hungrily, so when she withdrew her face Viktoria's vulva was fully revealed. Blushed, wet and swollen lipped.

As an ingénue in the matter of orgiastic sex, I could only follow the lead set by others. Freddie had by now begun to divest himself of his clothes, so I followed. By the time Lissa turned her heavy eyed and compliant face toward us, we were naked and very erect. Using the chain and collar, Viktoria directed her kneeling charge so that we two men shared the pleasure of her lips and tongue as she sucked, and we thrust. Not having a scenario to guide me I waited for clues as to the etiquette. Viktoria seemed content to allow Lissa to continue her fellation. She however, releasing the chain, began to fondle Lissa's buttocks and genitals, her fingers probing deep into the girl's cunt. This prompted Lissa to become more agitated in her attentions to our cocks. She fondled our balls, squeezed and pumped our shafts and altogether showed a desire to bring us to completion. In due course Lissa's body movements and gasps indicated approaching fulfilment. Freddie gripped her head and began thrusting his penis into her mouth with great urgency. He came, she gulped and spluttered and white froth dribbled from her lips around his shaft. Meanwhile, Lissa held my cock tight in her fist and once she evidently felt she had done Freddie justice she turned and closed her semen coated lips around me.

I was quite happy to fulfil my pleasure in this manner but Viktoria had other ideas. She pulled Lissa's head sharply away from its attentions. She stooped and closed her mouth on Lissa's with fierce intensity. Then releasing her turned to me and said, 'Fuck the bitch, fuck her.' On all fours her shapely buttocks striped from her beating, her cunt split redly amid the hair, breasts hung stiff tipped Lissa was an attractive object of desire. I thrust my prick into the welcoming cleft. Clearly, Lissa was no virgin. Rested on her forearms she pushed back to meet my entry with small exclamations of 'oh, yes, please, fuck, fuck.' As we enjoyed each other I was intrigued to see Viktoria and Freddie *soixante-neuf* on the floor. Freddie had recovered his erection and Viktoria seemed to be treating his penis and balls to a fairly severe oral regime at the same time crushing his head between her thighs and grinding her vulva onto his face. Well, Lissa eventually called time with a series of loud cries and I had an orgasm of well-deserved, well-received and generous intensity.

All passion spent we lay about in front of the fire drinking and being pleasant to each other in the way of general and affectionate conversation about how good that had been and how warm the room was. This sort of experience must change the dynamics of people's relationships and for the better, I hope. Even so, despite years in the business of providing environments for people to enjoy sex socially, I still wonder about the relative merits of group versus 'private' sex.

This first evening of sexual indulgence and rapprochement led to a small change in the order of things. The convention of separate rooms was sustained as a fiction to keep the servants happy, not that they cared. It is also good to have one's own quarters for the times when intimacy becomes oppressive. Mostly though, Lissa and I cuddled up very happily in my bed or hers, and our hosts and mentors abandoned any pretence as to their real affiliation. Interestingly, Lissa and I established an almost non-sexual partnership. We did enjoy sex together, but it was of a more cosy and conventional nature. What occurred in various contexts between us and Freddie and Viktoria, belonged to another set of conditions. These were perfectly acceptable and more, but they were outside the room in which we could collapse together and say, 'So how was that for you?' In fact we had become a couple.

Given the variety of Viktoria and Freddie's sexual repertoire, this was a much-discussed question. Dr Freud had not been widely read at this point. Had he been, doubtless he could have explained young Elisabeth's taste for domination and pain. My careless, if genuinely affectionate enquiries as to her past life, pleasures and so on were answered in the same spirit. If one could piece together a narrative it would combine strict Teutonic upbringing, conducted remotely under the aegis of nannies, a dose of Catholicism, much guilt and a well-developed sexual appetite. This last it seems being given expression through her pubescent acquaintance with Viktoria. All of which meant that she adored Viktoria, liked the male body and found having her bottom smacked pleasurable. Our present situation provided the perfect combination.

II

So we proceeded through 1917. Our days mostly comprised of the activities and duties common to landed gentry. Our evenings and nights were frequently enlivened by bouts of sexual debauch. The judicious blending of pleasure and pain and the indiscriminate satisfaction of our lusts with whatever combination of organs or orifices took our fancy. I learned to tolerate and sometimes enjoy being sodomised by Viktoria wearing a dildo, especially if I could immerse my cock in Lissa's mouth or elsewhere whilst this connection ran its course. Viktoria's tight cunt and sharp teeth both administered delightful agonies when she permitted access. More often, she liked to wield a dildo whilst one's cock was employed elsewhere. My penis was lucky to be admired by Viktoria. In more relaxed moods she would have Freddie, Lissa and I strip naked and enact different sexual cameos, so that she could sketch us. I think one can with practice become not merely inured to, but fully enjoy a surprising variety of sensual experiences. Having disclaimed louche behaviour following my one private encounter with Freddie, I have to own up to subsequent ones though these were promoted and supervised by the women. These were the only moments when Lissa and Viktoria combined on equal terms. It seemed just, given Freddie and my enjoyment of the women's homoerotic episodes. Viktoria's renditions of my virile part were certainly flattering and I still treasure the one sketch I managed to save.

Sheltered as we were, the external world had begun to impinge rather more on us. Freddie's injury had taken time to heal and he was still not fit enough to manage a horse in any demanding context. Neither was he anxious to return to the front. Forced to journey to Stettin for an army medical, he managed to persuade the doctor that he was still unfit but was given only another few months off duty. There was no doubt either, that Germany was in trouble. Increasing numbers of war invalids appeared even in the countryside, as beggars. There were continuous reports of political flux. These mostly seemed to revolve round confrontation between the communists and the nationalist parties.

War news was mixed. The Western front remained in bloody stasis, despite apparent mutinies in the French army. The Austro-Hungarian forces were in collapse. By mid-year, as I remember it, the Russians had a new government and launched an offensive in Galicia. Under the pressure of the German counterattack the Russian troops simply gave up and went home. In September, Germany also captured Riga. Freddie received instructions to join a Pomeranian unit being formed to move into South East Prussia in March of 1918.

Then the Russians had their Revolution and by December the armistice had been agreed and it was pretty much all over on the eastern front. In the spring there was a major German offensive on the Western Front, which seemed to be going well until the Americans joined in. Freddie reported to Stettin where he was told that his cavalry corps – redundant in major battle terms, was being reassigned in small units to what were effectively law and order duties on along the border with Russia. He lurked miserably in Stettin for several months.

During his absence, the erotic climate cooled. Viktoria still used Lissa for some girlish games, with myself as an occasional added player and model for her sketches and painting. Lissa and I became somewhat like an affianced couple using each other as a reminder of the quiet pleasures of the conventional fuck. She still preferred to be dominated though, and I was happy to oblige. I had only to stroke her thigh or nudge her with my cock and she would respond eagerly. 'Oh Willy, have me as you wish,' was her favourite response. We developed a very warm relationship and I grew to respect her intellectual capability. She was widely read and shared my experience of being in but not fully of, the ruling class. Intellectually, she was Viktoria's equal if not superior. This made for some interesting evenings as we sat around the study fire in conversation. I noticed that if Viktoria had been cornered by some remark – however innocuous, she would be especially severe with Lissa at their next sexual encounter. Indeed, conflict appeared to stimulate her desires. As they did Lissa's, for I noticed that she would often show herself deliberately provocative. In which debates her eyes would glitter and her breath come faster as if in anticipation. During my life I came across quite a number of women, and not a few men who appeared to relish pain and humiliation as an aid to sexual gratification. I read books on the topic, but candidly was none the wiser as to why.

By the autumn and winter of 1918, everything fell apart for Germany. The Kaiser was gone, the German navy mutinied and the Weimar republic sued for peace. Freddie returned to the Eisen *Schloss* with a small troop of Uhlans in the Polish Hussar uniforms affected in the historically ambivalent Pomerania. At least this is how Freddie explained their new guise. In retrospect it may have been a ploy to facilitate his subsequent activities. He told us that there was complete confusion everywhere. The army had disintegrated, there was great resentment about what was seen as betrayal by the government, and the officer corps was divided between anger at the Weimar and fear of the highly aggressive communists who had already attempted an uprising. The Bolshies had tried something approaching a revolution and although regional in impact and quickly suppressed, the conflict might grow much worse. He himself had been given carte blanche to use his troop to support law and order in the area and stamp out any Bolshevik inspired insurrection. It had also been rumoured that the Allies had drafted peace terms that would place the von Eisen estate in Poland. The 'flu epidemic, though severe, had seemed almost trivial by comparison to the other woes now overwhelming the Germans.

Freddie formally discharged me from my parole and declared me a free man. I thanked him, but said I was quite happy to stay on at the *Schloss* as estate manager if he was comfortable with that. There was in truth, little for me to return to England for, other than my back pay. Freddie declared himself delighted, but added gloomily 'I am not sure how long and how safely we can stay here. I have grave concerns for the future of my unhappy country, and to live under Polish rule is intolerable.'

When the Polish Corridor was eventually formalised and Danzig established as a free port under the League of Nations, nothing very much changed for us. There was sporadic trouble from returned and malcontent soldiery. Crime started to rise along with inflation. However, despite general mounting internal disaffection from and hostility to the Weimar Republic, local forces of order in terms of police and civil service maintained a Prussian discipline and loyalty to the old Reich. The Poles had more than enough to do further south and I cannot recall feeling their influence at all. Indeed, other than peasants, the area remained fundamentally German. Freddie and his twenty or so troopers galloped about usefully and were much appreciated by most citizens and the embryo 'new authority' – still in essence German, for providing genuine security. They were not averse to summary justice and looters, thieves and communists learned to keep away from our little corner of the Pomeranian Lakeland.

On the estate itself, my policies of enlightened self-interest earned their reward. Our Kashubs formed their own militia to protect our boundaries. Since they had livestock and hunting rights it was in their interests too, to ensure the growing number of ex-soldiers and urban refugees did not predate on our shared livelihood. Viktoria, who despised the Kashubs even more than Poles and Jews and Catholics, had the grace to admit my methods had been successful. 'I think it is the pragmatism of you English that is at once your most maddening and also admirable quality,' she said.

Fraulein von Eisen had become increasingly extreme and I was becoming a little concerned for her sanity. This was not only to do with her vehemence in regard to anything that did not conform to her Prussian nationalism. Both Freddie and Lissa were absolutely in her thrall. They were both willing to submit to what I thought were starting to become over severe physical experiences accompanied by emotional bullying in the form of habitual abuse of Lissa's racial and religious antecedents. This struck me simply as bad manners. The physical experience included whippings and restraints allied to performance of oral-genital acts that emphasised what I can only vulgarly describe as arse licking and pissing. I have no problems with a pretty girl's *cul*, nor indeed, with her piss if the passion takes us both that way. My difficulty was with the cold brutality of Viktoria's regime. This had ceased to be the licentiously playful indulgence I had first enjoyed. To find oneself fucking a woman in anger because she has just inflicted real pain on you is not my idea of fun although it may be others.

As they do, events brought all matters to a point and to a conclusion. I think it must have been late summer of 1919.

Freddie and I had been out riding, just to 'beat the bounds' and say hullo to our Kashubs. It was late afternoon when we got back and I went up to my room to bathe and change. I passed Lissa's door and heard a muffled sobbing. On entering, I found her lying naked, face down on the bed. She was clutching a rosary. Her creamy buttocks were covered in welts and I could not help notice, between her open thighs, that her vulva was swollen, livid and wet; her pubic hair matted with congealed semen. What does one say, except something like, 'what's the matter?' Her response was muffled and had to do with how she was 'a dreadful and sinful girl who would burn in hell for the pleasure' she took in debasing herself. She made it clear there was nothing I could contribute, so I retreated.

On the landing I met Freddie. He was in a state of great excitement. 'Quick, you must come to Viktoria's room now, she's in a most amazing mood - she wants us both.' My protests of needing a bath and a drink were dismissed - though at least Viktoria had schnapps in her room. I think she was already rather drunk, but it may have been a drug, since I knew her to on occasion favour cocaine if it was available. Since this was a seminal and terminal encounter, I am unapologetic in my impressionistic recall of our extraordinary collective coupling.

Naked and without her usual arrogant commands, Viktoria feverishly aided us to strip. Fallen on her knees she pulled down our britches, underwear, grabbed both our cocks and began pumping and sucking at each. As a breathless coda, she gasped 'Oh, Freddie, Willy, fuck me, oh Mother of Christ I need your cocks in me - today has been the most exciting fantastic day.' What she had in mind was something she had not asked before – though she had created the scenario for Lissa. Straddling me, she slid my cock into her cunt, and leaning forward spread her buttocks for Freddie. '*In meinem Arsch*,' she hissed. We paused for a moment. Viktoria was breathing deeply, Freddie and I could feel each other's cocks inside her. Everything was heat and flesh. I think Freddie could hear her too, as Viktoria murmured into my ear, 'Fuck me very slowly and I will tell you a story.' Her breath was warm and foetid.

'Oh, that debauched girl of ours, that Jewess, that absurd saint worshipper, that miscegenation. She went out you know, and I followed her. Guess where - yes fuck me together, how your cocks fill me! *Ja, gut*. She went down to the lake. I found her in the trees and she was watching your men Freddie, who were bathing and naked. I saw her feeling herself the slut. So I came up behind her and said to her "You jewwhore, do you want to fuck these men, do you want all their big fat cocks in you, do you want them to fuck you until their sperms run from your nostrils?" She just looks cow-eyed at me and nods her head and I tell her to strip herself. Then I find a birch stick and begin to beat her so she cries out. The corporal comes to see what has happened and all the men come from the lake. I say to him, "This bitch on heat wants to be fucked by real soldiers like you." And he laughs and says "Yes your ladyship." So we find a fallen tree and place the whore on her knees leaning on it. I say to her, "What do you want bitch?" and she says "To be fucked," and I tell her, "Louder," and she calls out, "Just fuck me fuck me." Then they fuck her, one after the other, in the cunt, in the arse, in the mouth until she is streaming and choking with sperm and I am saying "fuck her, fuck her," just like I want you to fuck me now, hard, hard, *Ja, ja*.'

Depraved as this may seem, when engaged with such a sensual woman the narrative carried great erotic force. Freddie and I followed her to her noisy and forceful climax before slipping from our respective burrows and reaching for the schnapps bottle. Later, after dinner, the womenfolk having taken theirs in their rooms, Freddie and I sat in his study and pondered life over what was the last of his brandy. He was concerned about inflation, the Polish thing in relation to his estate, the instability of Germany and the injustice of the Treaty of Versailles. I expressed sympathy with much of this but raised my own worries about Viktoria and Lissa. Our domestic situations apart I pointed out that discipline in his command had been prejudiced. He listened and then said, 'I agree. It has been very enjoyable, but safety, sanity and good order have come together. I intend to send them both away. We have a family house in Schleswig-Holstein and Lissa must go to relatives in Vienna.'

We briefly discussed the travel logistics for this. The escapade of the afternoon had made it impossible to provide either woman - especially Lissa - with an escort from Freddie's resident cavalry. He decided to drive them himself to Stettin in the car – recently acquired, and there secure a reliable means of seeing them to their final destinations. Whilst I could not hold official rank in relation to his troops, Freddie assured me they would be comfortable if I had an honorary post as his deputy. On my way to bed I called in on Lissa, who had, like Viktoria, dined in her room. To my relief she was composed if wan. I told her of the plans for her and Viktoria and made what I hoped would be comforting and uncritical remarks. These included assurances of my own affection and regard. She smiled and said, 'Willy, it has been very nice with you, and thank you for many things.'

A couple of days later, we loaded their trunks onto the estate's Daimler-Benz tourer and they left for Stettin some 120 miles away to the West. If Lissa was calmly resigned, Viktoria was almost ebullient. She had always hated the countryside here, and its people. In front of the servants we could only exchange politely affectionate embraces but Viktoria whispered 'I shall miss my Captain *Wilhelm*, come to see me in Rendsburg if you can.' I watched them out of sight down the drive and turned myself to estate duties. Despite the episode with the two women, Freddie's troopers remained courteous and disciplined. Their corporal, who was a good soldier, made it plain that he accepted me as Freddie's surrogate. In fact I enjoyed two or three very pleasant evenings in his company, and that of some of his men. The corporal's words to me allayed any doubts I had about the oddity of my position. 'A good officer is a good officer. We are all professional soldiers,' he said. We had shared a common experience; that of honest soldiers betrayed by stupid or careless generals. They did not feel defeated, any more than many of our soldiers felt victorious.

When Freddie returned he was in a determined mood. Having dispatched the women on their various journeys, he had spent a couple of days with the local military command. Everyone was angered by the government's treaty capitulations. Despite joining a practical political alliance to defeat the Bolsheviks the army was determined to preserve its independence. Some even proposed to restore the Reich. Meanwhile, numbers and materiel were being savagely reduced. As an alternative to resigning his commission - or whatever they did in Germany - Freddie had been offered an interesting option for continuing service.

Under another treaty, Germany had been asked to provide policing services in Livonia (wherever that was), whilst a plebiscite was conducted to determine who it should belong to. I must say, the further east you go, the more bizarre the tribal arrangements show themselves to be. Freddie could take his chaps and do that, but with a hidden agenda. Elements of the German High Command were keen to put out feelers to their Russian opposite numbers. The Huns had been told to hand back their best weapons and not have serious armament such as tanks. I couldn't follow the detail. The Russian did not, for obvious reasons face such problems. I think the scheme was that Freddie as a good Prussian would exploit his geographic position to establish some sort of liaison that might secure German access to useful contacts and indeed in due course, supplies. The upshot was that Freddie had decided he wanted to do this. He put it to his men and they all said '*Heil, mein Führer.*'

This left me. Freddie had thought of that. My mission was to close down the estate and ship all the valuables to Rendsburg, where Viktoria and her branch of the von Eisens would take care of them. After I had done that, I would be on my way home. The house and estate were sacrificed to politics. There being no market, they would either vanish into some titular limbo, or survive to be reclaimed. Gerhard and Birgit would stay on so long as I needed them, but had already decided to retire gracefully to Gerhard's hometown which was somewhere on the Baltic coast, safely in Prussia. Freddie's confidence in me was genuinely touching, and I told him so. He shrugged 'I think you are now part of the family. In any case, what choice do I have?'

Promises and commitments were made in high emotion. Freddie was anxious to reach his new, if temporary base in Königsberg up on Germany's far north-eastern Baltic coast before the weather became too severe. He had hopes of rail transport, but under present conditions could not guarantee it. I had to mention the problem of money. Whilst the estate enabled us to produce tradeable commodities and there were some nugatory rentals, to pack up and ship an entire household took quite a deal of cash, especially in these inflationary times. Freddie clapped me on the back, 'No problem old boy, the Hansa Bank in Danzig will have letters of credit backed by von Eisen gold – or what is left of it. I will leave you with your personal letter of authority. Do you think all my time in Stettin was worrying how to gallop about East Prussia with a bunch of mad dogs?'

He rummaged in his desk and produced a thick folder of documents that he thrust at me. I leafed slowly through them. My spoken German and Polish had now become quite fluent if in the second case heavily regionalised. My spoken German on the other hand was very smart thanks to my tutors. Reading and writing were much less competent. The gist of these letters was however plain. The bearer was who he said he was, and the fully competent agent of Ritter Friedrich von Eisen. He was to be afforded all assistance and resources on command and so forth. I was puzzled by quite who was 'the bearer'. This appeared to be one Count Magnus Pietrowski.

'He is you, you are he.' Freddie was delighted with his little surprise. 'Willy my dear friend. The von Eisens and the Prussians have been in this part of the world for centuries. Think of it as you English and the Scots.' He could never get the hang of Cornwall. 'So we have German titles and we have Polish titles. Not all of the Poles are peasants you know. So this is one of the small pieces of our family story. In fact, it is derived from this area and I believe the Eisen estate and possibly the entire area was originally in the Pietrowski name or something like it. We von Eisens are the parvenus.'

The idea was perfectly simple yet rather subtle. I was now provided with some very flexible identities: a freed British officer, yet the accredited agent of a good Junker aristocrat and also a scion of Polish aristocracy. My use of these was up to me. Freddie thought that given the new arrangements, there would be times when to be Polish could be helpful. He also remarked with a laugh, 'this will also help you explain your terrible accent.' How wise he was, how farsighted. He left the following day at the head of his little troop. I watched them down the drive and just before they were out of sight, he broke away and reined in facing back to the house. We saluted each other. There was something in the moment that had an air of finality. He was riding quixotically enough into dangerous territory in uncertain times. Friedrich von Eisen would have been a fine elder brother. Whatever his fate, he wouldn't die falling off his horse drunk.

III

If Freddie had been anxious to get on before the winter, so was I. The prospect of a solitary Christmas – or Yulefest, in the *Schloss* did not appeal, although it seemed inevitable. Gerhard and Birgit were very attentive in the days following Freddie's departure, but it was evident they were now looking to their Baltic seaside retirement. There was little time left before the roads turned to swamps in which to even establish let alone execute a major move. The key element was reconnaissance. I decided to drive to Danzig and see how this newly created League of Nations Freeport would work for me. It was of course also the place where the von Eisen money now was. I told Gerhard that it was very possible they could not leave until the following spring; but that I would make it very much worth their while to manage the house until then. He was content with that. I also had to visit my favourite Kashub; an aggressive old swine with whom I had many arguments and drunk many bottles of their local, vile, potato vodka. He had the simple commission to protect the estate, the house and especially my horse, during my absence. The reward would be in gold. It never fails really, especially in uncertain times. I had a dreadful hangover the morning after our diplomatic meeting.

The *Schloss* was indeed a dreary place in which to be alone. Gerhard and Birgit had their cosy servant's quarters, I was left to nurse my schnapps in the study or make my way along the empty corridors to a chamber peopled only with the ghosts of absent friends and lovers. The size of the rooms and the heaviness of the Teutonic décor added to the cheerlessness. Freddie and Viktoria's collection of erotica only served to remind me of more amusing times. So I occupied myself packing things up ready for the forthcoming move.

To reach Danzig was less problematic, though no less tedious than I had supposed. It must have been mid-October. Mellow September had given place to wet and chilly intimations of winter. The roads were bad and in the absence of a detailed map I relied heavily on my compass, instinct and the odd villager. I had no idea of the range of the Benz. Freddie had left me with the fuel cans he bought in Stettin - many litres - but was characteristically vague about the vehicle's consumption. Though he knew to the hundred grammes how much hay a horse needed each day. The distance as I recall, was only a little less than that to Stettin in direct terms; but inevitably, the route to Danzig from Lake Drawsko – at least on what passed for main roads, involved some deviations from the compass line. That said, I made Danzig with only one overnight stop and my fuel well conserved thanks to the availability of black market petrol from the occasional entrepreneur, at a price.

Danzig or Gdansk as it became was an extraordinary place. It combined the confidently ornate and powerful architecture of a Hanseatic entrepôt supplemented by the unique mixture of barely concealed criminality and oppressive bureaucracy that derives from war and being on the edge of disputed territory. The whole overlaid by the thin daylight and constant drizzle of a Baltic late autumn. I must say, that if it was my combination of languages that got me there, it was my identity tag as Captain W Myddleton that finally got me into the League of Nations office, albeit one staffed by a German official. We fenced around the major issues along these approximate lines.

'So Captain Myddleton, you are an escaped prisoner of war?'

'Liberated perhaps rather than escaped.'

'As you wish. Why do you come here also as Count Pietrowski?'

'I don't, those are simply my letters of authority.'

'They may be interpreted differently.'

'I'm sorry, I only show you what I was given.'

'I see you are authorised by Ritter Friedrich von Eisen.'

'Yes, I was his prisoner and then on parole to him.'

'Why are you here with these authorisations?'

'To protect Baron von Eisen's interests.'

'Where is the *Rittmeister*?'

'I believe in Königsberg, on official army business.'

We sat contemplatively for a while. He, looking at the papers in front of him, me looking out at the grey sky.

He said 'The von Eisens are a good family. They must trust you.' I agreed with him. He fiddled in a drawer and pulled out a form, the bottom of which he signed. 'You should fill the rest of this in, and take it to the Westerplatte free port, when you have decided everything. If I can advise you, I should sign as Count Pietrowski.' I stood up and thanked him. He asked where I was staying so I told him. 'Please, remain there for one or two days, I think someone will wish to see you, someone who will be helpful,' he added before I could ask any more.

I decided to make good use of the time. The Westerplatte was the designated Polish free port and I presented myself with my Pietrowski letters of patent. The official at the gates was more impressed by my Kashubian Polish than by the documents. Good relations established over a shot or three of vodka, we shook hands on the promise of my return, in due course and God willing, with fully completed papers. The bank was shut until the next day. I found a café and sat in it with a cup of real chocolate and the inevitable schnapps. This was where I met Jurgen Tost, mutineer, deserter and my business partner for the next eighteen years.

Arrived at an adjacent table he seemed hardly different at first, to many of the men I had observed around Danzig. A little gaunt, clean if roughly shaven, somewhat shabby but in his case with an alert and confident quality to his physical bearing. He had the air of a man who had something to offer, not one seeking a favour. Well, we caught each other's eye and nodded and ultimately began to converse. He smiled without deference at my identification, in Polish, as Count Magnus Pietrowski. 'Oh, one of those Polish things. I thought you might be German.' I switched into that language to say, 'It is a German title, owned by the von Eisen family.' He looked quizzically at me. 'That is very good, *Rittmeister*, but something tells me you are not what you seem. Does it have to do with why you were at the Westerplatte earlier today?'

There are moments when you have to trust to instinct in relation to another human being. This was one of them. Jurgen had style and I felt not merely an immediate rapport, but the sense of a much larger shared purpose. So it proved. Over supper in some cellar café of his recommendation we exchanged biographies. To the particular point, he had been a rating involved with the German navy mutiny in 1918, when the officers of the Baltic fleet had tried to order a last do or die excursion. Ashore, and uncertain as to whether he was mutineer or discharged he simply submerged himself in the ambiguous environment of Danzig. Here, his natural charm and commercial talents helped him exploit the new and fluid boundaries of authority. I told him of my mission and he was delighted. 'I can tell you Willy, this is possible. We can get all this stuff you have to move, and ship it out. With your papers and my inside knowledge there is no problem.' So, our partnership began, with Jurgen Tost as my *Herr Fixit* and me as the credential-bearing, wealth-generating, Pomeranian Count.

Chapter 4

'TIS TO GLORY WE STEER

I had booked a room at the Hotel Vistula, and transferred Jurgen there from his grim sailor's hostel. The Vistula was sensibly unpretentious. Probably a brothel for most of the war, it had managed to clean its sheets and repair the plumbing to accommodate a prospective new clientele of business rather than military guests. The effort had been only partially successful, and had definitely failed in regard to the staff and food. Though I doubt many English hotels would have done any better at the time. The morning after my encounter with Jurgen, I descended to the lobby to be greeted by a very British looking man in a quite well cut suit. He addressed me quietly saying, 'Good morning sir, I believe you are Captain Myddleton. I am Charles Hoddle, HM representative with the League Authority in Danzig.'

I hadn't spoken to an Englishman since God knows when, so I was very taken aback until I recalled my conversation with the official the day before. I stammered a reply of acknowledgement. He quickly explained himself as HM's local intelligence officer in addition to his official function. He turned out to be courteous, straightforward and honourable. I probably have him to thank for my little ship of enterprise being launched rather than sunk.

My first League interlocutor had of course passed me on to Mr Hoddle. Whether for official or other reasons I shall never know. We reviewed my circumstances much as I had already done. I made it plain that I had no great desire for early repatriation and felt honour bound to fulfil my mission for von Eisen. He listened without comment and asked if it would be convenient for me to stay in Danzig for a week or so. Since Jurgen Tost and I were only just starting to work out our plans for the shipment of a large quantity of valuables through the freeport, this was acceptable.

By the end of our first week, we had secured an ex-army truck and a good line of credit. Freddie's bank was very cooperative and as inflation was already gripping, a little hard currency – in this case, Swiss francs and gold coin, went a long way. We had also secured the promise of warehouse space within the Westerplatte. Mr Hoddle had not been in touch and I was anxious to be away. Then he turned up at the hotel one morning, apologetic for the delay, but with the reasonable excuse that communication with London took time.

We sat at a table in the hotel bar. He looked quizzically at me, fiddled with some papers he had taken from his briefcase and cleared his throat. I felt as uneasy as he looked. He said, 'Some bad news I'm afraid. Lord Broleigh is dead. He died two years ago in fact.' I noted he had not referred to Arthur as 'your father'. 'Ah' I said, 'I know he'd been very ill.'

'The thing is,' said Hoddle, 'when the Army first notified Lord Broleigh's representatives that you were missing, believed killed, they disclaimed any knowledge of a William Myddleton.' He allowed a pause. I said nothing. He went on, 'The Army is of course glad you are alive.' I thought fleetingly of the entire Army going 'Hurrah, Captain Myddleton is alive.' Hoddle added 'Whoever you are.' There was no point in attempting some kind of bluff. The ammunition locker of invention was empty. 'Actually, I am genuinely Lord Broleigh's younger son, but illegitimate.' The rest of the narrative took only a few minutes to set out.

Hoddle called to a waitress for schnapps. He waited until this was served and then said 'I'm very, very sorry to tell you that your mother is also dead. 'Flu, in the epidemic.' He let me absorb this and drink my schnapps. I felt nothing. Life had just come to a full stop. Hoddle went on gently, 'I'm afraid it was her death that found you out. She'd obviously dealt initially with all Lord Broleigh's personal post during his illness and simply kept the Army's communiqué back. When she died it was found in her possessions.'

'I don't suppose you can prove your paternity?' asked Hoddle. I shrugged. My birth certificate had 'not admitted' on it under that heading. I suppose mother's relatives might make sworn statements. It was all too complicated. 'The thing is,' said Hoddle, 'strictly speaking you should go back to England and face an Army Board. Mainly because you've been missing a long time and the circumstances need to be clarified. I mean, might you be a deserter and how did you get here?' 'Of course.' I replied. 'Actually' he went on 'the issue of your assumed identity is not that important to the Army. I mean technically it's an offence but mostly it is a civil issue. At least you haven't tried to embezzle money or anything.' He chuckled in a friendly way. I decided more schnapps might help. I noticed Jurgen had come into the hotel bar and was sitting across the room watching us. I waved at him.

Hoddle said 'A friend?' I confirmed this. Hoddle continued 'You had a good army record, a very good record. You did the family name credit.' 'I'm glad you think so.' 'Not me, the Army.' Ah, the bloody Army. 'Well the Army thinks it would be much more use if instead of dragging you back to all sorts of enquiries and procedural nonsense with the civilian authorities you stayed around and used your unique position to help us cope with the rather fluid circumstances in this part of Europe.' He read my question in my face.

'Intelligence is quite concerned about how matters are playing out after the war in Germany. Given your mission for the von Eisen's, some regular reports and some eyes and ears work on specific subjects would be very welcome and of course recognised.'

It didn't take me many seconds to agree. We met the following day and I received a briefing at his office. It was mostly about the technicalities of reports and message exchanges and the rest. Like the reporting procedures, the actual scope of my job was pretty loose. The reward was that I would be considered to have remained in good standing as a PoW and then on active service. The Army would ignore the slight irregularity in my credentials, provided I didn't embarrass them. They took the view that Myddleton was hardly an unusual name.

At the end of our meeting Hoddle held out his hand to bid me goodbye. There was something that looked like a twinkle in his eyes as he said, 'Ah well, these are interesting if troubled times. Good luck Captain Myddleton, or should I say, Count Pietrowski?'

Apart from the truck, Jurgen had also acquired a cook and a housekeeper for us. It was evident that we could not think of shipping things out until springtime and that the *Schloss* would remain our base until then. Nadia and Catherine were White Russian sisters and refugees from the Revolution. They worked as cook and waitress respectively in Jurgen and my favourite restaurant. Somewhere in their twenties, they had a typical Slavic calculated charm rooted in the need to survive. They came from good, but now dead families. That they had very adequate physical attributes made the offer of a job easy to make. This was of course accepted with alacrity but without any exhibition of pathetic gratitude. We all returned to Eisen *Schloss*.

Dreary as autumn and winter may be in that region, my recollections are of a pleasurable time. Partly due to Jurgen's invigorating and useful presence, Nadia and Catherine certainly added to our quality of life. November proved mild, so as we now had staff, Jurgen drove Gerhard and Birgit to Stettin, from where they could entrain to a well-earned retirement with a small but useful emolument in the form of gold coin.

There was much to do. We had to take inventory of our stock and begin the process of packing it up for shipment. I noticed that Jurgen and my Kashub headman had struck up a relationship. It turned out that there were a number of households around the border area who had need to either sell or arrange exit to safe refuge for valued possessions. We never asked why. In these and subsequent times, there were many reasons to remove assets from Germany and Poland. Whilst my primary concern was for Freddie's most valued stock, development was not to be ignored. I put Jurgen in charge of making the business decisions. When we would buy outright or charge a fee for shipment and storage. In the former situation our access to Swiss francs – later, dollars and other hard currency, guaranteed knockdown prices. In the latter, fees were the same, hard currency. Candidly, I didn't much like the responsibilities attached to caretaking other people's possessions. Jurgen just laughed it off and said, 'We'll work it out.' To be fair to both of us, in most cases we managed eventually to at least ship the stuff to a place from where the owner might collect it: provided we and they were able to keep in touch. A number did so.

In one way, the winter helped. December and January were bad - apart from the general shambles, those assiduous myrmidons of authority who might want to interfere had to struggle with the desire to stay indoors. Jurgen, his charm and his ex-army truck - a rather good purchase as it turned out - together with a bit of currency and the Kashub grapevine did the rest. By the spring, the *Schloss* and its outbuildings were crammed with valuables. They were real valuables. No one parted from, neither did we accept anything, that had not an impeccable claim to being worth a good price.

Meanwhile, back at *Schloss* Eisen, Nadia and Catherine provided the real comfort of our bleak albeit commercial midwinter. Perhaps impressed by the very gentlemanly way we conducted ourselves; after a suitably formal period, the girls did what all women do in the company of the most powerful and successful men in the vicinity; they threw themselves at us. Nadia chose Jurgen, Catherine me.

I do not quite remember 'first time.' That may have been the evening we all sat around the fire in the library, sprawled on the huge sofas and the girls just came and lay on us like cats. Or it might have been when Catherine tip-toed into my bedroom on a particularly cold night, candle in hand, and shivering, snuggled up next to me, wrapping her bare legs and arms around me, her face laid on my chest and her hand finding its way into my pyjamas. They weren't twins, but looked enough alike to be mistaken for such. They had high Slavic cheekbones, calculating blue eyes, strong jaws and full lips; the sensuality of which hid the steely nature of the survivor.

II

Whichever had been the circumstance, regardless of cynical perceptions as to motive, we refugees from hideous reality enjoyed ourselves. I doubt love was involved, but we had grown to like each other. True, when Catherine had her fist around my cock, she became somewhat less hard edged. Then, given how she had a particular trick of using her cunt to squeeze and milk my cock in small pulses just as she wanted me to come, I felt very affectionate during our shared moment of pleasure. Her predilection for cocksucking was matched by my taste for her savoury slit. We came to an unspoken accord on how in general we preferred each other to be. Her English improved a great deal, and I learned some useful Russian. They may have been two tarts on the make, but they deserved only the good things in life.

Mostly we fucked happily and privately with the girl who had, for her own reasons, chosen to our partner. Occasionally, and Yulefest was one such occasion, we found it more convenient or amusing to remain in the warm library with its blazing log fire and let the alcohol and the festive mood carry us along. People may suppose that the male with the biggest penis excites envy in his peers. This is possible, but Jurgen was perfectly well endowed and to judge from his relations with women, a highly competent lover. Whatever the case, at some point both girls decided they would like to swap experience of '*Villy's und Jurgen's grosse Schwanzen.*'

'You are both very nice mens,' pronounced Nadia one evening as we lay on the sofas in front of the fire. 'Very sexy, very rich,' agreed her sister. 'We are going to fuck you both together,' added Catherine. In a short moment, we were all four naked. Nadia and Catherine were strongly but leanly built. The firelight enhanced the curves and shadows of their torsos. 'Lie down Villy,' commanded Catherine. I lay back on the rug in front of the fire. Nadia straddled my hips and gripped my already half-erect penis. She began to pull on it and rubbed the head along her slit. Then Catherine knelt astride my chest facing her sister. Her buttocks curved and split above me. She moved back into my face. There was a whiff of cunt and arse. My now erect cock was swallowed in Nadia's cunt and she began to ride up and down.

There was only one thing left for me to do. I opened my mouth and began to run my tongue along Catherine's vulva from clitoris to arsehole. She sighed and let her weight come down a little. Then her whole cunt enveloped my face and I was fucking her with my tongue and sucking her clit and drinking her juice to stop myself from suffocating, drowning or both. I propped up her buttocks enough for her to grind away without killing me. There was a peripheral sighting of Jurgen between the two women who were competing to suck his cock as they pleasured themselves on my prone body.

These diversions apart, we had a task to perform which was to save the von Eisen hoard. At the same time, we had collected a significant quantity of straightforward art and craft that owners had either sold or wished to protect. By spring we began shipping disposable stock to the Freeport and on from there.

Whilst Germany was going through grisly upheavals and tribulations, and Poland much the same, we led a rather charmed life up there in the Polish Corridor. A degree of fleet footedness was required to be sure. There was a border of sorts to be negotiated from time to time. Numbers of violent political gangs to be placated or faced down in some German towns: as well as the array of mendicants, thugs, dispossessed and Polish official chancers that attempted to invade our estate or waylay our little convoys. In these matters we were helped by the relative tranquillity and homogeneity of the Pomeranian scene at the time; the fact we were in neutered if not neutral territory; and very locally, our Kashub allies. Overall, it was safest if pressed, to be nationalist and of the right wing. This enabled one to express broadly sympathetic views without risk of insult to specific party susceptibilities. Later on and increasingly, this became quite central to our dealings with bureaucrats and civil servants. Many were to lose their jobs; all suffered inflationary effects on, and even reduction of, their salaries.

Our command of hard currency in combination with our flexible diplomacy won us safe passages, access to permits and studied indifference to our irregular transactions. Jurgen proved astonishingly adept in getting us around difficulty and out of problems. He also became the key to securing a continual supply of materiel for our business from internal German sources. My role was in effect, external relations. I had the title and the legal authority. I also had the diplomatic contacts with the Freeport and the League representatives. Herr Richter, my first contact, became an expensive, but effective asset, as did in due course, the traders who came from Hamburg, Berlin and even Sweden, to look for opportunities in Danzig and en route make us wealthy.

Over the following year, our base of operations became Danzig, or for the Poles, Gdansk. The *Schloss* was stripped and shuttered up. We had a warehouse full of furniture and artwork in the Westerplatte. This became our trade centre as we gradually reduced our stock. I rented the whole top floor of the Vistula, so it became both our office and our home. Nadia and Catherine showed a useful talent for customer relations and I feel they more than paid for their keep in this regard. When Nadia eloped with a Swedish ship's captain and Catherine took off for Berlin, we missed them for more than their company in bed. They had a nose for business and for crooks. If they said '*niet*' then that was it.

The day they decided to go was memorable. We had noticed their growing distraction from our business, although we could not fault their attention to duty. Then one evening, in our quarters on the top floor of the Vistula as we relaxed after dinner, Catherine said 'We have some news.' Jurgen and I sat up in our chairs. 'But first,' said Nadia 'we want a good fucking with you.' We negotiated the news before the fucking. It turned out that Nadia had formed an alliance with a Swedish ship's captain and Catherine wanted to go to Berlin. They had decided to celebrate the severing of our alliance with a last shared sexual amusement. 'Men like to see girl with girl,' said Nadia, 'so we will do this and you can fuck us also while we do it if you like.' They stood up, embraced and stripped each other with a sort of ironic sensuality. Blouse, skirt, knickers, swaying hips and pouting lips. The descent to the double bed as their mouths writhed against each other and their bellies and breasts pressed close became less and less satirical. By the time they had turned and gone *tête-bêche*, thighs clenched around necks, there was no artifice. The sisters rolled on their sides still locked face to cunt. From where we stood, Jurgen and I had the erotic image of blonde hair between fleshy buttocks and a general mêlée of hands and legs as the women snuffled and suckled.

The bed wasn't huge but we chose a partner and snuggled alongside the woman with whom we had first paired months before. I slid my cock between Catherine's thighs under Nadia's nose. She licked the head and shaft squeezing my balls as she guided me into her sister's cunt. We fucked until the combination brought us all to a satisfactory and messy finish. As we lay laughing with affectionate pleasure, Nadia said 'You know, this is the best. Women can suck, men can fuck.' The next day they left. We envied the Swedish captain. Especially as the Berlin plan had been shelved because the sisters did not want to be separated. We both thought he would be lucky to escape with his ship. This was not least because the sisters had managed to embezzle a measurable, if tolerable percentage of our sales income over the months of our acquaintance.

By 1923 Jurgen and I had decided that our time in Danzig was at an end. The departure of our amanuenses was coincidental and fortuitous. We had grown tired of the constant ducking and diving necessary to survival. Moreover, Jurgen was finding it increasingly unrewarding to move into and around a Germany in a state of flux. We decided that Denmark would provide a comfortable and stable environment in which to set up shop; and the port of Esbjerg on the North Sea coast seemed ideal. It gave us ready access to England, the Netherlands and Germany – from which last, we still had hopes of business. In any case the Schleswig-Holstein branch of the von Eisen family was in Rendsburg not far from the border, and I was mindful of my unfulfilled obligation to them.

I warned Hoddle of my intention to leave Danzig. He was relaxed, even encouraging. Over the previous year or two I had kept him informed with general intelligence about 'the mood', and an occasional titbit concerning the devious trade alliances and the more notable protagonists we had come across. I hardly imagine any of it was of real value, but it seemed to please Hoddle and I hope kept bureaucrats back in England happy.

One aspect that may have been helpful was our connection with Berlin and the Weimar cultural milieu. Whatever the political and economic turmoil, 'modernism' dominated the intellectual scene. Our business and my personal interest made me alert to it. Berlin itself was a cultural centre where art and sexual liberalism created a bizarre atmosphere. Alongside the decadence was a brutal and violent undertone to the *zeitgeist*. Nothing expressed this better than the paintings of George Grosz and many others, who made rape and sexual murder the subject of their art. Given the Eisen collection's influence on our business, we rapidly acquired many additions to our stock. Much of it less artistic than pornographic, but marketable nonetheless.

Not that I recognised at the time, but the decadence at the heart of Weimar was shared in the 1920s across the Western world generally; that is if fun, sex and freedom are decadent. The overlay for Germany was the rage of that unhappy nation's post-Bismarckian evolution. I do not recall either, that I spotted the rise of Nazism. Hitler's appearance was of course remarked; but we were far from its originating epicentre and preoccupied with our own business. We did however, comprehend the total fury of most Germans at the consequences of Versailles and the perceived incompetence of their Government. I say 'we' since Jurgen was invaluable in his assistance as I compiled my sporadic reports for Hoddle. Given our geographic position the Bolshevik issue was more interesting to him than anything else.

It was Jurgen who brought me news of Viktoria von Eisen after a visit to Berlin. He had come across an eccentric art collector dealer and publisher with American connections called Putzi Hanfstaengl who was based in Munich, but visiting Berlin. He met Jurgen at an art gallery, where my agent was negotiating the acquisition of some controversial paintings and sketches from the Jewish owner. On the disclosure that Jurgen was in some sense an agent for the von Eisens, Hanfstaengl exclaimed, 'Then you must know the divine demoness Viktoria!' Jurgen had heard of her through me and as non-committedly as possible outlined my own business role in the person of Count Pietrowski.

Viktoria had become something of a star – or maybe notorious is better, among the Berlin intellectual glitterati. A supporter and promoter of artistic experiment in all media, she had the reputation of being a ball-breaker. She gave vent to her Prussian nationalism and Wagnerian predilections in flirtation with Jewish and Catholic writers and artists. Most notably she had suborned some of them to produce pornographic works that satirised their own race and religion. Her intellectual grounds were simply that such work challenged the hegemony of 'old thought'. Her other weapon was her sexual voracity. Jurgen acquired two paintings from Hanfstaengl, who was anxious to protect his reputation for political reasons. One featured Moses in some rocky landscape clutching a stone tablet in one arm and masturbating with his free hand. The other portrayed Christ being orally serviced by the kneeling Mary as he lay rather languidly in his tomb. Neither was in any way original in concept, but both had a crude energy and decent quality of technique that we thought would amuse an iconoclast collector of such things.

The word was that Viktoria was heavily reliant on drugs, increasingly extreme in her sexual behaviour and rapidly running out of money and favour. Jurgen had tried to establish contact, since if nothing else, we had some duty to help; but it seemed she was no longer in Berlin. There was a rumour that she had become enamoured of General Ludendorff, but I never knew the truth of this.

III

My thirtieth birthday found me bobbing up and down on a rusty old coasting vessel on my way to Sonderborg in Denmark. In the hold we had the von Eisen treasures and a great amount of our own. We missed Nadia and Catherine, but were glad they had been good entrepreneurs and found a new sponsor. Jurgen assured me that from his experience growing up in Kiel, girls from our region of destination – whatever their nominal nationality, were very friendly. It was a relief to leave Danzig. The voyage was therefore full of hope and excitement and we drank a great deal of vodka.

As luck had it, a small engine problem caused us to put into Rostock. Whilst the engineers fooled around with the ship Jurgen and I went ashore. In a bar we met Renata. She was Polish, penniless and very keen to get out of Germany. I have to admit that had she been fat and ugly, we would have simply nodded in sympathy and regretted our inability to help. Renata wasn't beautiful, but she had great vivacity, a sensual mouth and nice legs that supported her sturdy, but full breasted and definitely well shaped figure. To get her on board was simple; our captain liked our money too much to object. We sat around in our cabin eating sausage, drinking vodka and swapping life stories. Renata was almost in tears with happiness at her lucky escape.

The good will generated by our selfless action and liberality with alcohol prompted our guest to express her affection in a tangible way. So that around midnight, as the ship's engines throbbed into life, Jurgen and my cocks throbbed in Renata's welcoming embrace. Small as our cabin was, we contrived to make our guest comfortable on her knees as tits swinging, she gobbled lasciviously at Jurgen's cock and I buried the length of mine in her swampy cunt and vice versa. In these situations, where the liquor is enough to blur sensibility without damage to capability, there is a peculiar quality of abandon to the primeval.

What we enjoyed with Renata over the subsequent two days was nothing to do with 'making love.' It was basic fucking. It might be argued that she had prostituted herself for a safe passage, and that we had abused her vulnerability, and so forth. Well, Renata seemed very keen to keep both of us employed and spent her time in our cabin stark naked, sprawled like an odalisque on Jurgen's bunk crying 'More vodka, more chocolate, more fat sausage.' Meanwhile she fooled around with the thick black bush of hair between her legs and opened up her cunt for our delectation. We felt like schoolboys behind the bicycle shed when the local tart in training takes down her knickers for pfennigs. But then, women have a taste for exhibitionism. It excites them.

In the small hours of one night, with Jurgen comatose, I felt Renata pulling at my cock. She wanted a pee and a wash. Whatever its faults our vessel did have passenger quarters with their own head and shower. It was a small shower, and pressed up against a smooth female stomach, an erection was inevitable. Renata laughed and grabbing hold said 'Such a big bad boy.' Hardly surprising then, that we were soon kissing and fondling each other; Renata single minded in her pumping of my prick and me dividing my time between her tits and her cunt. At one point I was suckling on one of her generous teats - she liked that - when she exclaimed, 'I must make a piss.' I invited her to carry on and felt the hot flood as she released herself over my hand while I continued to fondle between her legs. Freed from inhibition and to the accompaniment of her cries of pretended shock, I let go a jet of my own over her stomach. After which we pushed our fingers up each other's rectums and began a mutual masturbation under the hot shower. There is something very sensual about water and sex in combination. The episode ended with a contorted *soixante-neuf* in which I had my tongue up her arse, my fist in her cunt and she was sucking the last drops of sperm in my balls from my sore and swollen glans.

Given my experiences with Julia and at the Eisen *Schloss*, it may seem strange to recall so vividly the brief passage with Renata. There was something to do with having drunk so much vodka that the censor who is the super-ego has abandoned ship and left the bridge to the id. There was also the effect of being on a boat and on the way to the unknown. Transients between life and death, voyagers in time, name your own idea of limbo. However arrived at, Renata offered us unconditional access to the pleasures of the female body and we gladly accepted.

With this in mind, we invited Renata to stay on with us as housekeeper. We were rather disappointed when she said 'No,' she planned to go to Sweden. That country's appeal seemed to affect everyone we met. At Sonderborg, we paid her off with a ticket to Malmo. So with hugs and protestations of amity, we parted.

Although we had left Germany, its presence was palpable and inescapable. Sonderborg, like our destination Esbjerg, had no fond memories of Germans. Both towns had suffered badly in some conflict of the nineteenth century. Sonderborg had been rebuilt quite prettily. Esbjerg had always been and remained a busy working port. But then, our location in Jutland was a practical rather than aesthetic choice given my sense of responsibility for Friedrich's possessions. In any case, news might have come through, and I had some hopes of meeting Viktoria whose perverse sexuality retained a lingering appeal. In particular, I recalled her prominent clitoris. Often a somewhat discreet element of female anatomy in relation to the local topography, hers would swell along its ridge and bare its glans like a miniature penis when excited. In such condition it became an irresistible tidbit and I could understand why Lissa was so willing to orally gratify her kinswoman.

The next few months were spent establishing our base. Apart from our formal credentials, we had to acquire premises and transport. Whilst not immune to the economic vicissitudes of the time, in contrast to Germany, Denmark was a tranquil backwater of civilized life. Our reception there was cordial, and residency easily granted. My ability to enter and leave Germany was more questionable, since the lack of a passport – which the Danes had made remarkably little fuss over in the light of my other papers and on production of my army ID – would certainly be a problem for their neighbour. Jurgen said he could fix a false passport. I declined. There might be a need for other things to be counterfeited and we had to have something important that was genuine. The passport was a detail that had been forgotten by Hoddle and myself.

The answer was of course provided by my connection with British military intelligence. Through the consul in Esbjerg, 'lines of communication' were established, with the result that I acquired my rightful British passport; delivered by the consul – himself a Dane – in a wax-sealed envelope that also contained a signal. The orders confirmed my status as a reserve officer (MI) on secondment for special duties. I had no specific orders other than in essence, keep my head down and stay in touch as appropriate. Still, I had the passport, as 'Mr' W Myddleton. Rather wittily, it described my occupation as 'Commercial Traveller'. I also acquired a Polish passport from that country's sympathetic agent in the same shabby dockside offices as those of my British representative. His not being Polish helped and my having the papers of a Count clinched the matter. In the aftermath of war, loss of personal possessions and documents makes ownership of anything, convincing. It was tempting to go for a full hand and acquire a German identity as well. Jurgen and I agreed that the risks attached to weak authenticity far outweighed any benefits.

Once we had become established, I felt it time to visit Rendsberg and the von Eisen family. This region of Germany was no more pleasant to be in than Pomerania; if anything, more volatile. The Nazi party was now visible and vocal, though yet to become a serious electoral force among the melee of competing interests. The crosscurrents of communism, socialism, nationalism and the various right wing factions together with numbers of paramilitary groups made a poisonous brew. I remain astonished that anything worked at all. We had acquired a touring car and in this, under the guise of English tourist and German guide - these being increasingly common despite the underlying uncertainties - we made our way south to Rendsberg. The possession of hard currency was as ever, invaluable.

The address I had in Rendsberg was that of a substantial detached house in the older suburbs of the town. Behind tall walls and wrought iron gates, it looked somewhat rundown and deserted but we rang the bell hopefully. After a long pause an elderly woman, evidently a servant, opened the door. We enquired after Viktoria von Eisen. The woman scowled and shook her head. We asked if any of the von Eisen family were in residence. This too was greeted with surly denial. Jurgen seized the initiative and speaking rapidly, smiling, bringing out his wallet, he explained something of our mission and indicated that reward would follow information.

After a short lacuna in which Jurgen visited the local stores for coffee, schnapps, cakes and so forth we settled down in the kitchen for a good old *Kaffeeklatsch*. Jurgen's charm apart, my own persona as Englishman and faithful friend of the beloved Friedrich von Eisen, made the old lady amiable and loquacious. The news, such as it was, was not good. Friedrich had vanished. He had indeed been on a mission for the German Army, to establish cooperative contacts with the Russians. Our Frau believed he had been murdered, by the Poles but had no evidence. She spat into the fire as she spoke of them, and again when we asked after

Viktoria. In this second instance she apologised for disrespect.

Poor Viktoria, drug-raddled and on the edge of sanity, had returned to Rendsberg and the care of her aunt. She was not an easy guest and quickly found the circle of dissolutes who formed the Weimar *'Kultur'* there. Our informant did not call them that but her scathing description identified them. They were much as one would expect; provincial quasi-aesthetes who dressed up addiction to sex, drugs and alcohol as part of artistic expression. After a few schnapps we were treated to graphic accounts of dreadful events that involved sado-masochism and ceremonies of appalling and obscene blasphemy. The aunt died of a stroke – attributed to these events, though not as participant – and Viktoria left for destinations unknown with the last of the household cash and a local political hopeful. I mentioned rumours I had heard about Berlin and the Nazis. The Frau shrugged, 'They were a weird lot as I have told you. We had officers and bohemians all together, whips, boots and naked bottoms. There was even a Swedish aristocrat among those awful people.' The news of Lissa was even vaguer. Viktoria had been heard to exclaim that 'The daft bitch has run off with a Turk.' It was later that Jurgen confirmed Berlin and some of Viktoria's connections with the more louche fellow travellers of the Nazi party.

We stayed the night, in chilly and bare rooms. There was no money for heating and the housekeeper was selling the furniture bit by bit to feed herself. In the morning, we left gratefully for Denmark. However, Frau Schmidt as she might as well be called, had some good cash in her pocket, we had an entrepôt in Germany for our business and I still had the von Eisen erotic art collection.

IV

With great respect to the Danes and to Esbjerg, life was pretty dull in our little backwater. Business was slow too. As happens, people became inured to inflation and the economy and the German mark improved too during the twenties, just in time for the great recession. Meantime, Jurgen wandered around Schleswig-Holstein and beyond seeking out trading opportunities. These missions paid their way but were decreasingly fruitful. I was not keen to develop the antiques and bric-a-brac side, preferring the more portable if specialist arena of erotic art and artefacts that had got me into this business in the first place.

Whatever the dramas in political circles and in provinces such as Bavaria some sense of normality had returned at least to our part of the country. Our trade had depended on fear and uncertainty. We were scavengers and pickings were getting thin. I had a touch of ennui.

Jurgen was happy to pursue our business in his native country. The liberal stance of the Weimar Republic had spawned a strong body of dissident and challenging art. Jurgen had struck up an acquaintance with an art and antique dealer in the border town of Flensberg. He proved a valuable intermediary for items too controversial or perhaps dubious in origin for conventional offering. This was to open up an interesting trade with Sweden, many of whose upper classes had strong Germanic affiliations, at least in cultural and political sympathy and frequently with an accompanying taste for the decadent and often perverse. I decided it was time to leave Germany behind for a while. That strange yet compelling country had absorbed enough of my life.

There were only two European cities left with prospects, so far as I could see. These were London and Paris. In both we had a fertile mix of post-war hedonism and a moneyed class. I also had, if Hoddle had told the truth, an army account with some back pay in it. A final contributor to my boredom was the absence of female company. Jurgen's assurances had proved false. As a port, Esbjerg was very able to provide a chap with a fuck of a sort but that wasn't it. I have never worried about pleasuring myself at need. This is a better alternative to a joyless encounter with a wretched, unlovely and probably unhygienic tart. If imagination or some well produced stimuli can't help, better to give up sex altogether. Which would also be kinder to the girls involved. In provincial seaports, you do not come across perfumed professional escorts who will offer witty conversation as well as physical pleasure. This being a service that can be provided at a profit by a decent urban brothel. My main point is however, that mere physical gratification was not the issue. The society of an accomplished and good-looking woman is one of the most desirable ingredients of the civilised life.

Accordingly I made my way to London and presented myself at the War Office in Whitehall. Dressed as I was in continental style and having acquired a slight foreign intonation, my welcome was circumspect. In fact it was somewhat chilly. I mentioned Hoddle, gave my London address as the Cavalry Club which slightly relaxed the atmosphere and the Major who had received me said he would get back to me as soon as possible.

I had never known London well, and it was not too short of a decade since I was last in England. It was like being in a foreign country – but delightfully so. Most of all, I thought I had never seen so many pretty women. Everywhere seemed to be bustle and colour and a sense of frivolity; although, if largely true of the West End of London this was something of a false impression. In contrast to the War Office, the Cavalry Club could not have been more hospitable. I had a decent room, and in the bar was immediately adopted into the circle of regulars. Some younger subalterns, others of my own generation or rank and several older and more senior officers; but all united in our common profession and experience. Though only from a Yeomanry regiment, my credentials and war record gave me adequate kudos and I spent many bibulous evenings swapping tales with my new friends.

After a few days I received a summons to the War Office. Here, I was grudgingly told that my position had been regularised and approved. I was in good standing, except for a reprimand on the record in relation to my tardy resumption of contact with the Army. It seemed pointless to argue the assumptions behind this and disclose the real circumstances. In any case, back pay would be in full up to the date of my capture, after which I would be on half pay until having left Danzig. Thereafter, and until further notice I would be regarded as a reserve officer. This meant no pay, but the Army could call me up at any time. My debriefing Major must have seen my dismay at this last. He looked down at his file and said, 'Not to worry old boy. I think the powers that be just want you to stay in touch in case you can be useful. Someone seems to think you're a bit of a card.'

The money was modest enough, but paid my uniform and some old mess bills that had miraculously been retained and I got my medals and replacement ribbons at last. I was struck by the way they had kept track of everything. This enabled me to cut a dash in the Club for a while, but I had decided to return myself to civilian life and as soon as possible assume the persona of Count Pietrowski. Retired Captains, however gallant had limited social currency. The final prompt for this decision was Dottie Scrimgeour.

We met by accident at the theatre, or rather, outside the

theatre. I don't even recall the show; some confection of a review I believe. As the audience dispersed I became aware of an altercation on the fringes of the cab-hunting cluster by the kerb. There was a girl's voice taut with annoyance and a man's angry imprecation. The words 'bastard' and 'bitch' were distinct. As my chosen course brought me in range as it were, I could see the girl, who was rather striking looking, struggling in the grip of a beefy, red faced type in evening clothes. It wasn't a moment of great wit and refinement. I enquired if there was a problem, the girl got as far as saying 'Yes, this man...' before he slapped her and told me to bugger off. Which is when I hit him very hard on the side of his head and he fell down. Since the English do not like a scene, and in any case the nearest witnesses made clear which of the protagonists they supported, I was able to take my new acquaintance's arm and lead her away into the bustle of Shaftesbury Avenue and the security of a taxi.

Dottie and I liked each other from the start. It wasn't especially my white knight act – though she said it had been as she put it 'dreamy.' Rather, we both just saw something we found interesting. As soon as we got into the taxi she said 'The Ritz,' to the driver. Then turning to me, 'I hope you don't mind, it's one place I know we shan't bump into anyone ghastly.' I think I knew what she meant.

Chapter 5

On Yonder Hill

The girl sitting opposite me in the cocktail bar of the Ritz was of a category my long absence from England had rendered quite foreign, if for no other reason than the progress of history and fashion. For that reason, worth considered appraisal, as opposed to the quite rapid summations possible with more recognisable types.

In one sense she presented as a 'flapper.' Bobbed hair, slinky short-skirted dress that allowed a glimpse of thigh above silk stocking top as she crossed her legs. The beads round her neck were ivory and jade and her cigarette holder tortoiseshell. Thus far she could be any little rich girl. Except for her manner. This carried a degree of impatient authority. Her features were aquiline and she was tall; pretty much my six feet and a little over, in her heels. Broad shouldered but with slender limbs, her legs shapely enough, bony knees and quite big feet. She had no need to bind her bust as was the style, since she didn't have very much of one.

It was Dottie's eyes that imbued her face and character with its instant charisma. Having said her features were aquiline, her eyes reminded me always of a sparrow hawk. Black and gold and piercing they retained a constant alertness.

Dottie flourished her cigarette holder and consumed cocktails and fixed me with her hawk's eyes. Expressions of gratitude and deprecation had been adequately made. It was time to move on. 'So who was the chap?' I asked. She exhaled smoke and waved her cigarette. 'Just a stupid masher who thought supper and a theatre ticket got him into my bed.' She looked at me. 'So what sort of chap are you?' Usually, one tends to be circumspect. With Dottie, as with Jurgen, candour suggested itself to be the best course. A choice not to be regretted. So I told her in as short a summary as possible of my little history; from bastard son of impoverished landowner to retired and ex-prisoner of war cavalry officer and art dealer with another identity. A few brief questions elicited information supportive of my credentials as gentleman of sorts. The obvious counter question was, 'So what sort of girl are you?'

La Scrimgeour turned out to be the daughter of of a Tyneside shipbuilder who had given one or other late 19th century political party some financial support and been ennobled for it, not unlike the Broleighs. She herself, as female and two brothers separate from inheriting anything, took her quite generous allowance to London where she enrolled at the Chelsea Polytechnic to study 'Art'.

This commonality of interest led us into a cocktail fuelled, exchange of thoughts about erotic art. Early on I confessed serious shortcomings in my academic knowledge of the subject. Again, this was the right stratagem. Women are no different than men in appreciating intelligent deference on intellectual matters about which they feel confident. Perhaps they are a little more pleased by it. It also occurs to me, how extraordinary had been the changes in the whole scheme of things so far as candour between the sexes was concerned, since my Edwardian childhood. My relations with Jenny and Julia had been exceptions in the general rule of social intercourse. My exile had precluded becoming aware of the changes in society. I suppose any soldier returned home from some years' absence would find the same. It was a shock, although a pleasant one.

Be that as it may, the waiters reminding us of the hour and

the necessity to eject non-residents curtailed her art lecture. In the street I offered to summon a taxi. 'No, why don't you walk me home across the park?' was her reply. Home was in a mansion block in that odd area south of St James's Park between Queen Ann's Gate and Victoria. So we set off through Green Park. As we did so, Dottie linked her arm through mine. 'I've asked you to do this because I want a walk so I get less of a hangover. Also, because I don't want to meet that fellow you knocked down.' This explanation was perfectly acceptable. I wondered aloud if this chap was a more significant player in her life than she had so far divulged. She stopped walking and turned to face me. We had crossed the Mall and were in St James's Park. 'My father keeps sending people to me because he wants me to marry. I have to be sociable. That person was one of his wretched candidates.'

We strolled on through the greenery and the streets, resuming the discourse on art and erotica until we reached the entrance to her block of apartments. There was no one else in sight, so I took her hand and made my farewells. 'No, I am really quite afraid he may try to get in. Please, will you come in and stay the night?' Her manner was both pleading and imperative. Given my history and experience it's possible my perceptions had been coarsened so that something else – something masculine and lighthearted in my innocuous response conveyed itself. Dottie turned and fixed her eyes on mine. 'I've asked you this and made myself vulnerable because I trust you. All men seem to want is to poke one.'

My denials of ulterior motive were rendered inarticulate by the difficulty of disclaiming lewd desires yet remaining gallant. They nonetheless proved adequate, so I followed her into the lobby and up the stairs to her apartment. It was very spacious and eclectically furnished in a mix of Edwardian and contemporary furniture. There were numbers of pictures on the walls of the hall of equal variety, with a preponderance of portraits of women, in the Impressionist style. In the drawing room above the fireplace was a Modigliani nude.

I commented on this. Dottie laughed, 'Well of course, not the original. A copy I made. I'm rather good at copying. Useless at anything original, brilliant at pastiche.'

She poured me a brandy and made us coffee. We had a brief guided tour of her artworks. She really did have a remarkable gift as a copyist. There was a moment of embarrassment as I opened the door of a room that turned out to be her bedroom. Other than the usual feminine disorder there was a glimpse of a male nude; a satyr with a rather large erection that hung on the wall opposite to her bed. Later I recognised its style as that of Egon Schiele.

'That's my room,' she snapped, and stalked ahead of me back to the drawing room. It was by now deep into the small hours and the events of the evening had been too stimulating for sleep. Dottie had something on her mind and I was determined not to let it go. 'If you expect me to play the gentleman protector Dottie,' I said, ' why don't you just tell me a bit more about these chaps who want to poke you all the time and why you paint pretty Modigliani girls and satyrs with huge cocks.'

Her reply was rather disarming. 'I like women much better for their conversation and in bed. The bed bit is just a small if pleasurable consequence of all the nice things that go with female friendship. Trouble is, I find men sexually terribly attractive, and it's mostly to do with their cock. Just the look and feel makes me go funny despite myself. But your sex is so boring most of the time. There is really only ever one thing and that's how to get our clothes off and stick that fearful organ into us as fast as possible. In addition to which, contraception is such a tedious process.'

This last delivered with a tone of aesthetic outrage.

This made me laugh. I reassured her, that her views seemed entirely reasonable. It had been a long time since I had met a woman as intrinsically interesting as Dottie. Sleep had now become a priority. Whatever business might be conducted between us would have to wait until morning. As I drifted into unconsciousness in her guestroom it occurred to me that this had been a serious encounter.

In the morning, very late, I was in my bathroom making the best toilette I could sans one's usual equipment. The door opened abruptly and in came Dottie brandishing a safety razor and toothbrush. I had turned at the sound of her incursion. We faced each other. Her eyes met mine, flickered downwards. Possibly we both blushed or went '*Aah*' in unison. I was of course, hangover and morning semi erect. Dottie recovered more quickly than I. 'Oh sod, I expect I'm going to have to have that,' and dropping the implements she had brought, to the floor, she exited.

My return to my room was also to Dottie sitting up in my bed, a silk wrap round her shoulders, but otherwise evidently naked. A tray with coffee cups and biscuits was on the adjacent dressing table. 'Coffee or having me pull you off first?' I dropped the towel round my waist and said 'You choose.' Dottie elected for me to get into bed, have a quick injection of coffee and then submit to her masturbation technique. 'I told you I have this dreadful weakness for the male member.' she murmured as she slid down the bed, rested her head on my chest and began fondling the object of her obsession. She had strong and clever hands did Dottie. I would have preferred a more involving scenario but it was very gratifying, especially while I still felt weak. I lay back and admired the shape of her shoulder and hip, the nape of her neck, the clenching of her fist as she pumped away at my prick.

Dottie may have preferred girls but she knew how men worked. She gripped and stroked, teased head and neck, dragged tautly down to the roots, fondled my balls, hauled the ensemble up until it almost hurt. Everything was done with affectionate skill. I suggested my appreciation by gentle caresses to her shoulders and back. It was tempting to take hold of her neck and urge her mouth towards the object of her attention. I was about to do this when, possibly sensing that urge or my approaching orgasm, she sat up and without letting go of my cock began a furious masturbation. 'God, I love this bit,' she exclaimed, her gaze fixed intently on the appendage in her fist. Well, my cock delivered in a generous series of squirts that she expertly directed up my torso and away from her person. She thoughtfully kept her rhythm until she was sure that the whole event was complete.

When she was satisfied on that score, she slumped back against me, her head nestled into my shoulder. 'That was nice.' She lifted her hand to her mouth and licked off the residual semen that had inevitably trickled that way. This was surprising to me. It is a measure of the rapport we had that she said unprompted, 'I like the taste of men's stuff. Sort of oysters and secret.' Then, 'Do you like women's taste?' I was glad to say I did. She sighed. 'I think we'll be very good friends.'

It was, at this pleasant moment of mutual understanding that another of her very good friends crashed into our room with an exclamation of, 'God, one day away and you're back rutting with some awful man.' This was Sybil. She shared with – or rather sponged – off Dottie, and had a room in the apartment. They were indeed lovers and in time we came to accept if not much like each other. Dottie Scrimgeour may have been muddled about her sexuality, but she was entirely confident of her ability to manage it.

II

Inevitably, people spring out of bed, there are exclamations and the battle transfers to another room. I do recall that Dottie's tight buttocks and athletic thighs caused my loins to stir as she pushed her chum through the door and into the hall. Their quarrel diminished shrilly. I dressed and prepared to make my discreet departure. Just as I was about to close the front door, Dottie appeared, sketchily dressed but reasonably covered. 'Sorry about that - shall we meet again?' 'I'd like to.' 'I want to paint you.' 'I want to talk about your painting.' 'This is a business deal?' 'Contact me at my club soon.' 'I shall, later today.'

The immediate outcome of our discussions was that I moved into a spare room in her apartment. There was a financial benefit, though I wasn't short of money and rather liked the Club. Living with a woman has its drawbacks. They tend to try and take over one's life. The real reason I agreed to her suggestion was that I had somewhat fallen for Dottie. That she was a lesbian did not matter. I had no fantasy about converting her, or indeed, three in a bed. She charmed me and I loved her physical presence. If all she wanted to do was wank me, that would suffice.

These considerations I made explicit as we forged our agreement. She laughed, and squeezed my hand saying, 'I'm flattered and relieved. Don't worry William, I expect you'll get that splendid thing of yours up me sooner or later.' On the business side, Dottie was going to start producing erotic art for me. She would do copyist work, concentrating on some of the best-known pornographic works but creating 'new' material in familiar styles. She had a couple of chums who she said were good artists who would knock out suitably titillating and sound quality originals in various genres. We thought explicit versions of some of the classics would be practical, fun and very marketable. The other big decision I made was to revert to my Count Magnus alter ego. I didn't have much feeling for the English market but since that guise had been so effective on the continent it seemed worth trying 'at home'. As it turned out, despite the liberality of the social scene in London – at least in circles such as those Dottie frequented – England was still deeply bourgeois and repressive in sexual matters. The erotic had a market of course, but in a country where even contraception was a virtually taboo subject the obstacles to publishing erotic material were huge.

In consequence, although we were able to establish a small and highly clandestine clientele, England only managed to cover its expenses. Even so, our investment in a range of works made a living for the artists and ultimately a decent amount of money for us, especially abroad.

Meanwhile, the weeks had gone by and in spite of our regular exchange of cables Jurgen and I needed to spend time together. I returned to Esbjerg where Jurgen had hired a private room in a restaurant and we got gloriously tight. There was also a very jolly tart called Irma I think whom Jurgen had picked up in his travels. She was perfectly willing to play with us both and I was almost excessively glad to slip into a hot wet *chatte* after a long period of deprivation.

Our mutual regard could not have been greater, so it was easy to strike the deal that was in any case self-evident. Jurgen had done a great job on the antiques and related objets d'art. He had also done very well in securing reliable access to Putzi Hanfstaengl, who was now a close friend of Adolf Hitler. At this point, Adolf was just another political aspirant albeit with a distinctive line in campaigning. Germany might have seemed a mess to me, but in England, as the war memories faded rapidly,

German culture and ideas were becoming perfectly respectable and even fashionable. The middle and upper classes swanned off to Bavaria and yodelled and slapped their *Lederhosen* and spoke of the need for national pride, discipline and identity.

Whatever the case, Putzi had things he wanted to sell quickly and also that he wanted to acquire. The purchase list included neo-classical subjects especially those that featured naked maidens and warriors in Wagnerian mode. These, Dottie and her chums could and did, knock out with great facility.

So Jurgen and I split the business. He took the antiques bit, I took the art and we had a supply and demand arrangement for original – however interpreted – paintings. It's a rare pleasure to have an honest partner. We went to the bank together and took out money and signed forms and shook hands. Then we returned to what was now Jurgen's apartment and had some drinks, fucked the ever-agreeable Irma and all went out to dinner. It struck me that a woman in company with two men, especially when she is fucking both is singularly elevated in spirit. She has an air of confidence and relaxed intimacy that suggests both power and cessation of struggle or dissimulation.

I returned to London a week or so later. Frau Schmidt had been in hospital - not expected to live - and the house in Rendsberg would doubtless need to be sold. Armed with the von Eisen papers and as Count Magnus I had travelled south and having watched the old lady die – her last words as she clutched my hand were '*Ach, Scheisse!*' – took train and ferry back to England.

Dottie had a studio somewhere near World's End in which she and her confreres churned out their sensual and pornographic pastiches. That's unkind. Original they were not, well executed they certainly were. Since she was not at her flat, I took a taxi over to

Chelsea. Her studio was on the top floor – the skylights obviously the key elements – and on the landing I paused preparatory to entry. Normally, people would burst in unannounced, but some atavistic sense of manners prevailed. Through the door I could hear the sort of sounds only attributable to sexual activity. I'd occasionally stumbled into one of Dottie's lesbian passages with Sybil, and sometimes other girls. She put herself about did Dottie. Apart from one or two earthy encounters of the *soixante-neuf* variety that invited voyeurism, these episodes were rather charming and delicate tableaux in which heads, hands, breasts, thighs, pudenda and buttocks revealed and concealed by sundry fabrics conveyed the femininity of the seraglio.

Like a jealous lover, I opened the door gently. There was a distinct smell of whisky, Dottie's drink of choice. Across the room her bare bottom wiggled. From this angle I admired the strong curve of her hips and the neatly coiffed, ovoid bulge of her vulva and its attendant clefts and curlicues. She was engaged in sucking the penis of a black man. In the modern climate, this may seem unexceptional. Then, it was a matter only to be whispered about.

Utterly sanguine, Dottie stopped her fellation and getting slightly unsteadily to her feet, flung her arms round me with 'William, darling, how wonderful you are back.'

The pressure of her naked body and the warmth of her greeting disarmed my slight resentment at the discovery. Drawing back, she fixed me with a steady gaze and said, 'My love, this is Cedric, isn't he divine? I found him at a jazz club.' Cedric waved lazily at me from his prone position. He was a nice looking young man. Dottie clutched my hand. 'Just look at his cock, isn't it amazing? I think it's bigger than even yours. I just love sucking it.' She must have sensed my lukewarm response because she continued, 'I think I have to go on and suck him off, but it would be delicious if you poked me while I did it.'

What can one say? I stripped off, found a drink and despite the odd nature of this scenario found myself caught up in its peculiar eroticism. Dottie had gone back to sucking her black cock. I watched her mouth and hand as she embraced and manipulated the very thick, very long erect muscle, her teeth barely able to close round the pink-pigmented neck. As it was my first chance to fuck Dottie, I was certainly 'up for it' as they say nowadays. I straddled Dottie's sturdy loins and prepared to penetrate the already moist gulf between her thighs. Nature is wonderful like that. Valleys are always moist and fertile. Then she stopped sucking and said to me, or the absurdly named Cedric 'Gosh, this cock is so nice, I think before I get poked, everyone should suck it.' Women have this habit of changing one's marching orders. I looked at Dottie and she looked back at me defiantly. I think 'You must be joking' was on my lips. She said, 'You suck Cedric or you don't poke me.'

This is how I found myself sucking a very large black cock. To be fair, it was a fine specimen. It had size and gloss and as I had found years before, there are worse things you can do. I gave things my best shot as it were and as I sucked and pulled, Dottie sprawled under me and gave me her oral attentions for the first time. This went on for a while, until Dottie decided she wanted to have her Negro back and so we resumed our positions and she sucked away at Cedric's cock and I slipped into her tight and silky cunt. It may not have been the best fuck ever, but it was hugely enjoyable. Cedric came before me, but he'd had a head start as you might say and Dottie spluttered and moaned and swallowed and frothed. I held her hips and fucked her with her own rhythms until some garbled cries and her body's movements told me to finish us both.

Later, at the flat and when Cedric had been dismissed, she came into my room. 'I'm sorry you weren't first, I mean, well, you know. You can have me all to yourself soon.' Turning to leave she added: 'It was super seeing you suck him. I think you rather liked it too, you rude boy.' I told her it had been blackmail and not to expect me to make a habit of it.

III

The ensuing couple of years were very agreeable. We turned out the product and our customers paid us decently. Jurgen and I enjoyed the working of our mutual business interests, augmented by the sense of freedom we had in running our own enterprises. London however, was in reality restrictive and therefore dull. The apparent gay abandon of the Bright Young Things was a mere shooting star in a gloomy firmament. The establishment that maintained the social and moral hegemony remained deeply puritanical. The deceptive tolerance with which the English ruling classes allow licence to opposition is a clever safety valve. These things can of course be overcome by and even stimulate dissidence; but it laid a heavy hand on the esprit of our little group of entrepreneurial sexual freedom fighters.

Dottie and I discussed these matters at length. Sometimes it was over a meal or a drink, more often, in my bed at the flat. This was her favourite place, since she refused me access to her own sanctum, preserved for Sappho. Typically, we'd spend the restaurant time discussing the issues without forming any conclusion. In bed she would deliver herself of her final opinion. We were in practice, joint venture partners. There was no formal agreement, but I was her distributor and she had the factory. Part of the deal was that she let me fuck her reasonably often. It suited her, because as she had always said, she liked a stiff cock, much more than a dildo for example. Equally, her own sex was what she preferred. She once confessed to a passion for younger girls, but found them limited except in physical presentation. 'Much like men and pubescent boys I suppose,' she said, somewhat ambiguously I thought.

In bed, she was a generous companion given her rules and reservations. She didn't like kissing – the girl territory – and had other little quirks that demarcated her sexual boundaries. Her ideal was to sit astride me, talking as we fucked and she rather liked me suckling her teats. Despite tiny, cone-shaped breasts, the nipples were unusually prominent if unremarkable in diameter. They would harden and suffuse to a portwine colour when aroused. These characteristics of prominence and suffusion were replicated in her clitoris. I could achieve her arousal by massaging her feet between my thighs as she used her toes to tease me into erection. Once we had engaged, she might at any point in the proceeding – other than that immediately before her climax – begin to deliver her verdict on the earlier debate; in one notable case following a discussion about a new base for our business. Astride me, she stopped her slow writhing, took her hands from my chest, unveiled her predatory eyes and said, 'I think you're right. Paris is the only place to be.'

This conclusion flowed from the numerous practical, and let us say erotic characteristics of that city. It was infinitely more liberal in social and artistic climate than London. Certainly for the writer or painter the opportunity to express ideas freely, to experiment and so forth was due to a refreshing combination of indifference and *laissez faire*. Most important, the French had a genuine respect for the 'arts'. In consequence, and in growing numbers, the international community of those who wielded pen, brush and chisel with varied talent, including their hangers on and patrons, colonised Paris. Subsequently, I discovered Dottie had her private agenda. The sorority of Sappho was much more numerous and less constrained in Paris than in London.

Of course, the consequent discussion - she still astride me, animated in commencement of her plans for our removal to Paris - caused my sexual urges to become suppressed. To be fair, I didn't notice. The idea had long been in my mind and I had recently agreed with Jurgen on the likely transport of my collection of art works straight to Paris when the moment was right. The import to England of most of what was in my store would have had me in gaol. I had always kept a special collection of works I knew could only increase in value and which comprised my insurance against hard times. These included what were possibly the most contentious for HM Customs and Excise and doubtless the House of Lords. The prosecution of Marie Stopes only five years previous had alerted us all to the issue of prosecution for obscenity.

Dottie continued to squat on my hips as she expatiated. Dammit all, I was in love with this wretched woman and as I nodded and murmured my agreement I looked up at her illumined face and pointy breasts with their stick-out nipples and down to her athletic thighs and almost absently, caressed her bony knees. My cock slipped out of her of course and she finally noticed and said, 'Oh, sorry, gosh, poor thing.' I told her it was nothing to worry about but she slipped down the bed and began licking it and pressing it to her cheek muttering 'Mmm, I taste nice.' For some reason I pulled myself up in the bed away from her grip, stroked her hair and said, 'Dottie, I love you. It's an impossible love, but it can transcend *coitus interruptus*. Let's focus on Paris and you can give me a fuck or something later.'

On reflection all these years later, Dottie was almost certainly the only woman for whom I felt real love. That is, love because of which, if asked, I would have done anything. Jenny of course, except we were so young and she never asked anything of me, even to stay with her. Maybe I was too callow and selfish anyway. Dottie never asked for anything either. She demanded some things but that's not the same. Nor did she probably much care if I loved her. Ironic, isn't it?

We finalised our plans for removal to Paris in remarkably short time. That said, these things drag on and it was I believe at least two years, thus 1925/6 before we were able to take train and ship to our new capital. The excitement was severely diminished by the ghastly paperwork and engagement with 'authority.' In this case, I also had the additional matter of dealing with my effects from Esbjerg and supervising their shipment. Jurgen was immensely helpful in their transit through Germany. His friendship with Hanfstaengl and other ideologically useful denizens of the German cultural jungle ensuring we acquired the necessary rubber-stamps.

In terms of where, this too involved a certain amount of tedious to and fro. In fact, Dottie and I spent some very amusing times in Paris in reconnaissance. This did not much involve sex, and I think we had by now become chums rather than lovers except occasional ones when affection or the need to satisfy an itch prompted an encounter. Eventually we discovered the Rue St Michel and the property that was to become my personal source of income for the next decade and more. A four-storey residence of the post-Napoleonic era it was run-down and had been used by the University to house visiting professors and lecturers. The rent was modest. Apparently the owner of the house was a benefactor of the University who no longer needed the premises. Dottie and I agreed that the location – also not far from the Senate, home of well-heeled and lubricious middle-aged men – was ideal.

Looking back I am amazed that the great slump of 1928/9 had little or no impact on us. In London, bus driving was a fun hobby for the young socialites. The rich, that is the cash or property rich, were rather well served. In Paris we noticed the crisis even less. Even so, it was a time for acquisition once more as many people sought to cash in some assets and cover stock market losses. For Dottie and I and our friends the artistic pretenders, life was very good. Some of this, maybe the most of it, was because Dottie and I were financially well founded. We shared responsibility for our artistic dependents and this further cemented our friendship. Whilst as usual I handled external affairs, she managed the small coterie of forgers and kept them in order. The house was perfect accommodation for the business and we isolated minions in the attics – where else?

If love was impossible, real affection was not. As she guided me into her cunt, or held me in her fist and sighed over shape and texture, I didn't mind it was my cock not me she wanted. Equally, when we had our moment and she sidled off to her own room and maybe another lover, her blown kiss spoke to me of the unique intimacies of our involvement.

Two significant disengagements and engagements accompanied our move to Paris. Dottie parted with Sybil, I re-engaged with military intelligence. The Sybil thing had been a long time coming. Despite her distaste for me – as man and Dottie's phallus bearing friend – she had accepted my presence and role in Dottie's life. This to the point that she would sometimes come to my room or in Dottie's absence the shared living quarters in great distress about her lover's promiscuity. Her plaint varied between '...not understanding,' '...she's such a selfish bitch,' and '...totally sex mad.' I found it very easy to sympathise. On the basis of our shared love for Dottie, my soothing noises and expressed desire not to compete with her, led Sybil to acknowledge that 'for a man' I had some decent qualities. Sybil poor thing was dumped nonetheless and I am glad I wasn't around to witness the scene when Dottie defenestrated her best girlfriend.

The other matter concerned my equivocal relations with the military. Soon after I had dropped in to the War Office to say I was planning to emigrate, my pigeonhole at the Club – always a safe address – contained an invitation to dine with an old chum. It was Hoddle of course, now based in London, and we met at the Reform.

IV

He was very genial, reminding me of the purpose of the Reform Club, which was to allow free thought. 'You can plot to overthrow the monarchy if you want, just do it quietly so as not to upset other members.' He also made me laugh by telling me of his acceptance interview when first a member. 'The club secretary said "We don't inquire as to a man's morals but we do ask him not to chase the waiters round the pillars."'

For the first part of our reacquaintance he gently grilled me about what it was I had been doing. There was no point in evasion. The proposed move to Paris concluded my narrative. Hoddle signalled to the waiter for more brandy and coffee. 'Will you go as Count Pietrowski?' he asked. I told him I thought it best. He agreed.

'Excellent, very good, well done.' His enthusiasm was

intriguing. I asked him to tell me what his interest was. So he did, more or less as follows.

'Well, you know, the Continent is a bit of a shambles really. The politicos have their jobs to do, axes to grind and so forth, but some of us have to look ahead: big issues with the whole bolshie thing, especially in Germany. Actually the inside view is that chap Hitler, is going to win out with his Nazi lot. Weimar is finished. This might seem sensible what with Russia and the communists but as you would appreciate only too well, Germany rampant is a dodgy situation. I don't think many people have seen what you and I saw in our time over there behind the scenes as it were. Hitler is another Bismarck in many respects. Poland and all those other Austro-Hungarian empire remnants are nothing but potential trouble and the French, well, decent enough in their way but not whom you'd choose to back you up in a dark alley.'

The general theme of this commentary was suspicion in 'professional' quarters that Hitler, so deceptively attractive as the potential provider of stability based on solid traditional values, was as dangerous as Bolshevik Russia. My removal to Paris and adoption of my Polish-German title gave Hoddle another set of 'eyes and ears' as he put it. 'Nothing fancy old boy, just settle in among the expats and drop us the odd post-card.' His theory was that Embassies and even professional spies missed out on the accidental insights that brought the real picture into focus. Paris was of course filled with White Russians, Jewish refugees from Germany, dispossessed Poles, Hungarians and others. He was especially delighted I was to be so close to the Senate. He had a dim view of louche and decadent politicians but as he put it, '...a chap with his trousers down has no secrets.' There was of course no money in this. On the other hand as Hoddle in his disarming and jovial way put it 'We can give you a bit of help should you ever need it.'

So far as I recall, we made our final exit from London on the Paris boat train not many months before the national strike: that is Dottie, myself and a fey young painter who could do Dutch school chiaroscuro classical pornography, with remarkable facility. His versions of Europa and Zeus, unsigned but convincingly attributed, sold for high prices to and still hang I think in several private collections. The remaining members of our little group would join us over the succeeding weeks. I think they were damned lucky.

There is something peculiarly pleasing about leaving England. It is possibly because we are a small island and know the true horror of the word insular. Across that little water lies the mass of possibility and adventure that is 'abroad.' The other great advantage is that once in a foreign country, you need not care very much about their internal affairs and problems. Such inevitable bureaucratic inconveniences as occur can be shrugged off. 'Well, it's their country, *soyez-vous tranquil.*' Unlike one's own native heath where cultural fluency and sense of justice as taxpayer leads one to consider violence on occasion. I smiled benignly on the French customs official as he scrutinised my passport – the British one, used for the last time for some years – and treated him to my best line in reserved but well-disposed courtesy.

Our arrival in France was thus one of pure pleasure. Delayed trains, surly porters, disobliging taxi drivers and a uniquely incompetent concierge failed to quash our delight. We surveyed our quarters, made our dispositions. For the first and last time, Dottie flung her arms around me in spontaneous delight and affection. Her lips pressed on mine fleetingly. 'Thank you, thank you,' she said. It occurred to me then, that whilst our friendship was secure, this was definitely a sexual goodbye. It was the kiss that did it.

Chapter 6

Where the Girls are so Pretty

In Paris, Dottie came into her full flower as artist, entrepreneur and lesbian. Although at that time still in its early days, the 'bohemian' scene was beginning to take shape. I concentrated on the task of setting up the working parts of our business, which included the shipment of our stock down to Paris. The remaining artistic crew arrived. We refurbished and furnished our establishment. Whilst offering good advice on the décor, Dottie simply went out and met people.

It became obvious that if our imported establishment of painters were to earn its living, they would face serious competition. Paris was full of artists in all media including photographers able to reproduce sexual images in exciting form and prolific quantity.

Much of this was due to the legitimacy of the bordello or '*maison close*' in which under the sanction of the law – with a few, odd restrictions – men and sometimes women, could enjoy themselves. Politicals, academics, lawyers and intellectuals frequented establishments of quality as well as businessmen. In consequence there was a ready-made market for our wares.

Various places, including ours, also catered for women who preferred their own sex. In which context although not consequentially, it didn't take Dottie long to bring home her first conquest – a rather demure looking brunette – who turned out to be extremely noisy when pleasured by her English lover. Our problem here being that Dottie and I had selected adjacent bedrooms on the second floor. Oh well, *tant pis* and all was to change. In addition, our portraitist of lewd classicism acquired a young friend who proved equally loud in their all too frequent bouts of buggery. By contrast, my own sex life had come to a standstill. Dottie was obsessed with her new amour and had discovered the delights of well-designed French dildos for functional needs.

That said, I was pleased with progress. Our book and art shop had an opening that was well attended. That the guests owed a little more to the left bank than the *grand école* was not the point. Or maybe it was. We needed to achieve a reputation if we were to attract the haut bourgeois establishment. Sufficient of these also turned up however, united in their desire for sexual stimulation. Dottie had done her job of networking, well. Everyone had a good time and our display of art and books met with approval from the serious buyers, as well as the 'trade.' I became acquainted with Girodias and the photographer Brassai. No one actually bought at the time; but over the weeks, more and more people started to drop in. They were very much the elite professionals we wanted including several Deputies and Examining Magistrates. Complementarily, we had artists offering their work or undertaking commissions. We provided rooms on the third floor as studios in return for a percentage of sales.

Valuable as was the income, none of this was high volume. Dottie was again the person who suggested we turn the upper floors into a bordello. The French had been brilliant in making these excellent places legal. Indeed, our location had already led us to sacrifice our personal quarters for what I suppose might be called '*chambres privées*'. Those of our customers whose domestic situation precluded possession of pornography would wander off with a few books or pictures for a quiet afternoon's contemplation. Some however, appeared with a tart. We had a rough and ready means of pricing these accommodations. They varied from free to good spending regulars to rather costly for unknown dissolutes.

Dottie decided we should put all this on a business footing. Together we financed the re-equipment and decoration of the building for its new purpose. I like to think we held our own with the competition, though we were not in the same league as such places as the famous *'One Two Two'*. We were however well remarked in *'Le Guide Rose'*. The bookshop remained suitably discreet and antiquarian in its presentation. This was appreciated by the bordello customers and of course our little house of pleasures became titled *'La Librairie St Michel'*.

In consequence, we chucked out the small English art community to fend for itself. They weren't too dismayed and continued to supply us with material from new quarters in areas such as Clichy and the Monts of Parnasse and Martre.

Dottie made a splendid job of recruiting sufficient *'jolie filles'* – rather than simply *'poules'* for our premises. Her idea was to avoid an exploitative *'pensionnaire'* regime. She thought, and rightly so, that our customers wanted to come and find people in whom they had confidence and whose company they could enjoy. Whilst the girls were free to set their own hours and indeed book their own customers they had an obligation to the establishment. As ever, there was a price for everything. Their relative liberty was bought by higher charges. We had an early difficulty when Dottie's pick up technique – approaching girls in cafes or on the street – ran foul of one of the professional *'placeurs'* whose livelihood was recruitment of the whores. A meeting was held and after consumption of several drinks a deal was done. There was no point in making enemies and alliances are less costly than wars. The gentleman in question seemed to think highly of Dottie's skills and offered her a job. What intrigued me was how easy it was to find willing girls, fresh to the sex business; and ones with some class as well.

The growth in Dottie's enthusiasm for our enterprise was as I said, paralleled by her decline of sexual interest in myself. She was very aware of this from early on and had decided to address it as part of her pursuit of our business advancement. I was not very bothered by this lacuna in my sex life. There were many things to do and to look for a fuck beyond my vain desire for Dottie was a distraction. In her terms, seeing so many available women was equally diversionary.

Quite where she found the charming Celine escapes me. Custom required the bordello to have a *madame* and Dottie realised she herself was not that person. We needed a native Frenchwoman. Celine and I had in common that we were born out of wedlock to poor mothers with rich or socially superior lovers. Her ambition had been and still was to find and marry a person of social and financial position and avenge her dear *maman*. This would best be accomplished with an older man whom she could kill with excessive kindness. Food, drink and sex were the appropriate media for this process of slow and agreeable murder and one that seemed very French.

The decision to find work in a decent *maison close* was entirely logical. However, Celine had grown tired of servicing men whose virtues were at best variable. The chance to rise to management therefore freed her from sexual vassalage and enhanced the prospects of winning the affection of the right sort of man. She rather favoured the legal profession, unless an aristocrat was available. When we knew each other better she told me how pleased she had been to hear I was a count and how sorry that I was 'too young' for her designs. 'It might have been a *bon mariage*,' she said. I thought about that comment but let it go. I think she meant well.

This intriguing woman, she must have been in her mid-twenties, had one other characteristic. Fellatio apart, she would only have sex up the arse. 'It is to preserve myself for my husband and to avoid babies,' she explained, 'My *cul*, it is nothing. But also, it is perfectly pleasant to have a man there. Everything is convenient.' In case one thought that virginity was a moral issue, Celine had a more cogent reason. 'Many men, especially older ones of good breeding, like virgins. So my chance is better.' This restriction had not affected her work as a *fille de joie*. As well as virgins, she found that most men liked her bumhole as much as any other part of her anatomy.

It has sometimes occurred to me that nearly all the women in my life have been somewhat eccentric in their preferences. But then, it's more likely that eccentricity is the norm. When you have such complicated biological machinery and an equally complex social role to cope with or manipulate there's bound to be a consequence in your sexual psychology. Leave aside the appalling effect of religious education.

Evidently Dottie and she had previously discussed and agreed our new *madame's* relations with myself as owner. These included looking after my personal needs if required. This addition to her duties she made explicit at our first interview, if that is what I can call the encounter in which Dottie introduced us. She herself had privately confided that Celine would be happy to fuck me if I wished. 'You need and deserve a sexy woman near to you,' she said. Celine's caveats about where she would be fucked were not mentioned, though I suspect neither woman would have wanted to declare it, Celine to Dottie for fear of losing the job, Dottie to me lest I object to Celine.

After the general and business talk of our introduction Celine said in a matter of fact tone, 'Monsieur le Comte must not hesitate to call me to his bed.'

Our new *madame* proved highly capable. Her comparative youth was irrelevant to the efficiency and authority she brought to the role. As our girls were mostly quite new recruits to the business they were glad to defer to someone of experience. Equally, on the occasions we accepted a more seasoned warrior, Celine's evident first hand knowledge of the 'game' earned respect. She also had a forthright approach that made her a delight to deal with on business matters. I was glad to let her run the bordello and adopted many suggestions she made for its improvement. Dottie got on with producing art and selling our wares and I sort of supervised our happy ship, mostly in terms of counting money and the consummation of particularly important sales or other business matters. As our clientele grew in quantity and influence, my presence to greet monsieur the Judge or Professor or Deputy was very much required. Dottie and Celine had their admirers, but I remained *Monsieur le Patron*.

We had invited Jurgen to our opening and he had stayed with us for several days. I was glad to have time with my old friend and business associate. We got drunk and visited a brothel or two, this latter a necessary piece of espionage of course. I confided my mission from Hoddle, to Jurgen. Given the failure of Hitler's putsch a couple of years previously and despite his recent release from prison, Hoddle's bet on the man seemed bizarre, not that politics interested me much. Jurgen disagreed. He thought that Germany, like Italy under Mussolini was headed if not for revolution, then for some form of dictatorship. 'Hitler is an extraordinary man. He's building a group around him that will put the Nazi party into power very soon. Believe me, the Bolsheviks and the Americans have between them created a monster counterforce. You English in your little island should choose your friends well. We Germans will come again.'

Jurgen still had our little office in Esbjerg. He said it was good to have a safe house outside Germany. Lawyers had disposed of the villa in Rendsberg. Viktoria, as the surviving beneficiary had been discovered in a seedy club in Berlin performing some grotesque cabaret act, fuelled by drugs. This made me sad. Perverse she may have been, but she had class and beauty. The von Eisens may not have been absolute Junker in pedigree, but they represented a branch of the noble Prussian tradition, albeit one etiolated by death and dissolution and now broken off. We presumed the money would be spent to support her limited life. There seemed little point in returning the von Eisen art treasures.; these and the existence of Count Magnus, having apparently passed beyond discovery. There was no news either of the hunting-lodge in Pomerania. Jurgen was vitriolic on this topic. 'Fucking shitty Poles,' he spat. 'I expect they've fucking turned it into a fucking pig-sty.' It did not really occur to either of us to visit the place.

II

The months went pleasantly by as our enterprise flourished under its trio of partners. The only sour note was Celine's manner toward me, which after a very cordial start became palpably off-hand. Eventually I decided to mention this. We were in the salon of the bordello at the time. 'Aha,' she exclaimed, 'you ask me what is wrong. What is wrong with me I reply? Part of my job is to fuck you and you don't want me. Many weeks go by and all we do is discuss the business.'

I had to laugh. Her small oval face, so French and so furious passed like a summer storm through its emotions until she began to smile too. 'I'm so sorry,' I said, 'I just didn't know how to ask you. You are a business woman I respect very much but you are also very desirable.' Mollified, she reiterated her enquiry about my lack of requests for her sexual favours. I pointed out that she was a colleague and I found it difficult, without invitation, to simply request sex. 'You're not a *poule*, we must have some exchange of signals that you are in the right mood. It is not good manners for me just to demand.' I said.

She gave a sniff and came up to me, put her arms around my neck and kissed me with great enthusiasm. 'Silly man, you are too English.' So much for my cover story I reflected. The upshot was that I shared her personal quarters, as an alternate to Dottie and my apartment in the 8eme. Our apotheosis as lovers was more than enjoyable. Celine had, in the intimate and entertaining dinner we shared that night, confided her sexual preferences. It makes things so much easier if people do this. The supposed 'voyage of discovery' is for any thoughtful man, a tension filled series of examinations as to one's competence or sensitivity. Women, one supposes, are too often inarticulate with reservation about the fumbling attentions of the hairy beast and the expression of their own specific desires.

There was no surprise therefore when I came into her room from my toilette. She lay face down, legs slightly parted. It is a convention to describe a woman's appearance. The length of leg, size of buttocks and breasts regarded as the necessary means to suggest desirability. However she might change as she aged, Celine at twenty-five or whatever had the delightful skin, firm flesh and the shapely formation of a young woman. If not perfect – she was stockily Mediterranean - then no less desirable in consequence. I never tired of mounting her strong haunches.

On her bedside table was a small bottle of olive oil. I greeted her and she turned her head and smiled at me. To use the oil to lubricate her *cul* was pure pleasure. She sighed and lifted her hips and welcomed my fingers and palm as first I massaged her buttocks and all the secret places between. This accomplished I knelt behind her and she raised her bum and I spread their cheeks. I was more than ready. Just above the temptation of her neatly trimmed but thick black bush and its wrinkle-lipped slit was the brown circle of her arsehole. Well, she knew how to do it, and so did I, so after opening her with my oiled finger, I let my cock nudge his head against her anus. It slid in with the tight yet easy fit of a piston in a well-engineered cylinder. I lay along her back, my face buried in her hair, softly kissing her neck as I lifted up and down. She moved against me and we found a slow rhythm together. Between her legs I could feel her fingers as she masturbated. It seemed important that she should be in control. Eventually, she began to breathe more heavily; I could hear her murmuring to herself, nothing coherent, merely disconnected sighs and expletives. When she began thrusting her buttocks up into my belly and her sphincter squeezed me convulsively, I let her hear my own groans of pleasure. Well, we finished off in a shared chorus of grunts and cries and rolled over and my cock retreated from her rectum. She turned toward me and laid her head on my shoulder. Her thigh lifted over mine, her hand on my prick's softening body. We drifted into sleep.

A woman's arse is a splendid place for one's cock. It is tight and hot and full of life. The cunt is of course delightful but the bum has its own unique magic. It was therefore no hardship to acquiesce to my new lover's dictates. She happily allowed me oral access to her cunt and indeed often climaxed that way, as she would perform a similar service for me. In fact *la tête-bêche* was a frequent variation of our lovemaking. Still, her bum became a resort of choice rather than necessity.

So well did our relationship flourish that with inevitable contrariness Dottie grew jealous. At the end of one of our regular lunches, having enquired after Celine, she said, '...Of course the minx has set her cap at you.' I made light of it, but with sharpened awareness did notice over the next few days that Celine had grown more solicitous and affectionate. She bestowed little looks and touches and was especially feline in bed where she would snuggle against me and seduce me with her hand at my groin and whisper endearments.

Another slight difficulty was due to my desire to sustain fluency in Polish, which had declined through desuetude in the preceding few years. This despite my making a point of finding books or newspapers in that language; not always easy in those days. By chance one of our girls was from Poland. I therefore engaged her for an hour a day for conversation and language tuition. She was a bright young thing, a graduate of Warsaw University. Like so many others, she had fled the miserable and chaotic wreck that was Poland, in search of civilisation. Neither Dottie nor Celine liked the idea of my consorting with one of the staff in this manner, so there was something of an atmosphere.

In such situations a man has to confront the problem. I called Dottie and Celine into the bookshop's office and in what I hoped was a kindly, but firm manner clarified my position. Dottie was my partner, also a woman I loved, hopeless as that passion was. Celine was a valued business colleague and a woman I held in great esteem and affection. I would never marry anyone. Rula – the young Pole – was simply my language tutor. I did not desire her, nor would it be good business to fuck her. They listened politely, said they understood and left. Dammit I thought I am in my 'thirties and I am entitled to run my business and live my life the way I want. It felt quite grown up.

When there is an imminent change in the weather, subtle shifts occur in the sky and the general atmosphere. Other than a resumption of our cordial relations, nothing obvious occurred as a consequence of 'our little chat.' But surrounded by all this femininity I had become more attuned to the barometrics of our social climate. Dottie became more and more a jolly chum and she confided in me her impatience with young girls and her desire for something more stable with an older woman. Celine and I sustained our collegiate and sexual partnership with no reduction in warmth. It transmuted however into what felt like a *mariage de convenance* and I noticed that she reserved her most sparkling manner for those of our customers who fitted her vengeful candidate list.

Rula proved a good tutor. She was highly entertained by my Kashub influenced vocabulary and pronunciation. Though increasingly respectful of my fluency, she warned me that I could never pass as Polish. In the guise of a German-Pole, long exiled, even foreign born, there was possibility and she was impressed by my experiences in Pomerania and Danzig.

Beyond these personal affairs, Europe ground out its sordid history. Economic depression, constant low level but significant bloodshed in Germany as communists and Nazis fought for control of the soul of the nation. Even America suffered massive unemployment and the near collapse of its economy. Yet in Paris, none of these matters much interrupted our lives. A few riots occurred and some friends vanished, their investments or businesses slaughtered in 'The Great Crash'; but for the most part we ate, drank, fucked and were very merry. As the twenties gave place to the thirties, the liners still delivered Americans to France and its capital became the sybaritic honey pot for all forms of artistic and licentious aspiration. Various refugees from Eastern Europe and Russia may have plotted counter-revolution for their benighted native countries. They mostly did so drunk on absinthe and with a tart on their knee.

My duty to Hoddle had not been neglected. Our clientele and the nature of our business gave ample opportunity to compose periodic reports transmitted via the British Embassy. At its kindest these were slight enough. Initially, they were merely dossier items on the sexual predilections of various alumni of the French elite. Now and again we might find ourselves with an overseas client, who if British and in a position of influence was worth remark. There were times too, when the girls would report an indiscreet comment or disclosure of possible interest. As the thirties progressed such bulletins began to assume greater importance. I would not exaggerate the value of such information as we were able to pass on but know for a fact that we had early warning of the growth of what was to become Vichy and the attendant collaboration. Such warnings did not much help the Jews in France, but I think they must have modified optimism about French sturdiness in the face of German aggression. If they got through to the right level, that is. Politics eh?

By the time we got to 1933, Hoddle's prescience was vindicated. In fact, he came over to Paris in that year and we had an agreeable luncheon together. He was about to be posted to the Far East. I believe he went to Tokio, but sadly, never heard from him again. He transferred my contact to someone called Wilcox, whom he described as 'young but a good egg.'

More significant to me was the approach of my fortieth birthday. An event I regarded with considerable horror. Had life carried me this far, were grey hairs emerging, was the deference with which the girls greeted *M. le Comte* due to my age and not my charm? I felt that everyone but me was progressing. Dottie had fallen in with a rich American lesbian called Grace Palmer. Though not this woman's favourite – she had a passion for the *madame* of one of our rivals - Dottie became a valued part of her circle, undoubtedly bedded her and became at least socially intimate with the group of literary, film and theatricals that included Dietrich and later Piaf. These people not only appreciated Dottie's talent as a Sapphic, but her intelligence and artistic skills. I watched her blossom in this hothouse of approbation and realised our time together was coming to an end.

Our own establishment never quite reached the pinnacle, but we could count some distinguished people among our clientele. We offered perhaps a more informal change from those acmes of perfection such as the *Sphinx*. Celine ensured that our range of delights encompassed all but the most degraded sexual tastes and that our clientele of both sexes was well entertained. She early on spotted the benefits of pornographic film for example, so the salon had a permanent showing. In fact a number of our girls featured in them. Though the premises could not cope with a restaurant, we had a kitchen in the basement from which elegant snacks and light meals could be supplied.

Celine had also found a potential victim. This gentleman, if we can be kind, was a highly successful, self-made retailer. Now semi-retired, in his seventies and suffering the consequences of over-indulgence he was more a voyeur than protagonist but with a penchant for being spanked and pissed on and he longed to fuck a virgin. He very early on made it clear that his continued patronage depended on Celine. She came to me and in her forthright manner told me she thought she had found her 'mark'. Of course, how could I protest? It had briefly occurred to me, that since Dottie was lost and Celine was such a splendid business partner and bedmate, we might after all get together. We were very kind to each other, and my diffident scouting of a possible alliance met with a courteous '*tres gentil – mais non.*' She really did want revenge and her chap's money was irresistible. The discussion was therefore entirely civil. The outcome was obvious. I had to recruit a new Madame. It took her three months before her prey proposed and the determined Celine eventually left for a new, and in the man's case probably abbreviated life, somewhere in Normandy.

The final event of my year – other than Adolf Hitler's accession as Chancellor of the Third Reich – was a letter from Jurgen to announce his marriage. Of all the changes occurring, this surprised me most. He merely described his bride as '...a completely charming and pretty Frieslander with whom I think I can spend a good life.'

None of these developments were simultaneous or sudden in their fulfilment. After their initiating announcement they meandered to their ultimate conclusion in ways that hopefully pleased the principals. To me, they merely loaded the passing of time to my fortieth birthday with serious foreboding. For the first time in my life I had intimations of mortality.

III

My first pleasant surprise in these cloudy days was to run into Julia. There I was on the Boulevard Edgar-Quinet and she appeared in front of me. It was raining, so after our initial exclamations we dashed into the nearest café. She had worn well had Julia. The slight chubbiness of a discontented young wife had been replaced by the leaner, more groomed appearance of a confident woman in her mature years. I mean, Julia must have been in her late forties. It strikes me I had never much thought of these relative ages and the passage of time.

The encounter with an old lover can be awkward or it can be a pleasure. With Julia it was the latter. Freed from the constraints of our first liaison, we could enjoy the intimacy of mutual knowledge it had provided. That we had both prospered helped. Her marriage to FitzMalpas had foundered as was inevitable. The Colonel, subsequent to the divorce on the grounds of his wife's infidelities, died in a shooting accident – not on the battlefield, but in a Shropshire copse.

She was aware of the rudiments of my military career. 'Actually, when you were posted missing believed killed I shed a tear,' she said. We had a mutual exchange of compliments, in my case enhanced by gratitude for her generosity. This led to a passage of reflection on the sexual experience we had shared. By which time and three Pastis later, her eyes had begun to sparkle and we both felt the desire to talk for longer and in more detail. We adjourned to a restaurant.

Julia had been in Paris for several years. As with myself, England, even London had become dreary to her. She had spent the war in America and had married a French diplomat there. When this ended back in Paris, for reasons I politely declined to pursue, she threw herself into the general cosmopolitan scene. At the time we met she was if not the mistress, then certainly a lover, of Henry Miller. 'God he can fuck,' she exclaimed. When she discovered that I was indeed '*le vrai Comte Pietrowski*' of 'La Lib' she clapped her hands delightedly and I think we almost fell in love again.

My account of my passion for Dottie was met with sympathy. 'Poor lamb, so difficult for boys faced with girls who can do without willies.' She was highly intrigued by my narration of the von Eisens and Viktoria and sad Lissa. 'Golly William, you did learn a lot. Mind you, you always did have a bit of bums and beating in you.' The affairs of my bookshop and bordello were also interesting to her. The problem with Celine's departure especially drew her attention. She offered to find a replacement. 'I know several rather good women who have the right experience,' she offered. I accepted with relief. My only complaint about Celine had been her failure to find someone who would have her professional skills.

The end of dinner came. I called for *l'addition*. We both drained our brandy and gazed at each other. 'You're a very handsome woman Julia.' 'Handsome enough to fuck?' was her forthright response.

In my apartment we picked up where we had left off our original affair as though the goodbye had not been said. Except this time we kissed passionately and made affectionate noises. We bathed together. Her breasts and belly and thighs had not defied age and gravity but they had acquired ripeness and sophistication of texture. She noted that my own torso was not that of a keen young cavalryman, but pronounced it well preserved enough with the solidity that befits an adult male of gravitas.

'Lust is so exhausting,' said Julia as she drew me into her embrace and her lips opened to mine. The perverse fury of her youth had mellowed. We spent a long time doing simple things with each other at a slow pace. She grasped my cock with a reminiscent sigh and inside her I let her dictate what she wanted. Our mouths closed together, with her fingers at her groin she had come softly almost before I knew it, her cunt pulsing gently. On our sides, half in and half out and me thinking, 'This is nice but is there possibly more to it?' She stroked my face and said, 'If you weren't such a selfish sod you'd make a terrific husband.' I could only kiss her and reply that all she had to do was ask me to marry her, and cross my fingers under the sheets. So she laughed and felt my prick nuzzling hopefully at her quim and realised it hadn't fully expressed itself. By way of variety she turned over me, lowered her bum onto my face and began to suck me off. Her cunt had the delicious *bouillabaise* quality of all female bits when aroused and used, plus Julia's own flavour that reinserted itself in my tastebuds. We came together, I am pretty sure it was both of us, and fell asleep in each other's arms.

The second pleasure was the surprise party for my fortieth birthday. By the time this dreary anniversary had arrived, Dottie was firmly ensconced with her rich lesbian coterie, Celine was on the brink of departure and mercifully, Julia had introduced me to Sylvie. As a protégé of the notable Margeurite Lemestre she was highly qualified to for the job and other than Julia the one comforting aspect of my current situation.

All four of these excellent women had however, plotted and arranged. It was very touching. Inveigled to luncheon I found Jurgen in my favourite restaurant. On my return to *La Librairie* in the late afternoon I discovered most of our girls in the salon, dressed in their best *déshabillée*, with champagne and applause. There too, were some of our most appreciated and valued clients. We had an immense party in which many good things were said and much esprit de corps expressed. Somewhat fuddled, and leaving Jurgen to the attentions of our young ladies, I was poured into a taxi and driven home.

One may fantasise about numbers of women in one's bed. In reality, drunk or sober, it is something of a challenge. Luckily for me, I was drunk enough not to worry, and sober enough to participate. They were in truth there to give me a present and to share a female joke of the grubby character only women can achieve without being appalling. That said, it was a generous and unbeatable experience. In retrospect I remain very touched. To be sure, they were not the average hausfraus. We were all people of particular experience and with shared business interests. Even so, as they leapt upon me I loved them all equally. I have read that good Moslems can expect lots of virgins if they die well. If the virgins are anything like the four women who greeted me, I am ready to die for Islam.

Actually, in the grip of determined and randy women the eroticism can only flow from giving in. I was bathed, massaged, laid down. A little cocaine was sniffed. Mouths and hands stroked and manipulated. Fingers went up my arse, cunts were lowered onto my face. I was presented with tableaux in which, with my body as platform, women pleasured each other. I have the indelible memory of Dottie, transferring her dildo-waving torso from I think Julia, toward me. It was big, black, glossy and anatomically very realistic. 'William likes black cock,' exclaimed Dottie.

There was no question I was going to be sodomised; but before I submitted to that experience there was another surprise. Sylvie, clad only in stockings knelt beside me and holding my prick against her cheek said, 'Celine told me of your shyness. Every patron should fuck his Madame. I am your birthday present.' With that she lay on her back, and opened her legs, all the while keeping hold of me. The other women cheered and as I knelt between Sylvie's raised thighs I knew what was about to happen. That was certainly the cause of an increased erection. Julia's stinging slaps on my bare buttocks enhanced it. The extraordinary sensation of Dottie's dildo easing its way into my rectum, as I prepared to shaft Sylvie created what felt like a monstrously engorged rigidity. I fucked deep into Sylvie's receptive *chatte* as Dottie fucked me. Both women gasped noisily and made sounds like rutting lionesses. Our depraved audience laughed and applauded. Sylvie came loudly and my erection still rampant I was required to bugger Celine and fuck Dottie who straddled my face and loins by turns to keep all parts of their nether persons amused. If I came, how and so on escapes me. It took hours for my erection to finally wilt. My own and Sylvie's buttocks showed welts for a few days. I think that was to do with our further exchanges as she and I rode each other variously posed to allow our bottoms access to the ministrations of the three Furies.

So I woke up on the morning after my birthday, with Sylvie, a dreadful hangover and a sense of extraordinary wellbeing. I sat up in bed and regarded my new companion, on her back, breathing a little noisily and of course *sans maquillage*. Sylvie was certainly younger than I was, but in her thirties nonetheless. Like Celine, she had neither the advantage of breeding nor the means to fully defend her body against the years and her way of life. Actually, she was a bit of a slut. Her armpits needed a shave and her reddish bush curled all round her arsehole and groin. Her figure was awkward too. She was not overweight but had a low slung behind, soft belly and pear shaped breasts. She looked like a whore that morning, puffy round the eyes and reeking of sex in the aftermath of our orgy. I loved it, and rolling her onto her stomach slipped my cock between her thighs and into her still slippery cunt.

Of course, being French, she was incapable of not being attractive. Roman nose, strong jawline, liquid brown eyes and haughty look, combined with excellent posture gave her presence. When she decided to melt for you, her face had a soft submissiveness that invited forceful sexual mastery. So on that morning, after I had satisfied myself my new Madame extracted me from her vagina with a decisive hand, got out of bed and went to douche herself. On her return, and when dressed, she asked Monsieur if he would get his own *petit déjeuner* as she had to return immediately to '*La Librairie*'. I took her hand, kissed it gallantly without any irony and expressed my gratitude and confidence in our working future. Her formality relaxed enough for her to smile and stroke my cheek with the back of her fingers. '*M'sieur le Comte* is truly a *Chevalier* even when not shaved. All will be well.' Perhaps she meant that as much for her own reassurance as mine.

IV

The first two or three years of my fourth decade were very pleasant. Paris had fulfilled the early promise of lively self-indulgence. Our business continued to prosper; our place in this supportive milieu well accepted. Most important of all, our girls and our clients had confidence in us. Sylvie and I forged a genuinely affectionate and solid alliance. To some extent it felt like a marriage. The seduction over and a feeling of security attained, Madame became brisk and practical. She indulged me readily enough, showing pleasure in fulfilment of her physical needs as well as skill in meeting mine. However, our sexual transactions, though regular, were generally begun without ceremony and any afterglow as it were, curtailed after a suitable pause by reference to matters of business. In this she was like Dottie. Actually I never did find women who just wanted to cosy up and whisper sugary endearments. Though very willing to suck my cock, Sylvie was conventional enough not to make her *cul* available and was not much interested in my oral attentions to her cunt, either. 'It is not so exciting to me,' she confessed. 'If you want these things, I am happy for you to look elsewhere.' I teased her about becoming pregnant. She was dismissive. 'I am quite able to look after such matters, do not fear.' Well, that's a French woman for you.

Dottie and I continued our friendship on a casual and lunchtime basis. My hopeless love had long been quenched. She apologised for buggering me on my birthday. I told her it had been a great experience. 'I sort of still miss your cock,' she said on one occasion, 'The trouble is, I feel if I go back to men again I'll never be a good Lesbian.' She had become obsessed with what we now call feminism, on which she gave me long lectures. As she consumed the wine and foie gras I bought for her I reflected on some of the illogical aspects of her position; though without doing more than lightly tax her when she became too pompous. Her provision of artworks had become markedly unisexual over the months. Erotic they certainly were and sold well to men and women. However, I had to remind her that my clients liked to see a real penis somewhere in the vicinity of a female hand, mouth or other part, however conventional. The appearance of dildos in her work was a poor substitute. This altered nothing, so when, at the outbreak of the Spanish Civil War, she and Grace and their little circle packed up and retreated to America I was sorry, but not much inconvenienced.

Julia on the other hand reassumed her role as the mistress whom Sylvie had clearly indicated I should take. The former Lady FitzMalpas was undoubtedly a fully- fledged libertine, entirely capable of all and any forms of sexual excess. Neither youth nor gender inhibited her. Even coprophilia was something she had experienced though as the donor only. She admitted to me that the only pleasure had been in '...doing something disgusting to a fat repellent wog.'

My role in her dissolute life was one almost of respite. We never went down that line of enquiry, but I formed the strong impression that dear Julia was a working tart. Or, put better, professional mistress. She liked to remember what she called '...more innocent days.' As if Julia had ever been innocent. Yet I suppose she must have been once. I had asked her early in our first affair about how she had lost her virginity and was told it was none of my damn business. Memory lane remained untrodden. Kindly, she also confided that mine was the most satisfying cock she'd ever had except possibly H Miller's and that she nursed an abiding affection for both of us. So she would call on me at irregular intervals and after a satisfying bout of lubricious behaviour, I would take her out to dinner where her conversation was always witty, intelligent and given my covert assignment often informative. We would most often return to my apartment – Sylvie living, as was her professional duty, at La Lib – and Julia would bathe and come to bed again. In which she would lie naked, arms spread out across the pillows, her eyes hooded but friendly, a slight smile on her lips. 'So, what has Willy boy got in mind for me now?' That was the other thing. Although she was scrupulous about calling me Magnus in company, she always reverted to Willy or William when we were alone.

Normally, I preferred women to make their desires clear. Julia and my acquaintance had been too long for this to be a problem. In any case I knew her predilections and also that she knew the sort of thing I would suggest. Our rules of engagement were for the activities that we had enjoyed before; not something surprising and perverse. Much would depend on previous encounters and over-use or boredom played a critical role in her acquiescence. She would therefore accept or decline my idea and express her own wishes. Since there were only three places in which I might eventually bury my prick, the main performance was easily settled which left only the support acts to fit in with mood and practicality.

In my view, sex becomes unutterably boring when it has constantly to be attended by the sentimental nonsenses normally associated with courtship or seduction. Once two people have gone to bed with each other or even decided they want to do so for the first time, what is the point of coyness? Of course 'feeling like it' is important. So you establish who feels like what and experience should tell you about how far a negative is a maybe. Jenny had always got to the point and I preferred lovers who did.

These gentle and gratifying rhythms in ones life were barely interrupted by rumours of war, the events in Spain and the doings of the Third Reich. We ejected the odd drunk Fascist or Russian from *La Librairie* – curiously, few if any Communists frequented us, no money I suppose – but other than an increased flow of tidbits as Deputies and others whispered burdensome secrets to girls in their post-coital candour, nothing much disturbed us. I had also built up a very respectable collection of artworks. Of varying authenticity, including outright forgery by my team, they nonetheless included some real gems. *Dix, Gustav Courbet – the Origin of the World* – as superb a rendition of a cunt as I've seen even as a copy. Dottie so loved doing it she made several versions: also, *Egon Schiele* via Jurgen, and *Louis Corinth* via Julia.

Then we got to 1937. A couple of years previous, Jurgen had written to me – in an execrable hand I could barely decipher – to say he and his wife had a son. This was nice for him if of little import to me. Still, I responded politely at the time to the confidence, still baffled by Jurgen's plunge into domesticity. More to the point he had also asked me to act in loco parentis in the event of anything happening to him. We met in Paris early in 1937 when he was passing through on his way to Spain. Business was not so good. Despite the growing emigration of Jews, the market for art and furniture had become very limited. Not least, because the sort of heavy German style that appealed to Jews had little appeal elsewhere. Jurgen had decided Spain in Civil War was a good place for vultures like us to alight. He told me that his wife Hedda was a lovely girl and he adored his son Bernd. 'I need to settle down, Willy,' he said. He never got the hang of calling me Magnus. He liked Denmark, but had become enthused about Hitler's grip on the German economy and social discipline. I told him to stay in touch, promised to look out for his family should 'anything happen' and he left with a hug and a handshake, one of my suits and five thousand francs 'on account.'

The unlucky devil was killed in Guernica. Despite propaganda about the 'massacre' – and the attack was indeed a poor show – there were only a few hundred deaths. How he managed to be there in particular, and why he had thought the whole trip was a good idea always escaped me. I can only surmise it was because the business was indeed in a bad way that he took a gamble. I suppose Spain even in Civil War felt safer than the wilderness of Eastern Europe especially for a German in pursuit of second-hand furniture.

Various letters were exchanged. Jurgen's agent and lawyer in Esbjerg, Hedda Tost, myself. By summer I was in Esbjerg again. It had been a long time, and the place felt dowdy and provincial. The office we had been so proud of was just a dusty little room above a warehouse. The warehouse itself was half full of generally ghastly furniture and paintings. I met the bank manager and the lawyer. There was a little money, enough for a small widow's pension. Jurgen had been surprisingly careful in that regard. The junk in the warehouse would fetch a bit more. Then Hedda arrived.

Despite her sombre dress, she was curiously attractive. She wasn't sexy, so much as possessed of a wholesome prettiness the anodyne quality of which was modified by an aura of determination and even passion. She reminded me of one or two Scottish girls I had come across, especially ones from the Highlands. Knowing me as Count Magnus she was polite without subservience. Later, she told me her husband always referred to me as 'Willy', explaining this to her as our personal nickname. We rapidly concluded the final transfer of Jurgen's affairs to her; since he had pretty much already done that. There was a small matter of my own title to one third of his business subject to various provisos only a lawyer could have come up with but which at the time had given us both a businesslike feeling. I waived all that because it wasn't worth much and I felt sorry for the young widow. She warmed up a bit and smiled at me for the first time.

We had to stay in town for a couple of days whilst bits and pieces of paper were prepared, signed, registered and made ready for burial in a file. I was in Esbjerg's best hotel and Hedda in a boarding house. After a short argument she agreed to transfer to the hotel. We dined together, which gave her the chance to find out more about Jurgen's business and my role in his life. She seemed to know very little, and to suffer from the delusion that he had once been in the French Foreign Legion. I did little to disabuse her and contrived something plausible using the small truths to disguise the big lies. She struck me as very intelligent and practical, if a little naïve in the ways of the world. Growing up in Frisia would explain the naivete.

Naturally, she was very upset about Jurgen's death. She controlled it well, which I admired, but occasionally her eyes filled with tears especially when referring to her baby son Bernd. How women achieve their best trick of suborning your help has always amazed me. You start, defences well prepared, see the attack coming and then hear yourself surrendering with the words, 'Don't worry my dear, I'll sort this out for you, it will all be all right.'

If Hedda Tost didn't know quite what she wanted, she knew exactly what she didn't want. This was to stay in Denmark, in Frisia and as a single mother bring up her son in a backwater rural community. She liked the idea of Paris. Bless her, she was a romantic. With the usual acuity of a woman making an argument in her favour, she focused on my comforting words about '... affection for and debt to' Jurgen. I should note that of course our dialogue was in German, being our shared language of, in my case, only relative fluency. The sort of nuances I could share with Dottie, Julia or any other English native would be entirely lost. No disrespect to German, but rich as it is as a language, my skill with the subtleties of its convoluted grammar had limitations.

In a last desperate attempt to head off her aspiration to return with me to Paris – as housekeeper she had decided, having discovered I lived alone – I declared the truth of my business and its operational circumstances. She was entirely sanguine. 'But of course, this is the way of life. You will even more need a good housekeeper.' My relations with Sylvie were dismissed with equal sang-froid. 'Why should she mind me? Who you sleep with is your business, not mine.' I was forty. I had fucked a lot of women with many of whom I had also enjoyed close friendship. I still didn't have the grasp of women's strategic and tactical skill with an objective in view.

Chapter 7

Away, You Rolling River

To resolve the paperwork issues that secured Hedda's and my properties' transit from Denmark to Paris was simple enough. More problematic from my perspective was her child. I didn't meet him until they finally reached Paris, but the acquisition of a family was more than I had wanted.

Still, they both arrived, and to give Hedda credit, she adapted quickly and took on her new situation with considerable competence. This included learning French. Whatever Sylvie's suspicions, she overcame them and offered Hedda a good deal of help, both in cultural adaptation and in finding a nanny for Bernd. This girl, having had two doses of clap and an abortion had decided prostitution wasn't for her. In reality she was a jolly, straightforward provincial who should have been a nurse and married to a pharmacist. The three women in my household thus came to their mutual accommodations and with the minimum of fuss we resettled into our routines.

Bernd proved perfectly amenable. Whilst mostly confined to our private apartments, in which he, his mother and Regine the nanny had their own quarters, she or Regine sometimes brought him over to the *Librairie*. He was a precocious but quite winning kid, so far as I could tell. The girls made a big fuss of him of course and I think this turned him into the annoying little bastard he later became.

Had we but known it, the next two years were to be the Indian Summer of our Parisian idyll. Like all such summers, there were hints of autumn. Julia fell ill. She would not be explicit but the inference was that her way of life had extracted its price. We had a sad little luncheon when she came to tell me of her impending departure for a sanatorium in Switzerland. There was genuine tenderness in both our voices as we acknowledged the difficulties of sustaining a correspondence. Even so, we also looked to some happy reunion and the like. I put her in a cab and went to the *Librairie*. The cheerfulness there was depressing, so I went home and got maudlin drunk on Scotch.

What I really wanted was a fuck. Life had undoubtedly coarsened me. Never very sentimental there had been times when my affections had been captured. With Dottie lost – and imminently to leave for America - Julia was a rare female whose inner nature as much as her sexual energies had somehow won what might be termed my 'heart'. She was also a last link with the pre-war past and my youth.

Sylvie remained available and perfectly willing within her rules, but in truth, our partnership made us too close for me to sustain the indifference demanded to give us both a really hard gallop. I took myself off to one or other of the better bordellos. The arrival of a competitive patron was at first regarded with amused suspicion. Such was the nature of the culture however, that my honest explanation of my malaise was greeted with sympathetic nods. Everyone understood. I was found a tough little filly responsive to a rider who would take her over the jumps.

It was at this point that we had a small contretemps with the authorities. Some mischievous person, competitor or discontented ex-employee or rejected client had made a complaint. It was risible, and concerned a regulation by which a man, even the owner, could not live in a brothel unless married to the Madame. The charge was thrown out even before it reached its first formal hearing. Both the senior police officer and the examining magistrate were regular clients and in any case the allegation could be disproved.

By this time it had become clear to me that our life in Paris was drawing to a close. The talk was only of when not if, the war would begin. At the Embassy, my contact Wilcox seemed a decent enough chap. My bulletins had become more frequent and more alarming, however trivial. They had assumed greater relevance with Winston Churchill's interest in the issue of Nazi Germany's growth and aggressions and the concerns of the military about French reliability. Approbation of Hitler was not uncommon among our political clients. Perversely, the tendency to Nazi sympathies was often accompanied by requests for Jewish or Negro whores. We told our girls to report any situation where this was accompanied by abuse.

If Sylvie had any concerns over my decreasing attentions to her body, she was much gratified by my offer to her of control of the business, gratis, when I left Paris. Word of my use of another bordello had of course reached her. She was not at all offended. 'Le Comte has shown great respect, I thank you,' when I concluded my narrative about control of *La Librairie*. The prospect of war concerned her not at all. 'Paris is safe, men will want women. *Plus ça change.*'

With the prescience of the purely self-interested, I had already made arrangements for our departure. Hedda's credentials were approved and she resumed her Danish nationality. More problematic was the necessity to bring my stock of art and books into Britain. Wilcox did indeed prove a 'good sort' and we had the stuff packed and shipped under diplomatic protection. Careless, even ruthless as Governments and administrations are, if you have found a niche and your file has some sort of approval mark on it, doors become open. Or so it seemed at the time.

So, everything was in place, Hitler invaded Poland and Chamberlain declared war. The night before our departure I was lying in bed and Hedda crept into my room. In a very small voice she asked if she could lie next to me because she was frightened. Being naked, I demurred, but she said more firmly that it didn't matter. She needed to be close to someone and I was her protector and so on. This was awkward for me. I'd never really considered Hedda in any sexual context. I enquired about Bernd, but he was asleep with Regine. As Bernd's nanny she had been offered a chance to come to London but had elected to stay in Paris as Sylvie's assistant.

We lay on our backs in my bed and she told me of her worries. They were of the usual sort. Danger, change, new country, how we would earn a living, where to live, little bloody Bernd: I wanted to tell her she was a lucky bitch. In fact I think I did say just that; this stricture mediated by reminders that in England I was very well connected, there was plenty of money and her darling boy – my friend Jurgen's pride and joy – would have the benefit of a great British education.

Being a woman she heard this out and then sighed and turned toward me. Her head nestled into my shoulder. There was a scent of flowers. Her hand was placed casually on my chest; her knee lifted over my thigh and of course, her nightdress had already rucked up around her hips. We rested thus and I patted her shoulder in an avuncular way. 'Jurgen said you were a fine man,' she whispered. Whether this observation was to do with my general conduct or the fact that by this time she had her hand on my dormant but by no means somnolent cock is debatable.

Some kissing must have occurred. Hedda may not have been the most agile or inventive of lovers but she had fine firm flesh and erotic instincts. Quite evidently, as a self-serving male, I'm not going to reject the advances of a pretty and grateful woman. I think she must have fulfilled, with less perversity, the role I filled for Julia. That is to say, she provided physical comfort seasoned with that feeling of connection to a more innocent world beyond the merely sensual. No, maybe not; this was just what occurred to me at the time. Having got me nicely stiffened up and with her guiding fingers, I was welcomed between her soft thighs into her comfortable cunt and reclined on her pliant form. We were attentive to each other, and the event was genuinely, as the English say, 'Very nice.'

It was the rent for both of us; I owed Jurgen, she owed me. That said, we had a good partnership. She ran our business with me, never complained or tried to make me take more notice of Bernd than I wanted. Our sex life remained one that was soothing if not wildly passionate. But then, I was on my way to fifty by the time we left France. Agreeable and soothing were probably higher on the agenda than before.

II

Our migration to Chelsea was painless enough. Our new home was in a square north of the King's Road. It was one of those late or neo Georgian, who knows? Stucco things on several storeys. The rental was cheap because it needed a bit of interior decoration. What with the so-called 'phoney war', the general trance-like sense of stasis and the fact I had real money; we managed to have everything transformed – albeit often by amateurs on the make, before the bombing started.

There was no chance of a bordello in London, despite the sub-culture of licence. The approach had to be one of a 'salon', together with a specialised library cum art gallery; of a very discreet nature. It being this area and England, we had the usual hypocrisies of real and covert conduct and regulation. It was of concern to me that although my stock had arrived, late but without evident scrutiny, its replenishment was likely to be difficult. I needed to eke out sales of what were in many cases some very valuable items with great care.

Hedda of course wanted to ensure Bernd had a good education. Without being mean, I did tell her that her pension and capital from Jurgen – not forgetting my own remission of his estate's debt – had to provide such resource. She proved rather tough in her argument that a proportion of my stock in trade came from Jurgen's efforts. We settled of course. She conveniently forgot my gift of my one-third share back in Esbjerg. I handed over title to a number of works from Jurgen's Weimar collapse period of collection. I retained however, commission on the sales value. Hedda was a nice woman and an enjoyable fuck but I only owed her so much. Neither of us would realise full value from the collection anyway. German bombs, our exile and the cost of setting up and maintaining our new business reduced our resources. I'm afraid she came off worse in that respect due to ignorance of art and quite what it was Jurgen – deceased – had a hand in. We were not much helped either by the parsimony of the British military. I was put on some 'special expenses' pay list but the income was nugatory. Wilcox had however been helpful in many respects; not least in the encouragement of our salon. *La Librairie* had impressed with the utility of information gained. The arrival in London of varied would-be freedom fighters – French, Polish, Norwegian mainly, but with refugees of other nationalities – presented as many problems as benefits for the authorities. Our guests from occupied Europe all tended to be schismatic, devious, perennially plotting and scheming, constantly on the take. Our little salon would be an ideal listening post.

Early on in the establishment of the enterprise I received a visit from a thin-lipped, sandy-haired and officious little shit from some obscure Government department he claimed dealt with 'civilian and military morale.' I gathered it had been set up to deal with the inevitable issues arising from young men and women of various nationalities and without regular partners milling about our cities in a state of sexual excitement. He declined a handshake, seat or refreshment. He cleared his throat and said something like 'I am aware that your business is sanctioned by Intelligence to serve a useful purpose in the war effort. I am also aware that you have imported under official auspices, a collection of pornography. How foreigners use it in the privacy of your establishment is their affair. I am here to warn you that we will not tolerate this filth falling into the hands of the British civilian population.'

We had a mild bicker about the definition of filth but I decided to give him the undertakings he demanded; without the slightest intention of adhering to them. He delivered his final insult as I held open the front door. 'I know of your former identity as a decorated British officer. I hope some of the honour attached to that part of your life still remains.' Good God, I nearly kicked the pompous swine down the steps. It hurt though. In the long marches of the night the past can come up to bite you.

There was really too much to do for me to take much notice of the transition from phony into real war. Fortunately, I was able to draw on many of the contacts I had made from Dottie's period in this part of London, as we were close to her old studio. In addition, I revived my membership of the Cavalry Club. This was a risk of sorts given my cover but the one or two members whose help I needed never betrayed the confidence I placed in them.

My largest concern was Hedda's role in the salon – or club as we decided to make it – given her lack of English. To give her great credit, she herself found an English tutor, an exiled Dutch Jew, and applied herself with energy and to impressive effect. She had a good grasp of the principles of running the business, partly from our Paris days, but also from natural pragmatism. English fluency was also only part of the requirement, given our primarily continental clientele. Her combination of German and Danish covered most northern European countries one way or another; her French was very competent. As the war began properly, we opened our doors as *La Librairie Internationale*.

Once you had the Free French in, everyone came. Our previous credentials were well known enough to generate word of mouth from a surprisingly large number of them. In any case, there was a very small selection of clubs of our type and sophistication outside the official ones, where people could mingle, in a relaxed and permissive atmosphere at relatively low cost. The mingling naturally included meeting girls. In this regard we only had one problem: to weed out the professional tarts. I had nothing against them, but we could not afford to be prosecuted as a knocking shop. Other than that, there was an astonishing and constant supply of military and civilian women, mostly good looking, intelligent and all as eager for the company of men, as the chaps were for the girls. How these contacts developed was their business.

We rapidly developed a clientele for whom we were a reliable and discreet place to establish liaisons and make assignations. We had a salon or drawing room, gentleman's bar, a reading room and constant light food service that replicated our Paris business. Bedrooms were not available, if only for reasons of space, but we had an arrangement with a hotel in Sloane Street to whom lovers with no other home could repair. War creates a febrile atmosphere. I used to watch the animated faces of the assorted continental and later, occasional Canadian officers and the sparkly eyes and intimate hand gestures of the women, with affectionate amusement. All they really wanted was a warm, happy fuck; to take their minds off war, to help them feel human.

To set this up had cost me a great deal of money. Revenues from club membership and the bar were in theory adequate, in practice always lower than they should be. Whilst our 'members', especially the French, seemed to have a lot of money, they were elusive about parting with it. Except in the company of a pretty girl. We became inured to the sad eyes of the Poles – and others from the eastern borders - as they greeted our reminder of their debts with a ritual 'alas, my poor country.' I became quite tough with such abuse of our hospitality and would frequently tell them in good country Polish, to 'Fuck off back to Poland and liberate it then,' prior to banning them until they paid up. They mostly did. Pay up that is.

The early adoption of *La Librairie Internationale* – or *La Lib* as it became – by the Poles as much as the French, may be assumed to be due to my ostensible origins. In fact Rula's advice proved prescient. For a start they were suspicious of a Count; and they were baffled with my odd if fluent Polish. My knowledge of Pomerania and the northern border country was however, patently authentic. The massaged biography involving being orphaned and raised by the von Eisens was accepted. *La Lib* soon became a favoured haunt of some of the more volatile Poles. They set up an informal and I thought humorous social club of their own, which they titled 'The Free Polish Legation'. This irritated the more politically sensitive of their countrymen and was to have profound long-term consequences for me. Its first manifestation was an invitation to myself and Hedda to a reception at St James's Palace as representatives of the FPL who had persuaded some Court official of their authenticity. I tackled one of the Poles about it and he laughed loudly and told me to go, as it was good for business and just a little joke.

The gathering was large, we avoided the legitimate Polish delegates and I forgot about it. Then Wilcox, who had seen our picture in the papers, called me in. He told me the official Poles were very annoyed. They described my 'chums' as Wilcox called them as '...hotheads, very dangerous.' He therefore thought the whole thing a great wheeze and told me to 'stay on top of them.'

Connections had also been made with the clandestine erotic art business and I had acquired some good clients. Art dealers are a reliably amoral lot. That said, prices were not high and I was forced to sell off rather good things for less than they should have fetched. As replacement was almost impossible, this meant my capital assets were becoming depleted. I had still, quite a lot of cash in the form of Swiss francs and gold coin. This was however, rather inaccessible being in Switzerland where I had sent it before leaving Paris. Even Hedda did not know about this, and I was certainly not going to divulge its existence to British bureaucrats.

Then there was of course, our intelligence function. Given the social ambience it was obvious that we should use the staff and the girl guests as our agents. I was 'front of house' but you need women for solid espionage. I hired a very competent and extremely amusing ex-landlady from Bermondsey. She kept our clients in order and her ears open. Obviously she couldn't deal with foreign languages, but very many conversations were necessarily in English given that is who most of the women guests present were. After a few weeks I, and she, also learned how to recognise and suborn those females who had jobs that predisposed them to become helpful: as distinct from the mere flirts. In return for free drinks and food and from a sense of support for their country they proved remarkably useful. The internecine squabbles of the Free French and the constant feuding of the Poles, whilst known widely in general terms, were often given specificity by our eavesdroppers and pillow spies.

Surprisingly, it wasn't the perennially drunk and volatile Poles who cost little Bernd his eye, it was a bloody Frog. This dreadful man was in the salon, somehow having escaped our barmaid's and my attention. I think it might have been around the time of Dunkirk, and the news was on the wireless. Suddenly he produced his revolver, shouted a curse and fired off a shot. Fragments of glass flew from a vase; poor little Bernd playing cards or something on the floor looked up and received a shard straight in the eye. Screams and shouts, blood, Hedda clutching her boy to her bosom and I was wresting the revolver from the Frenchman.

The little chap, Bernd that is, not the Frog, behaved very well considering. The optic nerve had been severed but other than a blank look and no movement there were no other scars. The Frenchman was barred, and, I am glad to say, we had a personal note of apology from General de Gaulle, though signed by one of his aides called Palewski, which sounded Polish to me. Even better, a rather nice man called Andre Roy undertook to ensure that Bernd's assailant was punished by some suitably unpleasant assignment. After this episode, Bernd was not allowed in the salon and the Free French became seriously obliging clients.

III

It may seem rather frivolous to say we hardly noticed the war beyond some bomb dodging. We were fully aware of it, but in general, we just went on running our club and finding things to tell military intelligence. I also run the risk of appearing uncharitable to Hedda, who continued to provide me with charming intimate company when it suited her. Nonetheless, surrounded every evening by merry people and pretty women many of whom were shortly about to go off and fuck each other, I again grew discontented with my lot. Worse, I was on the cusp of my fiftieth year.

The passage of time is grisly enough. When one writes a *memoire*, time collapses into a few pages. Where was that dashing young man? A pander now, condemned to the scraps of charm dispensed by girls who might find one of passing amusement – even if he's an old chap. In short, I needed a fuck, several fucks, with a filthy minded young woman of great sexual appetite. There was no shortage of mature females, many of whose men, sadly, had been killed. Sympathetic as one was, I really couldn't face long, falsely cheerful, ultimately sombre dinners and the attenuated ritual prior to a shy and guilt-infused consummation in a borrowed flat. The guilt heightened if the husband were not dead but a prisoner of war. Even worse, was the return to the former married premises and its hastily concealed mementos of happier days. Then there was the quite serious risk of being fallen in love with and the expectation of marriage.

As is the way, acts of will or imagination, produce a result. One evening I was in the bar talking to our wonderful barmaid Edith about her family and old times. It was a slow night. Two girls came in. One was in civvies, the other in uniform. I greeted them and they looked round the nearly empty room with a mix of disappointment and annoyance. 'Where is everyone?' asked the WAAF. I shrugged. 'If they've not buggered off to fight the war they must have overdone the weekend.' The WAAF stared at me. 'Aren't you Dottie Scrimgeour's bit of bloke from whenever?' she asked. Pure genius enabled me to find the answer in the depths of my memory. 'You must be her niece Dido.' I replied. This was the prize-winning response. The aggression vanished and sheer pleasure took over. The civilian was consigned to history – or at least the margins of our conversation; from which she quite quickly retreated. 'Don't worry about Nancy,' said Dido as her companion left, 'I don't know her very well. She's from the Midlands.'

I laughed. I remembered meeting Dido in Dottie's flat. Aged ten or eleven she had been sent by Dottie's sister for an educational visit to London; art galleries and so forth. Introduced to me as the 'lodger' I suppose, she had gazed at me and said, 'are you the man with the huge penis in aunt Dot's picture?' To my astonishment, Dottie had replied on my behalf, 'No, but he would have been if I'd met him earlier.'

The ice broken, I caught up a little with the past. Dottie and my exchange of postcards had been terminated by the war. Dido – whose real name was Deborah – had subsequent letters in which her aunt enthused about America and New York where she seemed to have settled with another rich female lover. 'She's such a role model,' Dido sighed. Earlier conversational gambits concerning her life had met with little response so I was left with the Socratic solution, to ask 'Why?' Once again, this proved the key. 'She taught me that women are infinitely superior socially and in emotional terms, but that men, can be very useful in all sorts of ways.'

There are a limited number of possible responses to that final assertion, and they may have been made. I believe we went out to eat. At some point that evening, I had the astonishing pleasure of fucking a WAAF officer in full uniform with skirt up, knickers hauled aside, regulation stockings crumpled prettily around her knees and suspenders flapping loose. As I plunged my cock with great enthusiasm into her tunnel of love, Dido and I exchanged fulsome compliments. 'Oh fuck Dido, you are sensational,' and 'Aunt D wasn't lying about your cock, don't shoot it 'til I tell you.' This may not be entirely accurate, but it certainly reflects the mood of our first engagement on a bench in what I recall as Carlyle Square.

Dido had emulated her Aunt's lesbian philosophy. Unquestionably bisexual, she had no inhibitions about enjoyment of male company, albeit with a particular object in view. I don't know whether Sappho had a big following in the women's armed services – although the military did have real worries about that but Dido almost invariably came to the club in the company of another female, never with another man. However, on most such occasions I noted that this companion was abandoned quite ruthlessly if Dido had decided I was to conclude her night out.

Hedda of course soon became aware of the situation. She was very good about it, only saying rather wistfully that she supposed that 'that woman is more exciting than me.' I acknowledged there were things Dido and I liked to do that Hedda did not, but that Hedda retained my respect and affection. This seemed to comfort her and if our bedsharing declined in frequency she still came to me from time to time. 'You are so good for me,' she would sigh. It was no hardship to fuck Hedda, unless Dido had recently given my dick one of the truly lunatic thrashings to which she was prone. Falling on it like a tigress on its prey, she would bite and pump or grind away with every muscle in her body. 'Woe betide' me, if I should lose control before she was satisfied. I had to begin again. I once observed it was as though she hated my cock and wanted to kill it. 'I do,' she replied, 'that's exactly it. I want the pleasure and I want him dead. Then later, I want him resurrected.' This struck me as somewhat religious in imagery. It turned out Dido was indeed a left-footer, educated in a seriously strict Roman Catholic school.

So dragged on our war. Little Bernd went to school – initially several, as he turned out to be a smart, but challenging child. I would say dreadful little toad, except he had charm and I admired his strength of character. Then Hedda found a prep school locally and a young master of whom she became very fond. I don't know if they had an affair, but he looked after her and Bernd, which left me free to pursue my own interests. Apart from Dido, this mostly involved the FPL and military intelligence.

Our little group of hotheads had taken to borrowing a spare room in the basement for long evening meetings. In these, they alternated intense discussion with bursts of drinking, the ordering of food and singing Polish songs. Their main preoccupation was plotting ways to get back into Poland and sabotage the German war effort by fomenting revolution. My understanding of the tenor of the group was that they were left wing if not rabidly Communist. They deeply mistrusted the official Polish leadership; whether rightly or wrongly I neither knew nor cared. There were however several Jewish Poles in the membership.

They appeared to regard me as a mentor and person of influence. How else they reasoned rather astutely, would I be able to run this club and get all this food and drink. Hence I was constantly being badgered to use my supposed contacts to arrange secret flights and parachute drops and to give them grants of money. To be fair, there was one evening of enormous excitement when they claimed a great coup. Subsequently I understood it had been something to do with the capture in Poland of an Enigma machine but their part in the matter was probably fantasy.

Wilcox was visibly grateful for my reports, but very reticent in comment. Whatever the scares about Communism, 'Uncle Joe' was on our side. At this point in the war, the putative political complexion of our Eastern European neighbours was irrelevant. More helpful were the current squabbles that enabled us to play one element of our uncomfortable defeated nation pensioners against the other. For whatever reasons, the only Americans we ever had in the club were black. True to type, they were polite, well behaved, got on with everyone and occasionally played jazz for us with great facility. Since even Peers' daughters, were physically accosted in the street by white American soldiers, I am glad we were spared their presence and any contretemps.

IV

Eventually we got to the point when it looked as if we would win. Except the poor old Poles, who however annoying at times, had style and a country they felt strongly about; which was first to suffer one of the last grisly revenges of the dying Nazi scorpion and then to become swallowed by Stalin's Russia. They were not of course alone.

Our hard-core clique of Polish members became smaller as one by one they moved off to fight their war. The more casual visitors had usually been airforce types. The 'residents' as we thought of them were much more likely to be politicals and intelligence officers. This explained why they were very keen that we had no published members' list, and wished to trust my discretion. In case this proved misplaced they of course identified themselves under assumed names. So did the French come to that. It early on occurred to me as I researched Polish history as part of my own authentication, that the Zaluskis, Staszics, Koperniks and Skorewiczs were also Polish heroes from the past. But then, foreigners often have limited name repertoires.

So as the allied advance brought Russia and the West closer to the heart of Germany, more and more of our old chums vanished from London; Dido included. She left a note saying simply, 'bye-bye Magnus. It was big fun. Take care of yourself.' On VE day, with Bernd at his new boarding school and the club closed, Hedda and I retreated from the riotous jollity and sat in our salon sharing a bottle of champagne.

At that moment I felt very fond of her indeed, and said so. 'It's been good Hedda, we've done well. You've done very well. Jurgen would be proud.' She looked at me and gave me one of her Frisian Island smiles. 'Jurgen would be happy with you. I think we have had a good coming together.'

I think we both had tears in our eyes. Possibly, we shared an intuitive sense of change. Or maybe, since she knew of a visit I had made to Wilcox the previous day and with some insight into my manner, had realised something serious was in train. The upshot was, we finished our champagne and went wordless to her room where we made love. I think it is fair to use what is for me, such an anodyne term. In this instance, and probably for the first time in our partnership, we genuinely looked into each other's eyes; making our conjunction with warmth and mutual understanding. This wasn't my cock and her cunt. It was Hedda and Magnus – even if Jurgen was lurking around at the back of her mind – and we were saying thank you and goodbye to each other. It was indeed a good coming together. Three months later, in Paris I heard a rumour that Hedda was pregnant. Well, if that was what she intended, I'm glad it had a result.

The visit to Wilcox had been most instructive. I always knew I had had a lucky run. Now it was time to pay the bill. Politics can be so convoluted and when not dull, totally vicious. It seemed that although some echelons were frightfully grateful for my efforts and would love to retire me, there were a few embarrassments in relation to some other aspects of my business. Other sections thought I should still be 'kept in play.' This chess metaphor made me laugh. For reasons that now elude me, the proposition was that Hedda and Bernd would be free to stay and become British and so on; but it would be 'helpful' if I left the country and followed my barmy Poles as they connived their way back to their own land. The alternative was that the certain interests might seek to prosecute me as some sort of spy or traitor, having nurtured a dissident group of alien and probably communist, and also Jewish agents during the war. This was without mention of my suspect conduct in, or after, the Great War, and as a pornographer.

Without fully understanding the matter and its implications in detail, I grasped the necessity to leave England and prepare myself for a new future. I thought briefly, 'I am a decorated WW1 officer, over fifty years old, and the British establishment seems determined to persecute me: just at the point I should have another medal and a pension.' Of course, there in the file was all this other material, irrelevant except to the strange and dreadful culture of secret English governance. I said to Wilcox, 'Why are you doing this to me?' He replied simply, 'I am under orders.' 'I thought we just fought a war about that,' I said bitterly and that was that.

I was given two weeks to arrange my affairs. These really

only concerned Hedda and our property. I told her most of the truth about why I was leaving. The settlement was equitable, we had a few tears and a hug and that was it. Wilcox came up with a new British passport for me that he insisted I use to cross into France; and another, apparently official Polish one for Count Magnus to replace my old pre-war version. There were the usual bollocks about contacts and letterboxes, but it was all so perfunctory I felt no one cared much. Two Military Police then politely saw me onto the boat train. International travel in 1946 of any sort, let alone the ostensibly civilian, was difficult enough. From London to Warsaw direct was impossible. So Paris was my first destination and also that of several of my old FPL chums.

Other than the correspondent office of my Swiss bank, my first call was to Rue St Michel. It was all shut up. In the nearby café where I used to have my morning coffee I was greeted with gratifying warmth by the patron. He had a good moan about the war, and told me Sylvie and several of our girls had been given a rough time by the Free French and their cohorts after the liberation. This was of course because like most other bordellos they stayed open for business: some, who played both ends against the middle more successfully, escaped censure.

His wife had Sylvie's address and I went off to Clichy. Her apartment building looked decent and I sat in the café opposite the main door until she appeared. Our reunion was cordial but not effusive considering the pre-war relationship. She turned out to have been soured by her treatment by the Free French. 'It was nothing to do with you Magnus,' she said eventually. 'You were generous and fair and the war was not so bad, despite those German pigs. In fact they were often perfectly good customers.' After a couple of drinks, she cheered up and said she had been able to put away some money from the war years and so her apartment was assured. She worked now in a hotel as a receptionist. She was not complimentary about the politicians who had closed the bordellos. Life in Paris was still raw, she told me and her hair had only just recovered. She asked me about my visit to Paris. I said simply, 'I am no longer allowed to live in England.'

She was appalled. Her manner softened as it used to and she put her hand over mine. 'Poor Magnus, how unjust.' Well of course, two more drinks later and we were in her modest, but congenial apartment as she prepared herself for me to take her to dinner. Afterwards we took a taxi to St Lazaire to collect my luggage and she suggested I stay the night with her.

Dear Sylvie, nearing forty, she retained the timelessly self-confident carriage of all French women – well, most of them - and the languid way of walking that works the hips and buttocks. Her body was much the same too. A little less hair in the armpit, and a little softer and fuller round the hip and belly, maybe a trace of vein in the thigh: but not much. Undressed, we slurped cognac and kissed experimentally – Sylvie as ever, was chainsmoking Gauloise Bleu, but I liked that - and then she had me in her grip and we are rolling around with grunts and groans like people who haven't fucked for a while. The best part of it was that we were so familiar.

So I moved in with her. There was rent of course, and an agreement not to 'presume' on each other. My occupation of her spare room however, was a formality. Sylvie and I liked sharing a bed, regardless of what went on in it. Our previous relationship had evolved. Over the succeeding eighteen months or so I think we both thought about setting up some business together and eventually retreating to the country. There was so much we agreed on. Except my fucking her in the arse. Well, it was never that vital. Then again, although I was well into my fifties, she was only a decade behind and we were rather compatible, especially as we did not want children.

Meanwhile I spent my time tracking down and getting acquainted with, the local Polish community and my wartime chums from the FPL. This had many longeurs. Not the least of which were evenings spent in expatriate clubrooms in dreadful suburbs singing ludicrous songs and having vodka sodden exiles and maniacal soi-disant patriots slobbering over you with their sentimental rubbish about national revival.

One may think I was a rotten agent. Actually, that is true. I had absolutely no interest in the nuance of whatever it was my puppet-masters cared about. I was observant though. My indifference of course made me ideal, since no one suspected me of anything. My re-engagement with the FPL as reject from Britain of course won me acceptance. There were clearly issues that now sub-divided the group. I thought Jewishness had something to do with it. The unifying factor overall, was Communism. There were major reservations about Russia and Stalin of course, but whatever the nationalist and Catholic opinion, heavy Socialism won overall.

Then the French decided to deport me to Poland. I had been prepared for something to happen. When I first reported, as instructed, to the British Embassy I was briefed on the necessity to get me to Poland. Timing and method were unspecified. The pretext was of course to do with my real national identity and my connections with pre-war corruption and communist Polish dissidents. Who knows? I bade farewell to Sylvie and had an immensely tedious, supervised journey through Austria to the point I was handed over to the Russians in Vienna and ultimately arrived in Warsaw under the auspices of the Polish Intelligence Service known as the UB. In my later years, I reflected on the extraordinary quantity of paper and personnel it must have taken to deliver me; and on a fiction. I was also told later, how lucky I was the KGB, who were clearly the real players here, hadn't taken me first to Moscow. I must have been in some backwater of espionage and was in any case a very trivial pawn. The British were leaking secrets at every level; Communism had a big recruitment drive on. Where else would I go than Poland? Wilcox and chums had just chucked me out like a tadpole in a pond to see if I became a frog.

Political classes become obsessed with history. Individuals such as me concentrate for the most part on our personal survival and the most immediate circumstances in which we find ourselves.

These notions remind me of a post-war, Russian dominated Warsaw of grisly destruction. The foot stamping soldiery and the prolonged document scanning of sour officials – every society appears able to produce them on demand – eventually led me to a shabby office in the less derelict end of what might once have been a distinguished building.

We had an interesting conversation, my new interlocutor and I. He was a Pole in the UB. He ran through his file on an 'it says here' basis. His tone was cool and sceptical. It was of course his job, and I had lived too long on the margins of identities to worry much. I told him the truth; my whole damn history. I invited him to go to Pomerania and talk to the Kashubs. I told him how fond I had become of my Polish communist friends and that as an illegitimate peasant, I was sick to death of the establishment in my own country because they had betrayed me. I told them my transition had been engineered so that I could spy on the Poles; but that it had been the only way to get out and fight for continued socialist revolution. I warned them that Atlee's Labour government was a charade. It would never supplant capitalism and the right wing would return. I wanted to fight that. It was such an inspired rant that I convinced myself. He and his Russian fellow inquisitor looked at each other, nodded and I was in.

They found me a small flat – in truth one room, but as a privileged foreigner I had my own bathroom – in a 'protected' enclave off-centre of the city. Attached to the ministry of information I was to translate Anglophone intelligence of various sorts into Polish. There were many other things; including the construction of misleading reports to my supposed British paymasters. I found that part of it quite fun. Much of the disinformation material came from the USSR of course. It was dressed up as having been passed on through Polish dissidents. Either way, the material was workaday stuff that combined bits of political and other gossip with morsels of military and even medical science developments. What did surprise me was the degree to which the British Communist Party and the Trade Unions were willing to collaborate in this often fraudulent, if occasionally I suppose traitorous two-way traffic.

Sadly, the females whom I met were extremely dreary. Middle aged Slavs and lumpen in figure they were also severe apparatchiks. Dressed in sombre socialist fabrics of clumsy cut and unsubtle colour they clumped about in sullen receipt or return of ones output. No hairdresser, cosmetician, depilatory consultant or corsetiere had addressed their status as women. Even the most rabid lesbian feminist of my acquaintance in the 'thirties had taken some pride in a well-groomed appearance.

Then, on my way out of my office building and in the street on the way to the hard currency store, I met Rula. This was no accident. She may have been a genuine refugee whore in Paris. In Warsaw she was there to keep an eye on me. To find a coffee was not easy. We walked around and caught up on our lives. What regimes of any sort, let alone totalitarian ones forget, is how real people relate. Mostly of course they don't care; so long as the mass behave in some prescribed mass way and don't cause trouble.

Paranoia had no substance. We were both too lowly to have anyone following us. Trust was vindicated simply by results. Meanwhile Rula, now a real grown-up civil servant in the Communist Party and I, now a real middle-aged male foreign spy, got together again and went shopping.

Chapter 8

LIKE A BIRD ON THE WING

Rula's sojourn in Paris and apotheosis as whore had been entirely accidental. She had come to study at the Sorbonne, found it impossible to get in and had to earn her living. She had no intrinsic objection to fucking and the money was all right if you found the right place. At the end of the war she had avoided the pillory meted out to many of her French colleagues but was deported very rapidly as a collaborator.

Luckily, she had long been a member of the Communist Party and this, together with her language ability secured a place in the new regime's army of civil servants. Imagine her surprise then, when my file came across her desk and having declared she knew me, she was deputed as my 'minder.' She herself expressed astonishment at my arrival in Warsaw. I stuck to the story I had told my first inquisitors. It was perfectly credible even to me and Rula nodded sympathetically. She said, 'I always knew there was something different about you.' This is it you see; a spoonful of truth to one pound of lies and everyone thinks they have second sight.

Unlike myself, as genuine Polish citizen and despite her civil service role, she had no access to the hard currency shop. Nor did she have a flat with its own bathroom. Warsaw had only just begun its reconstruction programme. Other than my personal charm and our historic acquaintance, these functional attributes including use of my money brought her to my apartment carrying a decent supply of food, soaps and other items only women think essential. I reflected on the rather modest capital I had released from Switzerland and into the People's Bank of the USSR - Warsaw Branch - minus ten percent Moscow handling charge.

Could I afford Rula, or could I afford not Rula?

In the light of such concerns, for me, the evening began with slight anxiety. Rula engaged fully with the bathroom and the unguents we had brought home. I opened tins and boiled dried pasta and made the best meatballs in tomato sauce I could. Fresh vegetables of course were unobtainable other than for members of the Praesidium who didn't much care for them. Rula emerged from her bath dressed again in her office clothes and proceeded to work her way through my little culinary creation with impressive and gratifying energy. We also consumed probably two bottles of very well made Polish vodka. This was the only thing in the entire country that was well made.

During our meal, Rula took some time expatiating to me on contemporary Poland and her vision of its future. I felt encouraged. All women, especially one who has been a whore, strike me as pragmatists. This does not preclude idealism. Pragmatism is about the art of the possible. As one of my own staff had said to me, 'Of course I am romantic, if only the *mecs* let me.' Rula confided to me that her superiors had told her they were satisfied with my attitudes and work but felt I should be watched, 'just in case.' They said she should become as close to me as was necessary for this purpose. Rula leaned forward and flamboyantly waved her once more empty glass in my face. 'Magnus, as close as necessary.' I rescued the vodka bottle before it fell to the floor and refilled both our glasses with the dregs. 'Wonderful, Rula. What do you have in mind?'

Rula had a sharp little face with dark brows and darker eyes. 'Have you ever been fucked by a Polish Bureau of International Affairs Section Manager?' she asked fiercely. I admitted innocence. 'Well, you are so fucking lucky,' she said and fell off her chair. I picked her up, she was very light and slender, and placed her on my bed with the coverlet over her. Then I cleared up and still dressed laid down gingerly beside her. The bed was small, but the fabric-covered planks that masqueraded as a two-seat sofa just wouldn't do. I was quite pleased though that my Polish was holding up and she had been very complimentary about it.

In the morning I brought her coffee and sat quietly until she had made herself ready to leave. She came to me with hand out in formal farewell. 'Will you visit me again?' I asked, before she could speak. Her stern yet bashful expression turned into a smile. 'Yes, please. Will I wait for you this evening?' 'Of course, Rula,' I thought, 'as you will every night for as long as is necessary.' That said, she was quite a good-looking woman and the nights could get lonely.

She was outside the office next day and we revisited the hard currency store. The food and drink were one, or rather several things. It was the other two huge bags I found less comprehensible. To make light, I remarked on women and shopping. Rula turned on me. 'You have no idea. You can't even buy sanitary towels here if you are a Pole.' I held my hands up and said sorry and she relented and hugged my arm, saying what a very nice man I was. Nothing changes really, so I relaxed and looked forward to the evening.

Rula wanted to show me how good a housemate she could be. So she prepared her own version of the meatballs and pasta dish. These were the only palatable sort of thing available even in our privileged outlet. A choice of tinned vegetable and condiment of course gave variation for the imaginative. By unspoken consent we limited the consumption of vodka to sufficient instead of excessive. Whilst I washed up, Rula bathed. She came to me naked. This was good, as her body was much more enticing than her underwear. Although I know that women look at men with some desiderata in terms of their musculature, hairiness and so on I can see how they must suffer from the idealisation of their form in a way that despite Michaelangelo's *'David'* our sex has escaped. But possibly it hasn't, and both genders through love, lust and realism, accept and embrace the limitations of the object of their affection.

As a practised tart, Rula had few inhibitions, and whatever there might have been disappeared with a decent amount of alcohol. She posed prettily for me in that timeless manner wherein women raise their arms, turn their bodies, tilt a knee and say the equivalent of 'ta ra!' I clapped her and laughed and told her she was beautiful and wasn't it time she and I got to bed together after all these years.

She was a skinny little thing, even in her late twenties. There were ribs and tendons and the da Vinci-esque delineation of stomach and muscle. Her skin was very white and the hair of her eyebrows and armpits and at her groin was thick and black. Moles dotted her back. As she turned into me I stroked her thin but silky flank and within the softness of loin and buttock were the ridges and declivities high inside her thighs. My exploration of her form made me feel like a horse trader or a butcher. I wondered how she felt about me. Not fat, not thin, a small amount of hair on the chest. Her practised hand fondled my balls and her lips looked for mine. There you are then; it's another fuck. Except it isn't. Here in this miserable country with its ludicrous history and oppressed people Rula and I merely carried out in our own fond way the same revolutionary ritual that has always denied totalitarianism. Well, we had a very good fuck. Its subversiveness may be arguable.

I was always struck in my erotic art dealing days by the historic preference for plump women. Maybe fat was a sign of wealth as for the Chinese. I now realise, that despite having learned quite a lot in my childhood, I am very unread. I don't know what plump meant symbolically in different eras. Fat is not for me; even though some fullness of female breasts and loins is attractive. If it wasn't for my passion for the female sexual part, I might think myself homosexual. Rula's cunt proved voracious. It demanded to be licked, sucked and penetrated with great diligence. As we squirmed about I found the contrast between her thin white body and the hot liquescence of her cunt dreadfully exciting.

Privately, I wondered how long it would be before she decided to move in permanently. It took six weeks. During which time she was very attentive. That is, she fucked like a polecat. I deliberately forebore to take the initiative in any of our domestic arrangements. In due course, after she had been notably lewd in the matter of access to her orifices and her use of my semen, she snuggled up and asked me if I didn't think it a much better idea if we lived together. Apart from the simple convenience of her being available all the time, she pointed out that she would save on rent and her room would go to someone more needy. It was a good case. I wondered what our respective bosses would say. She laughed delightedly. 'Oh, mine thought it an excellent plan, and so did yours.'

Despite the poverty of post-war Poland, it was remarkable how quickly my socialist flat acquired things. Little bedside tables, and a new bed to go with them, new flowery curtains, soap racks for the bathroom. To be fair, Rula was a good housekeeper. I was no sloven, but she made the place sparkle. We even obtained some paint and there we were, in our bourgeois home together. In bed, she was still affectionate and fun, but took to reading at night and I realised, as she turned out her light and kissed my brow affectionately, that we might as well be married.

It would be unfair to categorise my years in Warsaw as durance vile. I had a decent job by the standards of the regime, a liveable apartment and little Rula, who was a jolly companion mostly. I also made some friends. Inevitably it was these who caused the first small squabbles. In a year or three I had become properly accepted. As my Polish got better and better and word went around I was politically safe, people began to stop at my cubby hole where I pondered the leader columns of The Times or some obscure bundle of Trades Union internal memoranda; and chat. Then they began to invite me to drinking sessions in someone's flat or an illicit bar. Despite constant teasing over doddery old Churchill and the failure of the British economy with its imminent collapse, they were very intrigued by 'the West.' As Communists, they were convinced it was only a matter of time before we had a proper revolution in England, and France. Both of which countries they pointed out, knew how to do it. I nodded and smiled and proposed toasts to the overturn of capitalism. As Poles, they were very aware that Britain had finally gone to war because of them and had given safe haven to many of their compatriots. The acknowledgement was mediated by a sense of grievance over what they saw as parsimony and self-interest by the British authorities. We skirted round the question of Russia and usually diverted into some anti-German discourse in which my age and war experience, together with my time as a prisoner in Pomerania caused more vodka to be drunk. Somewhere, somehow, my London club's hospitality to the FPL had also become known. This too had respect and called for more vodka. Poor everyone might have been, but the vodka never ran dry.

Such evenings out, terminating in my arrival home a trifle unsteady possibly, but perfectly compos mentis, were an irritant to my volatile live in tart. We would bicker away for a while until one or other would apologise and life would go on. I pointed out to her that I could hardly reject friendships made in the course of work. She responded that she too had a demanding job and social opportunities but chose to come home and wash my clothes and cook my dinner. So I would then suggest she had some evenings out with her colleagues and she would say I would be jealous. Which would lead to an examination of our relationship and the fact that she was a graduate and not just a whore and I was a traitor and having a big cock didn't mean I was perfect.

We made our quarrels up of course with the usual mixture of embraces, tears and promises of amendment. After one of which, prompted I think by some earlier sub-conscious premonition and an ongoing sense of Fate, I said lightly, 'You know Rula my love, we might as well be married.' Perhaps my Polish was still imperfect with regard to irony. More probably, Rula heard what she wanted to hear. 'Oh yes, yes, darling Magnus that would be wonderful.' At least, that was the import of her hugs, skips and claps of delight. Naturally, she suborned my libido to her cause in an especially lascivious demonstration of female concupiscence.

II

Whilst my liaison with Rula had brought knowing winks, nudges and lucky old dog remarks; the marriage created general hilarity. 'She's got you now old boy,' would capture the gist of sentiments expressed. We had a functional civil wedding. The witnesses were our respective bosses who beamed corpulently on either side. There was nobody from Rula's family. They had all been killed during the war. Probably by the Germans, but maybe the Russians. Everyone seemed very pleased by our union. Then we went off to a small official restaurant and had a small official buffet comprised of gherkins, dried fish and even drier sausage on desert dry black bread. Luckily, the vodka was supremely more plentiful than the cheap official *mousseux*.

Several jokes were made about Rula's accession as a Countess. Her wedding gown was a frock saved from her pre-war Paris years. Whether or not 'in fashion', it was very well cut and she looked terrific. I told her so, and must have communicated my sincerity. She gazed at me, her eyes suddenly tearful and she said as tenderly as she had ever spoken to me, 'Thank you Magnus that means very much to me.'

So began my married life. Shortly afterwards I realised I would soon be sixty years of age. My wife meanwhile was somewhere in her mid-thirties. Children were not in her plans. She had no desire to populate Poland, merely to better herself. Our marriage rather improved our ability to behave in a mature way with each other. Her supervisory role in terms of my 'soundness' had long withered as a reality. Marriage negated the whole concept. Instead, I was put under the nominal supervision of a Russian KGB officer attached to our bureau.

Gregor Volnikov was a nice young chap; Georgian by birth with a degree in economics. He had the good fortune to join the Russian Army late in the war, aged fifteen and had stopped in Poland. Nonetheless, our shared military background, however disparate gave us something in common. My age also meant I had some sort of credibility as a genuine ideological refugee. Why else would a sixty year old defect?

We met formally every week or so for a debriefing on the exchange of intelligence in my sphere. Given the extent of the Russian network, my role was extremely marginal. That said people appeared to find my comments, insights and translations of value. They also liked the facility to channel material out through my still functioning 'dead letter' drop. This was a small park in which a bench served as the monthly depository for a paper bag ostensibly containing a sausage. In return, I would usually find a newspaper in the folds of which would be some coded message of small import that took me hours to decipher. I used to give these to my KGB friends who had greater facility with this sort of thing. It all struck me as nonsensical. Other than these clandestine exchanges I had no personal contact whatsoever with London for nearly eight years. I remained impressed nonetheless with the perseverance of bureaucracy.

In Britain it had recently been decided the nation was to embark on a 'New Elizabethan Revival.' All sorts of pride arousing events, not least the end of rationing had confounded expectations of imminent collapse. The Communist Revolution continued the ideological struggle around the world. In the United Kingdom too, trades unions and intellectual establishment alike retained strong Soviet sympathies. Nonetheless, by 1956 even Poland had its episode of objection to the heavy hand of Stalinist Russia and large numbers of workers went on strike.

Apart from sounding me on my Polish colleagues' political views in these strained times, especially in relation to the Hungarian brouhaha, Gregor became increasingly interested in my own connections in the 'West'. My rarely accessed Swiss bank account – as an originally legitimate business vehicle and in its later secrecy part of my dissidence from British oppression – fascinated him. With rudimentary subtlety, over the weeks he established what he needed to know. The proposition was simply, that in exchange for a transfer to the Russian Embassy in Paris, I would make my Swiss bank facility available to Gregor and his associates. The implication being they had access to hard currency and wanted to get it out. With a few precautionary caveats built in, this struck me as a very sensible plan for us both. As he kindly pointed out, I was old, junior and if I walked out of the Embassy in Paris and claimed asylum, who would care?

The older one gets the more routine supplants adventure. I had spent ten years in Poland. It had become perfectly bearable, probably too much so and I had hardly noticed the passage of time. Now I faced old age, and this shocked me. Worse, in a short while I would be forcibly retired. This was not a good prospect in Eastern Europe. Thus Gregor and I put our conspiracy into play and within a few months I received orders to transfer to the Russian Embassy in Paris as a 'Cultural Liaison Officer Grade IV', or something.

What astonished me was how simple everything was. When the time came, a year or so later and my work for Gregor's little financial scheme had been completed, I visited the British Embassy. After weeks, in which signals were exchanged and I had several meetings with intelligence staff, I was shown in to see some official. He did a lot of 'Good Lord' and 'Extraordinary' and then issued me with a new passport and a bank draft for back pay that was modest, but very acceptable. Evidently my record had been wiped clean and I was again persona grata. I was told that of course, I was now retired and should regard myself as a civilian. I was to provide details to enable payment of a pension. He read me some piece of paper thanking me for my services. Then, and bless him for it since it was obviously unscripted, he stood up, shook my hand, saluted and said 'Thank you sir for all you have done. You should have had more.' I left with a lump in my throat and glad that my efforts for the USSR had clearly been useless in the attempted destruction of British *civilitas*.

This was later. Meantime, Rula had been politely dismayed

at my transfer. She knew it was forever, and she didn't know about my Swiss money: only the local account that I left for her. We had a professionally executed and very satisfying farewell fuck. Of course we were fond of each other. It had been a long time. Still, she now had the apartment, access to the hard currency store and as the wife, or soon ex-wife no doubt, of an ageing foreign intelligence officer in good standing, opportunity to bed some suitable apparatchik: hopefully, an advance on her previous liaisons. A recent promotion virtually guaranteed that. She wouldn't have my cock however, and I think it was that for which she reserved her most lingering farewell kiss.

In Paris, I had a wonderful period in which as Count Magnus Pietrowski I arranged Franco-Russian Cultural Exchanges. These were, we all knew, designed to create a context in which as many western politicians as possible became verbally if not physically compromised; it is astonishing how drink and sex accomplish this so easily. I went to Switzerland quite often, and at Russian expense ostensibly on official business connected with those we had suborned. Whilst there, of course I had to manage my private arrangements with Gregor and his associates.

I was in my sixties, but I was fit and in a position of influence, even at my modest level. Stalin had vanished and Kruschev taken over. The Cold War was still in serious operational stance, but the atmosphere, if you were on the inside, had lightened. The Russians were and are clever people. I had done my time in Warsaw and now they released me to do what they knew I was good at. The restrictions of accountability or place of residence were no more onerous than in the Army; in fact less so.

Meanwhile, as I mentioned, visits to Switzerland were easy to manage and officially justified by my cultural role. Swiss banks would do anything you wanted and not tell anyone else.

I shipped the great part of my money into a different bank, and then made the facility of my original company account open to Gregor and friends. The result was a huge influx of hard currency, mostly dollars over the next eight or ten years. The purposes and pretexts were I am sure ostensibly authentic, but I lost track of whether they were fulfilled. A modest percentage found its way into my possession. I would never be rich, but I would be free. Trust is a wonderful thing.

I didn't even have to make a 'walk out' break for freedom. Just before the Cuban missile crisis began, I was called in to see one of the senior embassy staff who pretended not to be KGB. He simply said, 'Pietrowski, you have done well. It is time for you to retire.' He gave me a medal; 'hero' of something and added '... you are free to go home at your own convenience. I regret you have not been granted a pension.' As I reached the door, he said more softly, 'Your friends are grateful. They will stay in touch.' So that was how it was done. He hadn't specified where 'home' might be.

III

I had no desire to return to England. Paris was a city I liked very much and in any case, I had formed an attachment to a viola player. It was absurd of course. For one thing she was only in her 'twenties. We old men are such fools. Then, I knew nothing about music, except of course what I liked which was primarily Baroque, Bach, Mozart at latest. All I had to offer her was my influence as a cultural attaché, a winning way and a still potent cock. But good manners demanded I wait until invited out. A sexual jaunt at my age with a young woman, especially if instigated by me seemed unlikely. My surmise that she might like me as a man was just instinct based on her flirtatious manner. That said musicians and ballerinas are often lacking in visible sexual energy, in my experience. Unless you get at it through their art of course.

Artists are also permanent mendicants. They will do almost anything for a free meal, a paid performance or the chance to show off. Whether they will fuck for it is an arguable hypothesis; but serious 'Art' demands serious seduction. In this case, Sophia O'Malley – Irish-Italian to clarify – was the one who took the initiative to inveigle her charming presence into my life. We'd met at a pretentious little soiree hosted by the Ambassador's wife of a second rate but aspirational country. I think it was Greece. Young and deceptively shy, she hovered on the fringe until with innocent intent, I noticed and brought her a drink and some food. Disclosure of my role at the Russian Embassy animated her. She stared into my eyes, moistened her lips, touching my arm lightly as she fired an array of questions. 'Interesting', 'fascinating' and 'exciting' were well-used responses to a narrative I tried to keep economical. Women so much expect a man to love nothing more than blathering on about himself. I like to disappoint them in that respect. That said, there's also nothing like a good story.

Heaven knows what rubbish I told her. None of it mattered, provided I could get her work, or a place in an orchestra, or a grant to attend a high class post-graduate music school or whatever it was young viola players need. The Russian cultural programme was obviously of interest. Actually we got on rather well; she was a sparky girl. I probably revealed more than I should. She might have been a KGB agent. I was very careful though never to speak unkindly of Russia. Parting from her on friendly terms with an exchange of cards, I told myself I was a long way off stroking her viola strings.

A couple of intimate lunches and faithful attendance at sparsely attended amateur concerts in which she performed at least gave the illusion of friendship. I managed to get her an assignment with a visiting Russian chamber orchestra whose best viola player had defected in Helsinki on their tour. This made me her mentor. At the point when I was looking for the cues that might, as it were, bring my own part into the symphony, I was demobbed by my Russian chums.

Following my principle of relative truth speaking, I advised my protégé over a pre-dinner drink that my time as Soviet cultural panjandrum was over: she needed to look elsewhere for patronage. She was nice about it. 'So what Magnus? You still know everyone, you've got the gift of the gab, just carry on. We'll be fine.' The annoying thing about this was that she had just effectively made me her agent: on the basis of one lucky fixture. I told her I had very little expertise in her professional sphere; that she should look for a younger, more widely knowledgeable sponsor or manager or whatever they were called. 'Sure Magnus, I've met them and they are full of shit. I trust you, and now you're out of work what else will you do?' Then she waved at the waiter and we had more Ricard. Sophia became electric with her plans for her future and my part in securing it. It occurred to me she was really talking to her Dad, who was I had inferred, away with the fairies in Ireland.

My dismissal from Soviet service also meant I had no home. Luckily, Sophia knew of a spare room in the apartment house she shared with several other musicians that I could occupy for a few days. Flat sharing was not something I wanted to do and Montparnasse was already in my sights. By a fluke, the very day of the conversation just recounted, I ran into an acquaintance I knew as Peter Romanov. He was a genial old stick and apparently a member of that unhappy family so thus a bona fide count if not Prince. As a distant cousin his part of the clan had been out of Russia at the time of the slaughter. Whilst he was quite remote from contemporary Soviet affairs, the Embassy used him for small diplomatic cultural missions. We had coffee, he congratulated me on my 'release' and I told him about Sophia. There should be no problem, he told me. So when I arrived at Sophia's apartment I was able to tell her she had an interview, recommendation and possible place at the Paris Conservatoire. Her reaction was touching and slightly overwhelming. I went to my room and lay down for a while. A young woman's body pressed to one was a long unencountered pleasure. I suddenly missed Rula.

We were both busy for the next few days. I found my apartment at the top of a house in Montparnasse. Sophia had her successful interview at the conservatoire. She burst into my room with a shout of, 'Magnus, Magnus I did it, you did it,' and hugged me again. I was able to tell her my own good news. She decided that the following day, she would come with me to make sure my new residence was suitable and then take me to lunch. Her father might have been a bit flaky, but her mother was the daughter of a serious Italian olive oil magnate. I was not so badly off myself, but it's pleasing when a woman can match one franc for franc at the dining table.

Such happy denouements put our friendship on a more than positive footing. Success is a splendid facilitator of good fellowship. Sophia chattered happily about her history, and freed from the KGB, I revealed a little more of my own. She was highly intrigued by the brothel years and moved by my account of my horse in the war; which involved owning up to having been a British officer. But then, it didn't matter any more. 'You're a bit of a dark horse yourself Magnus Pietrowski,' Sophia said, her hazel eyes fixed on mine.

In my apartment she gave everything careful appraisal. The paint and furnishing needed work, the roof terrace was very promising, the view stunning. 'God, I'd move in here myself,' she said. I couldn't help it. 'You'd be welcome,' I responded. There was a silence. I remained leaning on the guardrail of the *terrasse* and bit my lip. 'How old are you Magnus?' I heard her ask. 'I won't see sixty again.' 'I'm twenty four.' 'I know.' Her hand touched my arm and she turned me to face her. 'Good thing I like older men then, isn't it.'

We had a very long kiss. Then we went out and had a coffee and agreed there was no real future in it for us. There was her career, she certainly didn't want to look after an old man, and there were loads of other people like up and coming conductors, she might fancy. On the other hand, she had no one around at the moment and felt in the mood, if not for love, then some paradigm of it. All in all, I had passed her test as temporary bedmate.

Without being specific about our intentions, we bought food and drink and coffee and many other necessaries for occupation of a new flat. I remembered the poverty of Warsaw without regret. It took a while for us to create an acceptable environment; but to get near it in one post-lunch rush is rather impressive in my view. The most poignant moment was when we made the bed with fresh, crisp sheets. We didn't need to say anything, but Sophia leaned across and patted my cheek affectionately. 'See what you get for helping a girl in her career.'

So much for all these domesticities: there was a casserole in the oven and Sophia in the bath. Baths are an excellent facilitator for seduction. She invited me to join her. There is one thing about my cock, it's not a monster but it is impressive. 'Mother of God,' said Sophia as I stepped into the bath; at the tap end of course.

I repeat; anyone who thinks women aren't interested in size is deluded. It may not be the only thing, but believe me, if they have you in mind for a fuck big is better than small. We sat desultorily abluting and smiling shyly: soap and water ran glistening over her breasts. I had the foresight to bring some wine into the bathroom and we drank a little. Sophia's toes found my cock and trapping it, began to play. 'Well,' I said, 'this is nice.' Sophia lifted my dick out of the water with her foot. The swelling head popped up like a dolphin. 'It's certainly promising,' she replied.

If it were possible to predict how someone would behave in bed the oracle concerned would make a fortune, Despite her apparent forwardness she was a pliant companion. She knew how to use her hands though and this produced a pleasing result for both of us. Even so, as I was used to sexually assertive women, this gave me pause for thought. We rolled around for a while. She clutching the object of her desire, me discovering the textures of her body. We paused at one point, her fist still clenched round my cock. I felt we were going nowhere. I said, 'Sophia, you are beautiful and sexy and talented and I want you to tell me what you'd most like us to do for each other. Anything goes - not for me but for you. Think of it as music.' Or maybe I simply said, 'Just tell me Sophia, what do you like most?'

Muffled against my chest she said, 'Kiss me down there Magnus, kiss my *chatte*.' There it was once more. Be older, tell a girl you ran a brothel and show her a big cock and suddenly she is yearning for the experience and skill she supposes comes with this knowledge. I was glad though, because I was already headed that way. Sophia turned out to be sweet and liquid and spicy. She opened her thighs and let me bury my face between them and enjoy her. I was well rewarded. Whether experienced or not, Sophia opened herself up to me and meanwhile licked, sucked and whispered to my prick with convincing affection.

The fuck was more equivocal. Possibly because she had had a noisy and bed-testing orgasm as I licked her cunt. Maybe, since she declared a real interest in a fuck, because neither she nor I had any practical means of contraception. I suggested an alternative. She demurred on the grounds of previous poor experience, a not unfamiliar objection. But she wanted a fuck and had traditional RC practice to draw on. So we fucked, and it was delightful and she came first because she knew about masturbation as a means of keeping control. I held my nerve until she had gasped and heaved her satisfaction and then we laid my shaft along her belly so that she could stroke and jerk away. Older men don't squirt as far as young ones, but Sophia expressed herself very content with the whole exercise and took a while to squeeze and watch all my sperm spill onto her stomach. Overall, I think everyone involved found it a satisfactory evening.

We paid each other some loving and sincere compliments, dozed, bathed and went onto the terrace to look at Paris by night and drink cognac. Other than discovering more about each other we reconfirmed our equality. I wasn't her absent father, or her mentor or manager. She wasn't a surrogate anything, let alone fantasy of youth. We were just real friends. In the morning, we had breakfast in a café and she went off with a kiss and a wave. It felt sad, but comforting. In fact she moved in for a while and it was very pleasing in the manner of an intimate friendship with some relaxed, sensual moments. Then she met someone at the Conservatoire and moved in with him.

IV

Students were the main occupants of the apartment building I lived in. They were of diverse ages and disciplines, if the latter is the right word. They spent most of the time in disputation, fornication and demonstration. We got along perfectly well together, and I rather enjoyed what were to me lunatic ideas and the general freedom from inhibition. My rooms on the top floor were rather more an atelier than apartment, since there was a good deal of sloping roof and to take a bath involved a lot of stooping. I never took a bath without thinking of Sophia. On the other hand it had the roof terrace of good size. The previous occupant had erected trellis and placed plant pots around the edge. I watered these regularly and the plants in them flourished over the years.

In warm weather this garden was a resort for the students, who used it to argue, read, drink cheap Algerian plonk, smoke cannabis (that they also grew in a discreet corner) and fuck. I had evidently inherited a long established custom. Since they were polite to me and careful of my possessions I was happy for them to be there. I reached my seventieth birthday stoned in their congenial company.

We thus became amiably habituated to each other. Often they would invite me to sit with them, and perhaps as a tease, seek my opinion on some obscure aspect of existentialism or communist doctrine. Frankly, I failed to understand most of it. What I did grasp struck me as fanciful and overblown nonsense, but I respected their idealism nonetheless. My experiences in the Great War and subsequently in Poland were of considerable interest to them; which was flattering. They of course countered my critique of communism in action as simply a perversion by Stalin and imperialist Russia. My time as a brothel keeper in

Paris caused lively dispute as to whether I had exploited women or not. The girls more than the men usually felt not; maintaining that provided no one was forced, women had every right to sell their bodies. This always ended with someone shouting 'So what is marriage but legitimised prostitution?' Then we would lurch into a savage denunciation of the Catholic Church, all religion and the rest of it.

Frequently too, I would return from lunch to find a few girls sunbathing naked. They would merely go ''Allo Mag,' and relapse into somnolence and I would sit in my deckchair and read. Only occasionally stealing a fond glance at the breasts and pudenda or buttocks on display. I think they didn't give such frankness a thought and I was glad of that for many reasons, not all of them self-serving. Still, it did cause my loins to stir reminiscently.

The cast list changed of course. Although the length of study courses on the continent gave great continuity. One of my regular sunbathers was a student called Natalie. She was a flirtatious girl who usually had the best looking boy in tow. If not the cleverest student in the group, I marked her as likely to be very successful. She could sense which way the conversation or debate was going, pick up the leading points and leave everyone with the impression she had made the most important contribution. I came on her one afternoon as I had with others, *in flagrante delicto*. Usually when this occurred, the girl would wave and even blow me a kiss and I would tiptoe back into my living room until they had concluded. Then the couple would appear, the chap a bit sheepish, she insouciant with a 'Sorry Mag, *cherie,*' and off they would go.

On this occasion, Natalie looked across at me over the shoulder of the man whose bum rose and fell in foreground view. She rolled her eyes and made a moue indicating boredom. Then slapped her mate on the buttocks and said 'For God's sake hurry up

Eric, Mag's here and wants his terrace back.' After that, whenever we met, she would give me a look and say, 'Can we borrow your terrace?' and we'd both laugh. This became shorthand in the group for any remotely awkward yet funny experience expressed as '...a bit of a *terrasse* moment.'

One night, in what must have been 1968, our acquaintance took a more personal tone. It was quite early in the evening. Paris had been in uproar and at a standstill. I knew something was going to happen because 'my' students had spent days on the roof talking revolution. There was banging at the door and I heard Natalie calling 'Mag, Mag, please be there, let me in.' She fell in, slightly hysterical and very dishevelled. I noticed her cheek was scratched and bruised quite badly. Her jeans were torn. She leaned on me, her hand on my shoulder. 'Those fucking bastards, those fucking bastards. Look what they did to me.' With that, she turned, pulled her sweater and shirt over her head and presented her back to me. It was covered in livid welts. They looked very unpleasant. 'Fucking CRS,' she snarled. I suggested a doctor or the hospital. She sneered. 'Those swine will turn me over to the cops.' Then more pleadingly she turned back to me and said 'Mag, be an angel, run a bath for me, and if you've got any ointment or something.'

By the time I had done this she had stripped naked and stepped into the bath. She lay with the warm water lapping round her. Her pubic hair waved like seaweed in the foam and the raspberry bumps of her nipples broke the surface. I thought she looked very beautiful but said, 'The ointment is here, it should help.' 'Yeah, you can put it on later if you don't mind.' 'Do you want a coffee or a cognac?' 'Both, great, thanks, thanks very much Mag.'

Before the bathroom was a trail of her clothes. Just outside the door were her briefs. I collected everything and put them on the kitchen table. Except the briefs, which somehow I couldn't put down. They were innocently functional enough: some kind of nylon, a rather odd lime green and with decorative trim round the leg bit. I sat down and stared at them and then lifted them to my nostrils. So this was what Natalie smelled like: a trace of piss, sweat from the crack of her arse, a small smear of secretion from her cunt. This was the recipe for her personal musk. I dropped them on the table and went to pour her coffee, now ready in the machine.

She looked up from her bath as I came in and gave me a wide smile, reaching out to take the cup. 'Wonderful, you are a very nice man.' I stooped forward to avoid the roof and my dressing gown fell open. It was evident I had been thinking about sex. Natalie seemed barely to notice as she took the cup; but I saw her eyes widen and a small smile stayed on her lips as I fumbled to close my errant robe. 'Sorry,' I said, 'bit of a terrace moment.' Natalie laughed and turned her attention to her coffee.

I was sitting in the kitchen at the table, trying to read and not to think how much I wanted to fuck Natalie. I had put some eggs out and was going to make her an omelette. She walked out of the bathroom wearing her towel saying 'Did you get my clothes, oh yes, you did.' As her voice died away, I began saying, 'Let me make you an omelette.' She picked up her knickers, so evidently lying away from the pile of her outer garments. Our eyes met. I think we both took a deep breath. 'This is probably more than just a little joke,' she said.

Coming in close she stood looking down at me and dropped the towel. If her body was not perfect, I could find little fault in its appearance. She raised her knee and with considerable aplomb parted my robe with her foot. My cock was in mixed mode. One minute obsessed, the next chastened, now hopeful. 'Well Mag, does your omelette taste as good as your cock looks? I hardly know which to have first.'

She opted for my shrugging off my ridiculous dressing gown after which she straddled my thighs and took hold of me. 'If I'd realised what this fellow was like [she called him a '*mec*'] I'd have been either more careful or more careless on your roof.' I held her hips and she let me suckle her raspberry teats for a while as she pulled at my cock and massaged it against her belly. Then she got its head between her thighs and rubbed the shaft along the hairy and fleshy gully of her groin. She sighed and with her arms round my neck stroked my head and kissed my brow affectionately. 'You may be an old man Mag, but I think you're worth ten of some of the creepy types who want to get into my knickers.' The mention of knickers led her to seize her own from the table and hold them to my nostrils, 'Sexy old sod,' she said affectionately.

I felt her heat and moistness. She raised herself, found me '*en plein forme*' and slid my cock into her cunt. It was bliss. She was tight, he was taut and he pushed on and buried his head deep in her *chatte*. I cushioned her buttocks as she rode at a slow canter up and down. She held my face between her breasts, which was at times a little painful since breasts are soft but the breastbone isn't. Women often forget this. This did not disrupt the intense pleasure of all the sensations I felt. As we enjoyed our ride, she expatiated on the events of the day and how thrilling and awful it had been. I was reminded of Dottie. She had last seen her comrades being hurled into the back of a police van and had only just made her escape, writhing free from the grip of a baton-wielding mob of thuggish CRS fascists.

The narrative evidently acted as accompaniment to the course of her sexual fulfilment. As she struggled and broke away from her quondam assailants, so she began to gallop and pant astride my lap. I kept a light hold on her flanks as she rose and fell. Looking up I enjoyed her gorgeous face with its over large mouth, too long Roman nose and by now, closed eyes as with harsh gasps and grimaces she expressed her staccato extremis. Her cunt pulsed and her tits shook, I was being given a tremendous workout. Well, she came, I came, everyone relaxed and my nose was once more crushed into the hard centre of Natalie's chest. *Tant pis* as they say, there could be no better moment anywhere, let alone a *terrasse*.

This was inevitably, one of those singular passages. Ones that I hope remain as fond secrets, *billets doux* from unconfessed lovers in the treasuries of female memory. That said, I noticed the students who came to inhabit my *terrasse* in subsequent months were, if male, rather respectful, and if female at once slightly flirtatious and more reserved about bodily exposure.

These things do not last forever. Our community had a tradition and we were selective in our choices of resident; but in the end, time overcomes us. I had decided, as my eightieth year came nearer, to remove to Menton. I had the pleasure of visiting it after one of my excursions to Switzerland, to deliver some cash to a French Communist politico. Something about the place appealed. Less vulgar than Cannes and crowded than Nice, it had just the right mix of small town French reserve with undemanding cosmopolitan tolerance.

Then, as it does, life took its own course. Or rather, to quote a poet of my acquaintance '...*now are the mines laid in earlier years, sprung upon unwary travellers alone.*' To continue poetic reference, the first sign of the 'best laid plans' thing came on my return to Paris after a jolly week in the South of France, checking progress on my new home. It was an invitation to attend the retirement party of 'Simon Wilcox CBE.' The venue was Brooks's, and the date two days hence. I noticed that the envelope was addressed to 'Count Pietrowski c/o British Embassy Paris,' and had been redelivered by hand. The handwritten name on the invitation was to Capt. W Myddleton MC.

V

Not for the first time I thought to myself how perseverant is bureaucracy. One part of me wanted to tear the missive up. The past is just that. The other part whispered 'Go on, you're bored and this is an adventure.' After a couple of brandies during which one's mixed feelings about '*recherche*' and 'land of forefathers' churned about, I discovered the clinching argument. I had never been in an aeroplane. We were now in the age of the jet. The growth of popular aviation had arrived whilst I was buried behind the Iron Curtain. Flight had never occurred as an option and my trips from Paris to Switzerland had been enjoyable and leisurely train journeys. So I determined to revisit London and do it by air.

London was as alien as it had been after my return from the First World War. The girls' skirts were even shorter than in the 20s, but then 'swinging London' wasn't the only paradigm of female liberation. For me, the real problem with the place was simply unfamiliarity, including language. Around me in my sequestered first class seat, very smart people discussed parochial business and cultural matters about which I knew little. In the taxi on the way from the airport my driver asked 'So where are you from?' I had given 'The Ritz' as my destination, without any idea as to whether this was really where I needed to be. 'I am English,' I said. 'Of course Guv,' he responded. I was compelled to add 'I've been abroad quite a while.' 'There's a lot of things changed mate, and not for the better,' he replied in friendlier tones. As we reached Knightsbridge I decided that the Cavalry Club would be the place to stay. 'St James's', I told my driver.

Apart from being a little more shabby, the club was much the same. Declaration of my identity resulted in scrutiny of ledgers and then a smiling 'Welcome back sir.' Sadly, the welcome did not extend to the offer of a room. These were all taken. 'It's been a very busy month, Captain Myddleton.' So I had them book me in at the Ritz after all. In truth, the real value of the club was the bar. The bedrooms were not up to much in comparison to the Ritz.

I had a busy afternoon. My wardrobe had become aged and attenuated. The Paris years had supplied me with a good suit or two, but after retirement my apparel had tended to the casual. The club supplied a regimental tie and in nearby Jermyn Street I found shirts and shoes. Britain had just converted to decimal currency, which was simpler but made everything seem very expensive. In my hasty departure I had of course changed only a small amount of currency at the airport. So I visited the West End branch of the Credit Lyonnais, who were my bankers in Paris. Here I spent a ridiculous amount of time prising more money from their bureaucracy. Later, refurbished and fuelled by a glass of champagne, I strolled round the corner to Brooks's.

The years abroad had distanced me in many ways from English culture. Brooks's was curiously familiar. I wondered why, as I stood in the lobby and watched the to and fro of the members. Then I realised. I was back in Edwardian England. I nearly laughed aloud. Upstairs in the library a steward offered me a drink and I spotted Wilcox across the room. My name was announced and he immediately came over to me. 'My dear chap,' he beamed and shook my hand energetically. We exchanged pleasantries about 'wearing well' and then other guests arrived and he passed me on to a nearby group. As we transited he took my elbow and in a lower voice said 'Where are you staying?' I told him. 'Good, will you come back here and have lunch with me tomorrow? Things to catch up on.'

The company was affable enough. No one was very inquisitive about my connection with Wilcox who seemed very popular. Most of the gathering was military or civil service. The women were, so far as I knew, wives although I met no Mrs Wilcox. My residence in Paris was interesting to the women. For the men, mention of France simply led to derogatory comments about de Gaulle and lavatories. The wine and canapés were in good supply, certainly better than Poland. Though why Poland came to mind God knows, I'd been to enough smart receptions since then. I thought fleetingly of Rula and Sophia. Then I just thought about women and decided to leave. I reaffirmed my luncheon with Wilcox and went back to the Ritz where I had a discreet consultation with the concierge.

Meriel – though I doubted this was her real name – was a very attractive young woman. Tall and nicely proportioned she inhabited her well cut 'little black dress' with aplomb. Her long blonde hair was both genuine in colour and equally well tailored. It framed a face of regular features, generous mouth, neat nose and intelligent blue eyes. Her one concession to flamboyance was the collection of silver rings and bracelets that adorned her slender fingers and wrists. Acting on the prearranged recognitions we greeted each other in the bar with delighted cries of 'William darling', 'Meriel my love'. For some reason our intermediaries deemed these charades necessary. It's typical British hypocrisy.

My guest endeared herself immediately by ordering a dry

martini. From then on we had a very fine evening. Whilst I flatter myself I can be an entertaining companion, there's no doubt that my pre-war career in particular put us both on a different footing to the normal client-callgirl relations. So by the time we reached my quarters after a very indulgent dinner we were definitely the best of friends. I ushered her into the sitting-room portion. Friends we might be, relaxed she was, but she was a professional.

'So William lover, what's it to be?'

'What do you feel like?'

'Sweetie, don't be coy. It's your choice. The night is young.'

I managed to persuade her to join me in the shower. Her one demurral of the evening made me glad the Ritz had provided adequate hair protection. The brief power struggle that had resulted from my proposal resolved itself once we were naked and she had been reassured the shower cap looked fine. It had been a while since I had been so close to such limpid and silky female flesh. I've always loved the proximity of girls in water. It makes them so very sexy. Warm and soapy liquid does something not just for their skin but also for their sensuality. Luckily, my appreciation had communicated itself to my loins. So far, Meriel had taken her cue from me. I hadn't grabbed her and pawed her body or made lurid comments. So we had undressed with relative discretion and re-met in the shower.

'This is nice,' said Meriel as she lifted her face to the spray and ran her hands unselfconsciously down her torso. Then she remembered what her purpose was and turned her attention to me. She ran her hands over my shoulders and chest and lifted her face for a kiss. 'Mmm, nice.' Something must have registered because she looked down and said, 'Oh, wow!'

After that it was slalom all the way. 'Jesus fuck,' Meriel said vulgarly at one point in her preliminary examination of my cock. Her refined accent had slipped a little. 'This really is a good one.' She may of course have been overexcited by my attentions to her cunt. 'Show me,' I had demanded when she first began to slide down my belly and I still had my fingers high between her legs. Before I let her suck me, I made her spread her legs and let me open her up with my eyes and later tongue. After that, the commercial aspect was forgotten, and we concentrated on having a great night out. There is an expression about 'going round the world' that refers to everything you can do sexually. Meriel and I did it. Her cunt and her arse were equally sweet and receptive. Her mouth was as generous as it had first appeared. Having got myself fully in the saddle as it were I was reluctant to use all my ammunition and die.

'Not yet, not yet,' I recall saying

'Go on lover, do it, I want it,' she replied.

Then even in the subsequent quiescence, she took hold of me and caressed me with her tongue and played with me skilfully until I was stiff again. She lay on her back, spread her thighs and her cunt took me in and she ground the juices out of me. We lay together, she sprawled, thighs akimbo, eyes closed, her hand affectionate on my hip. Myself breathing heavily, trying to avoid putting my whole weight on her, and more at peace than I could remember.

'Thank you,' I whispered.

'It was lovely, Billy Boy,' she whispered back. It was clever of her to remember I had shared that old sobriquet with her.

In the morning we had a very relaxed breakfast served in my small suite. I like to think Meriel was a less than perfect actress, and hence her warmth of manner genuine.

'Oh dear,' she said, as we drained our champagne glasses in

a final toast to each other, 'there is a grisly bit of commerce.'

I found my book of traveller's cheques, signed one and handed it to her. 'Fill in the amount yourself Meriel.'

She went to the writing desk and scribbled briefly. Her lips brushed my cheek as she showed me the slip. It was for quite a lot of money, but no more than I thought it should be for a whole night and less possibly, than she deserved.

How delightful is a life lived at leisure in fine hotels with no imperatives other than lunch? Well, it all depends on what happens at lunch. I had forgotten 'club lunches'. Somewhere there still existed, chefs with a deep understanding of upper class English palates and a smattering of nineteenth century French cooking. On the menu, potted shrimp vied with *'crevettes Marie Rose'* and lamb chops with *'rognons diable'*. As expected, the food was adequate, the wine excellent and the port impeccable. Wilcox chatted away and we exchanged subtle accounts, explanations and (on his part), apologies for shipping me off to Poland. The only sad note was his report that Hoddle had got out of Tokyo just before Pearl Harbour only to end up in Singapore where he died at Japanese hands.

By the time the cheese and port arrived I had said, 'So I expect I'm wondering why you asked me here?' Wilcox laughed and said 'Yes, that's the thing.' Then he told me.

The Paris riots were a sideshow compared to the growth of violent terrorism. Various groups such as the Red Brigade and a highly militant IRA were fed by a Russia intent on destabilisation of the West. It was all bollocks to me but I had no case to dissent. I was thinking, 'Why is he telling me this?'

He said, 'Your apartment in Paris has been identified as a resort of revolutionaries.' I was stunned. 'I mean, for Christ's sake these are just students being what they are and why the fuck do you come to pick on me?' I also wondered why he was involved with this when he was retired.

'We in the Service never retire,' he said as if reading my thoughts. 'Not you either,' he added, 'I mean, you're not much under suspicion, but we do need your help.'

I thought of the students drinking and fucking on my terrace and Natalie covered with welts and riding my loins, her tits jiggling.

'You people seem to have things covered; what's left for me to do, and what does "not much under suspicion" mean?'

Wilcox refilled his glass from the decanter and pushed it over to me. 'You always were a canny bugger,' he said. 'Don't get me wrong, the war stuff was good but you were brilliant in Poland.' There was a pause. 'I mean old boy, some might think that to survive and get out you played both ends against the middle.'

'Implying what exactly?' My mouth was dry and I reached for the decanter.

'Nothing, except you have a talent for dissimulation.'

'Oh for fuck's sake, I spent ten years in forced exile at the arse end of the Soviet Empire reading Trade Union minutes and passing messages between you lot and the KGB'. Which was when he suggested we retreat to the Ritz and my suite.

'Very nice.' Wilcox said as we entered. I recalled the previous evening in regretful contrast. I poured us both a drink from my bar. 'Actually, I was teasing about the students. The French were helping us over the IRA and mentioned Count P. That said, we felt you went rather quiet when you were transferred to Paris.'

'I was about to retire.'

'Maybe. Tell me about Gregor Volnikov.'

'My KGB controller in Warsaw.'

'That's the chap.'

Wilcox put his glass down and got to his feet. 'He's quite a big wheel now. He thinks very highly of you. What's the Russian for 'jolly useful chap?'

It was probably the brandy but my brain had ceased to operate. Wilcox had reached the door. He smiled amiably. 'I've got a nice little house down in Cornwall. I'm having two or three houseguests this weekend. I'd like you to come too. Chance to see old stamping grounds.' He rummaged in his jacket pocket and produced an envelope. I took it. 'It's all in there,' he said, and was gone.

I was beginning to regret coming to London. Something told me that chickens were about to roost in my backyard. The envelope contained a First Class rail ticket and a brief instruction to 'detrain' at Bodmin Road where I would be met.

The 'Cornishman' Express was a cut above Polish State Railways. I settled into my dining car seat and decided that whatever sinister purposes Wilcox had in mind, a good lunch would fortify the spirit. The carriage filled up and a youngish man seated himself opposite. We exchanged the ritual gestures of request and acquiescence and got on with the menus and the drink orders. I covertly studied my fellow passenger and rather took to him. In his early to mid thirties one guessed. He had a definite military air but a certain civilian relaxation in his haircut and clothes. There was something familiar about him. Being *tête-à-tête* makes a degree of dialogue inevitable. A few banalities over and our shared destination declared, we rapidly established our Cornish credentials through answering the question 'do you know that part of the world?' From this, it was a short step to our military backgrounds. Mine simply declared as cavalry, First World War; his, just as circumspectly as Chief Petty Officer, Royal Navy, supplemented after inquiry by 'well, let's just say one of the odder branches.' We chatted happily about life in the Services past and present. At some point introductions became necessary. So we reached across the table, shook hands and announced ourselves.

'William Myddleton' I said.

He smiled, 'William Corey, sir' he replied.

We had got to the cheese course and Plymouth. The train stopped and people milled about. The interruption allowed us to think our thoughts.

'You wouldn't be related to James Corey from St Manion?' I asked. He smiled. 'It's a common enough name, but my grandfather was James Corey and my father was a James William.' Only one question was needed to confirm this discomforting coincidence.

'Is your grandmother's Christian name Jennifer by any chance?'

William laughed, 'Nana Jenny, yes indeed.' Then he suddenly grew solemn, yet eager in one shift of expression. 'You must be "cousin Billy" who went missing in the Great War?' I felt I was in a trance. Life goes forward not back. Young Corey was illumined. 'Good Lord, Nana talks of you often, so does the whole family, you're a myth, a fable. I mean the story is that you were killed in action but then weren't and just disappeared.'

'That's just about it.' I said.

He was such a nice young man. 'Gosh, Nana and Dad are going to meet me at the station, they'll be so surprised.' There was no answer to that. Grandfather James Corey had died a few years before. Sadly, so had William's mother. There were however numbers of family, including young William's siblings who would be thrilled to hear my story.

'So what does Nana Jenny say about me?' I asked. 'Oh, she

says you were childhood sweethearts and then you had to join the army and she fell in love with Grandpa.' He paused. 'She says you and your mother had a difficult time given your, you know, situation.'

The train was winding a slow way through the vales that led from Plymouth to Bodmin. I contemplated jumping off. 'Oh, it wasn't really so bad' I said lightly. William began to question me. I fended him off, perhaps a bit abruptly with 'I have lived abroad since the end of the Great War.' As for my reason for visiting Cornwall, it was 'just some business.' He was rather crestfallen and I thought how young he suddenly seemed. To make him feel better I said, 'It's pretty bloody weird to run into one's past you know.' He smiled again 'Of course, I can see that.' The train slowed more definitively as we rounded a curve. William leapt up and peered through the window. 'It's Bodmin, gosh, there's Nana and Dad on the platform.'

I don't know quite what I was expecting. Of course, the image in my head was of a Jenny sixty years younger. Instead, from the train step I looked downward at a comfortable broad-beamed matron with ruddy cheeks and permed hair peaking out from under a slightly dated hat. Father and grandmother gathered William into their arms and I hovered uneasily on the carriage step. William broke free, turned and waved me forward. 'Look who I met on the train!' he announced. 'Oh my Lord' whispered Jenny, 'It's Billy.'

A handshake seemed too cold, a hug too presumptive. Both of us had our arms slightly raised as a preliminary to some further greeting, so I stepped forward, took her hand and bent over it, my lips lightly brushing her fingers. Our eyes met and we remembered and lived our lives and regained the present in one brief exchange. Then it was James' turn. At sixty, he had the look of a hard-working but prosperous farmer. There was much of Jenny in his eyes and general features. The mouth was familiar, like his son's. I tried to think, where else I'd seen that mouth. My mother came to mind. The thought was lost as I shook hands with him. He was friendly in a baffled way. As we stood smiling and nodding uncertainly, a smartly dressed chauffeur wearing a peaked military style cap and black gloves appeared beside me. 'Mr Myddleton sir, your car is ready when you are.' 'Where are you staying?' asked William. I shook my head helplessly. William fumbled in his pocket and found a pen and a piece of paper he tore from the magazine he had been reading. Armed with his telephone number and nodding assent to his demand I call them soon, I gratefully followed my rescuer to the black Rover car parked in the station yard.

VI

Wilcox's 'nice little house' was a substantial manor in a valley and about ten acres of grounds. Originally early eighteenth century it had been much fooled around with in Victorian times. I knew it quite well, having been there several times on business for Lord Broleigh since his and the owner's estates ran alongside each other. Luckily the plumbing had been modernised in the 1960s. No one was about. A housekeeper showed me to my quarters and told me that 'drinks will be served in the library at 1830 hours'. There was a decanter of whisky and I recovered myself with a very large neat one. From my bedroom window I could see the lawns and the hedges of a small maze. Two figures were walking away from me toward a tennis court. They were deep in conversation but neither looked like Wilcox.

Feeling refreshed from a shower but slightly squiffed, I

walked into the library about five minutes late. An attendant offered me a dry sherry. Across the room I saw Wilcox, two vaguely military looking types I didn't recognise and Gregor Volnikov. 'Magnus *tovarich!*' exclaimed Gregor and almost ran to greet me. We embraced; or rather he embraced me, babbling in Russian. Luckily I had put down my sherry before he got to me. I recovered it and followed Gregor to join our host. Wilcox looked amused, his two colleagues less so. One was quite elderly, the other much younger. I don't recall their names and their function was only loosely described as 'Intelligence.' 'You must regard yourself as bound by the Official Secrets Act' was Wilcox's opening remark. Volnikov himself was considerably more heavily built than when I had worked with him. He was also much more elegantly clad.

Wilcox was uncharacteristically brisk and direct. 'Mr Volnikov is, or rather was, supposedly a Second Secretary at the Russian Embassy in London,' he began. Gregor seized my elbow and whispered to me in Polish, 'You got to Paris, I got to London, goodbye Warsaw,' and laughed. The younger Intelligence man snapped, 'Keep to English please.' Wilcox continued, 'there are two issues that materially affect Mr Volnikov's application for political asylum in Great Britain and they are both to do with you, Mr Myddleton.'

Well, I thought I had a pretty good idea what was coming so I waved my glass to indicate the need for a top up. This was supplied and I turned back to Wilcox and looked enquiring. Malfeasance part one was my role in suborning weak-minded capitalist businessmen and politicians whilst in the service of the KGB. Part two was my Swiss bank account and its use as a money-laundering device for the KGB and tax evasion for me. During this narrative Gregor shrugged at me and said 'Sorry

Magnus, what could I do?'

By this time we were seated round the dinner table and tucking in to a very good piece of beef. The resident young bully said 'You are in serious trouble Myddleton, we can throw the book at you.' His elder companion said mildly but firmly, 'There's no need to be disagreeable. Captain Myddleton was a distinguished soldier and has done his country great service in the past.' 'Before he became a crook and traitor' was the unabashed response. I put down my cutlery. 'Someone here has to decide what the rules of this game are. For my part the little shit opposite who has been using the wrong knife shouldn't be allowed to play.' Gregor laughed and even Wilcox smiled fleetingly.

The deal emerged. Dated as they might be, the names of the people who had been blackmailed in consequence of the various cultural activities with which I had been engaged in Paris were still of interest. If provided, my failure to pass them on to my British Embassy contact in a timely way would be overlooked. This was unproblematic. I kept a log of everything I did in that line and it was in a safe deposit. I forebore to score a few points by telling them my original debrief had been cursory, their Embassy intelligence officer had made no attempt to keep in touch and anyway, I'd been signed off with a pension and a twee ceremony yonks ago.

The Swiss thing was a little more complex. Gregor said in Polish 'It's fine, tell them everything. I am covered.' He was pissed. Management had clearly been briefed to provide vodka and his personal bottle reduced rapidly. I translated but left out the last sentence to see if anyone noticed. We were probably being recorded though. I didn't care. I told them about the account and the money that came in from time to time. Although Gregor was the main conduit for both deposits and outward transfers I had always been the account holding authority. Only I received the periodic statements, also stored in my safe deposit. This was the information my 'team' wanted. Since, as an agreed fee, I took a small percentage of the throughput in the account and transferred it to my personal account elsewhere, I was not anxious just to give them a bundle of paper.

'I want immunity for any spurious British tax evasion charges,' I said. 'In writing before you get the documents,' I added. Gregor said, 'Good move, Magnus my friend.' There was a nasty look from our young tiger, but Wilcox and his ageing chum seemed happy to say 'yes'. We discussed arrangements for my return to Paris, a visit to my Bank for the safe deposit contents. 'Don't be funny' was the response to my suggestion of my apartment as a handover rendezvous. The heavies left Gregor and I to catch up, like old lovers.

We both got smashed as rats and fell about laughing. Anyone listening would have learned nothing except about our delight. In a garbled mix of Russian, Polish and English we drank to our good fortune in escaping death in war and crucifixion by ideologues. We'd played the system and won. I believe we were helped to our rooms and I know I slept extraordinarily well. It was probably the last evening that I felt truly young.

On Sunday I woke late but in a surprisingly fit state. In the morning room, Wilcox was finishing his breakfast. I joined him with my own plate, laden from the sideboard.

'Good show,' he said. We discussed arrangements. The others had already left by car. I was booked on the sleeper to London, that night. I would be back in Paris by mid-week and we would meet up and deal with the business. Wilcox said 'You have a driver available today if you need one. You know, to catch up on anything.'

It was William who answered the phone when I summoned the courage to call. He sounded very pleased to hear me. 'Nana's out just now. She said if you rang, to ask you to come to lunch. We'd all love to see you.' I wondered who 'all' might be. Nothing for it, though, but to accept. Luckily 'lunch' was at a civilised two thirty.

Everything went surprisingly well. Over a dozen assorted Corey children, grandchildren and cousins sat around the big table in the farmhouse kitchen. James, Jenny, young William and I grouped at the head. I entertained them with a carefully edited version of my adventures and they eventually trooped off with waves and cheery salutations. 'Well, that was very nice,' said Jenny. 'The Boys', as she called her eldest son and grandson, had ushered us out into the kitchen garden. I gazed out over the fields. A short way off the chimney pots of Broleigh Manor showed through the trees. 'It's a posh country house hotel now,' said Jenny following my glance. Beyond, forming the horizon, Rough Tor and Brown Willy were silhouettes in the misty early evening sun. There were lots of things that might be said, but they all began with 'why' or 'if'.

'You've got a lovely family.' I said. 'I've had a lovely life and been very lucky with all my men,' she replied. 'I'm glad,' I replied with sincerity. There was a silence.

'I like young William,' I offered, 'James too of course.' Jenny laughed. 'I know what you mean. James is the complete Cornish farmer. He and his Dad really did wonders with the farm. William is thrilled to have met you. In fact I often think you and he have a lot in common. Adventure, another horizon, a romantic streak.'

It had gone cool and Jenny shivered. 'My car will be coming soon,' I said. 'I have to get the train to London tonight. Then I'm off back to Paris,' I added unnecessarily. Jenny laughed softly.

'Poor old Billy, I know that slightly trapped tone.' Her hand reached for mine. 'There will always be a home for you here if you ever wanted.' 'That's good to know.' It was good, but both of us knew it was just a way of saying everything was all right. My car was waiting outside the front door on the farm road. I shook hands with James and William and we exchanged expressions of goodwill. Jenny and I had a clumsy but affectionate hug and bumped noses in an uncertain kiss. The whole weekend had been exhausting.

Back at the Ritz I called the number Meriel had given me. Since it was only about ten in the morning she wasn't too thrilled to be woken up, but agreed to join me for supper and so forth. 'I can't stay the night,' she said. That evening I had a couple of cocktails, ordered a light supper for about nine and waited for her arrival. She appeared punctually at seven and accepted a dry martini. I thanked her for making time for me. 'No problem, I'm just sorry it has to be a short visit.' She enquired about my weekend and I told her. 'Sounds like you need a simple therapeutic fuck,' she said. We dispensed with preliminaries.

Both of us stripped naked. She knelt on the bed; hips raised and knees wide. I knelt up behind her, cock in hand. In the valley between her buttocks the pursed roundel of her anus winked at me. She had shaved nearly all her pubic hair and the soft flesh of her cunt glistened. I opened her up with my fingers so that the anemone pink interior was revealed. She was supported on her elbows, her face turned sideways resting on the pillow. Her breasts hung full and round and dark tipped as ripe figs. It was a fine sight. 'You look good,' I said. Her tongue flickered. I thought of Julia. 'Fuck me then Billy,' she said. I watched my cock stretch the throat of her cunt, slide in between the clinging lips until my balls banged against the small tuft of dark hair she'd left at the centre of her pubic mound. She sighed, wiggled slightly to secure her position. Her cunt contracted around my shaft. I gripped her hips and began to fuck her.

In a sense she was entirely passive. Eyes closed, one hand resting by her face on the pillow, the other between her thighs, lightly touching my balls as they slapped against her. I admired the curves and textures of her shoulders and the creamy stretch of her torso. Mostly I just lost myself in the tight, hot, liquescent embrace of her cunt. It was a totally selfish engagement. As every nerve in my body focused on my cock I began to fuck with increasing vigour. I grunted with the force, she gasped in reaction. Her tits swung with each impact, her muscles tensed as she held her position against my thrusts. She knew exactly how to pace things. 'Come on sweetie, give it to me, love that cock, spunk me hard!' How right she was. I let go with almost painful intensity and a short series of blasphemies and fell forward breathless over her body. She let me lie there for a short while before gently extracting my softening cock from her vagina. 'There,' she said soothingly, that was lovely, wasn't it?' 'Thank you nurse,' I said and we both laughed.

The next day I flew back to Paris with Wilcox. We went to my bank and I handed over the files he wanted in return for my letter of immunity. For some while I had been increasingly disenchanted with Paris and my apartment whose inhabitants seemed coarser and less agreeable. It had been a tedious process but the place I had found in Menton was eventually ready and it was with few regrets that I saw the van leave with my possessions and myself taking a taxi to the railway station.

FINIS

Envoi

Some might think Menton dull, but it suits me. I have a pleasant routine in which my walks keep me fit and my favourite cafés and restaurants supply society. I read a lot and fool around with my *memoires*. There is an English lawyer who is a neighbour. He's a good chap and I've given him charge of my affairs. It gives me great pleasure to think that this comfortable way of life has been bought with what some might call ill-gotten gains. Bloody *well*-gotten in my view. I wonder how Gregor is doing. Someone's ringing my doorbell down in the lobby. It's probably that ghastly American widow who is pursuing me. In a weak moment I let her suck my cock. It was a real case of 'shut your eyes and think of England'. Disgusting at her age and I shan't let her in again. Now, that Angélique in the Café des Sports, she's an attractive woman and she flirts with me outrageously. On the other hand I'm not stupid enough to think she'll ever ring my bell. Sorry, old cock of mine; it's just you and me and the view from the balcony. We remember though, don't we, friend? Oh yes, you reply, stirring slightly, we remember it well.

Menton, October 1985

Author's Postscript

The Count's story does not of course end quite there. He died aged 97 asleep on the balcony of his apartment overlooking the Mediterranean. He is buried in the English section of *la Cimetiere du Vieux Chateau*. His headstone records: 'Capt. William Myddleton MC 1893 – 1990.' Not far from the grave of Webb Ellis, inventor of Rugby football, his other neighbours include several Russian and Polish exiled gentry. He must have known and appreciated that. On the memorial is also a short inscription in Greek that translated reads: '*Sweet and cruel Calypso, I dwelt but briefly in thy vaulted cave and now am in mine own forever.*'

I am indebted to Alan Morteson, of solicitors Morteson, Harkness and Trimble for providing me with the manuscript of these *memoires*. Alan had met Magnus, as he then knew him, when they both visited Menton on holiday in the early 1970s. His firm also had a professional interest in the area. This being the time when Magnus had begun searches for a new home. Subsequently, Alan bought an apartment in the same small development and they became neighbours. Despite their wide age difference their friendship grew and Magnus asked him to help with tidying his affairs.

Magnus ended his life a moderately wealthy man. He was frugal rather than mean, but nonetheless had purchased a quality apartment on the edge of Menton and dined out every day, albeit modestly. He also walked for several kilometres each morning, along the front, only in his last years using a stick. Alan recalls many luncheons, often including his family, for which Magnus insisted on paying. On the other hand, the question of professional fees always seemed to be gently avoided.

There was little left of his former art and book collection.

Alan confessed himself rather shocked at what there was; as he had been by the *memoires*. Apart from some very foxed Olympia Press editions of de Sade, what were probably the last of Dottie Scrimgeour's phallic forgeries graced the walls of Magnus's bedroom. If his Presbyterian sensibilities were offended by Magnus' career, Alan admitted that he much enjoyed his company. 'Witty', 'interesting' and 'iconoclastic' were words he used to describe the old man's conversation. In his guise of a wealthy Count in exile, there was no shortage of female attention in Magnus' declining years, from divorcees and widows of a quite wide range of ages.

On Alan's account, such attentions were rejected politely but firmly. 'He'd say to me, "Another of those harpies wants to clip my wings, I shall tell her to keep her knickers dry. I can keep good company with myself."' Magnus would not of course say this directly to his suitor. Indeed, Alan suspects that one or two of the more forward divorcees may have slipped under the radar. His only reason for supposing this is the occasional comment Magnus let slip along the lines of 'The thing about new money old boy, is it will suck any cock that is likely to squirt cash.' Alan was torn between horror at such vulgarity and amusement at the outrageousness of the remark. Even Magnus had thought he had gone too far with his friend. He had apologised saying, 'Sorry Alan, I'm a very old man, and still a peasant at heart.'

With Alan Morteson's professional help, Magnus had set up a Trust for his assets of which his friend was the Executor. As his client put it, 'I've only got remote relatives and no great causes. Let's just leave it lie until you get bored with it and then give it to a horses' home.' Morteson was wondering about this very thing when my biography of Bernd Tost was published. He only came across it because a friend of his son, who was staying with them, happened to be reading it and left the volume lying about. Morteson flicked briefly through the opening pages and the name 'Pietrowski' caught his eye.

Whether Count Magnus or William Myddleton or Billy Jones would have approved I don't know. He had known of Hedda's pregnancy but had made no further references to Hedda or his possible child. He had also left in his *memoire* a hint that Jenny's eldest son might not be a bloodline Corey. His dismissive reference, ('*if I have left any bastards myself*)', to the possibility of descendants and in general to his Cornish relatives was curious to say the least. We decided that the estate should be divided between the two children Magnus almost certainly fathered with Jenny and Hedda respectively, and held in Trust for their grandchildren. I hope that in due course some of them will go to see his grave.

Caussens, October 2007

By the same author

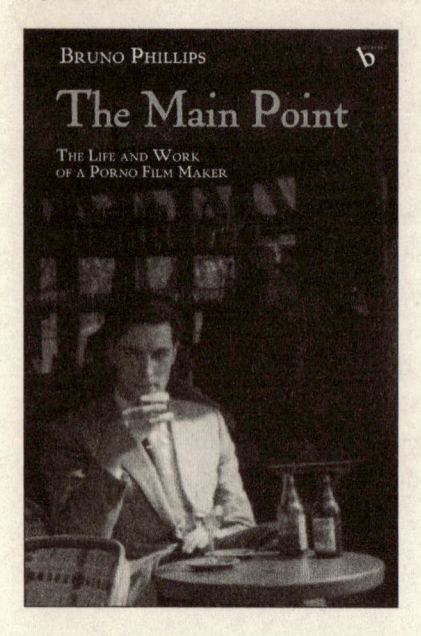

The Main Point
Bruno Philips

The story of Bernd Töst and his career as a porn-movie auteurs is as colourful and strange as any in the history of pornography. Gathering together stories from the stars of his films, his family, and the great man himself, Töst's erotic biography is the most fascinating expose of the early porn industry and its players since *Boogie Nights*.

£7.95

Some more titles available from the ER Books:

The Diary of a Sex Fiend   £9.99
Christopher Peachment

If you're a serious subscriber to political correctness, then this book is probably not for you. But if you are a genial, intelligent and well balanced Renaissance man or woman (as most of us are), then you can do no better than to order this book. In return you will receive a vast repository of acerbic wit, sharp wisdom and an astonishing amount of pithy sexual fact written by the Erotic Review's top columnist, Christopher Peachment.

Rogering Molly & other stories
Christopher Hart

From the small market towns of mid-Wales to the narrow streets of ancient Babylon, from a lofty Singapore penthouse (with a rooftop pool the size of Surrey) to a woodland shack deep in the forests of Transylvania, the sexual predators are afoot, and... they're hungry. With an extensive cast of wickedly erotic characters, Hart shows himself to be a subtle master of the genre in these 25 lubricious tales.

£7.95

Dirty Habits and Other Stories   £7.95
John Gibb

From fairy tales and fighter jets to religion and royalty, John Gibb uncovers erotic potential at every turn in this brilliant collection of 30 tales. He is able to manipulate the most innocent elements of everyday life and turn them into passionate moments imbued with sensual power. Every tale is intriguing, surprising, and completely different form those that have gone before. Some are dark and tense, some quirky and humorous, but none will disappoint in their ability to arouse and excite.

Orderline: 0800 0262 524
Email: leadline@eroticprints.org

WWW.EROTICPRINTS.ORG

Bruno Phillips

Billy's Long Game